James Patterson is one of the best-known and biggest-selling writers of all time. He is the author of some of the most popular series of the past decade: the Women's Murder Club, the Alex Cross novels and Maximum Ride, and he has written many other number one bestsellers including romance novels and stand-alone thrillers. He has won an Edgar Award, the mystery world's highest honour. He lives in Florida with his wife and son.

Praise for James Patterson:

'The man is a master of this genre. We fans will have one wish for him: write even faster' *USA Today*

'Patterson knows where our deepest fears are buried . . . there's no stopping his imagination' *New York Times*

'Patterson boils a scene down to the single, telling element that defines a character or moves the plot along. It's what fires off the movie projector in the reader's mind'
Michael Connelly

'Makes Kay Scarpetta's lot look positively fairytale' *Mirror*

'A novel which makes for sleepless nights' *Daily Express*

'Skilfully put together' *Cosmopolitan*

'Patterson's action-packed story keeps the pages flicking by' *The Sunday Times*

'A fine writer with a good ear for dialogue and pacing. His books are always page-turners' *Washington Times*

'Patterson is a phenomenon' *Observer*

'Brilliantly terrifying . . . so exciting I had to stay up all night to finish it' *Daily Mail*

'Awesome' *Independent on Sunday*

'I can't believe how good Patterson is – he's always on the mark. I have never begun a Patterson book and been able to put it down' Larry King, *USA Today*

4th
OF JULY

JAMES
PATTERSON
AND MAXINE PAETRO

headline

First published in Great Britain in 2005
by HEADLINE BOOK PUBLISHING

This edition published in 2009
by HEADLINE PUBLISHING GROUP

3

Cataloguing in Publication Data is available from the British Library

ISBN 978 0 7553 4929 6

Typeset in Palatino Light by Palimpsest Book Production Limited,
Grangemouth, Stirlingshire

Printed in Great Britain by
Clays Ltd, Elcograf S.p.A.

HEADLINE PUBLISHING GROUP
An Hachette UK Company
338 Euston Road
London NW1 3BH

www.headline.co.uk
www.hachette.co.uk

4th
OF JULY

Our thanks and gratitude to top cop Captain Richard Conklin, Bureau of Investigations, Stamford, Connecticut Police Department and Dr Humphrey Germaniuk, Medical Examiner of Trumbell County, Ohio, a great teacher and noted practitioner of forensic pathology. And special thanks to Mickey Sherman, Criminal Defence attorney extraordinaire, for his very wise counsel.

We are also grateful to Lynn Colomello, Ellie Shurtleff, Linda Guynup Dewey and Yukie Kito for their excellent research assistance on the ground and on the Web.

PART ONE

Nobody Cares

Chapter One

It was just before 4:00 a.m. on a weekday morning. My mind was racing even before Jacobi nosed our car up in front of the Lorenzo, a grungy rent-by-the-hour 'tourist hotel' on a block in San Francisco's Tenderloin District that's so forbidding even the sun won't cross the street.

Three black-and-whites were at the curb, and Conklin, the first officer at the scene, was taping off the area. So was another officer, Les Arou.

'What have we got?' I asked Conklin and Arou.

'White male, Lieutenant. Late teens, bug-eyed and done to a turn,' Conklin told me. 'Room twenty-one. No signs of forced entry. Vic's in the bathtub, just like the last one.'

The stink of piss and vomit washed over us as Jacobi and I entered the hotel. No bellhops in this place. No elevators or room service either. Night people faded back into the shadows except for one gray-skinned young prostitute who pulled Jacobi aside.

'Give me twenty dollars,' I heard her say. 'I got a license-plate.'

Jacobi peeled off a ten in exchange for a slip of paper, then turned to the desk clerk and asked him about the victim: did he have a roommate, a credit card, a habit?

I stepped around a junkie in the stairwell and climbed to the first floor. The door to Room 21 was open and a rookie was standing guard at the doorway.

'Evening, Lieutenant Boxer.'

'It's morning, Keresty.'

'Yes, Ma'am,' he said, logging me in, turning his clipboard to collect my signature.

It was darker inside the 12 x 12 foot room than it was in the hallway. The fuse had blown and thin curtains hung like wraiths in front of the street-lit windows. I was working the puzzle, trying to figure out what was evidence, what was not, trying not to step on anything. There was too damned much of everything and too little light.

I flicked my flashlight beam over the crack vials on the floor, the mattress stained with old blood, the rank piles of garbage and clothing everywhere. There was a kitchenette of sorts in the corner, the hotplate still warm, drug paraphernalia in the sink.

The air in the bathroom was thick, almost soupy. I swept my light along the extension cord that snaked from the socket by the sink, past the clogged toilet bowl to the bathtub.

My guts clenched as I caught the dead boy in my beam. He was naked, a skinny blond with a hairless chest, half sitting up in the tub, eyes bulging, foam at his lips and nostrils. The electric cord ended at an old-fashioned two-slice toaster that glinted up through the bathwater.

'Shit,' I said, as Jacobi entered the bathroom. 'Here we go again.'

'He's toast all right,' said Jacobi.

As Commanding Officer of the Homicide Detail, I wasn't supposed to do hands-on detective work any more. But at times like this, I just couldn't stay away.

Another kid had been electrocuted, but why? Was he a random victim of violence, or was it personal? In my mind's eye, I saw the boy flailing in pain as the juice shot through him and shut his heart down.

The standing water on the cracked tile floor was creeping up the legs of my trousers. I lifted a foot and toed the bathroom door closed, knowing full well what I was going to see. The door whined with the nasal squeal of hinges that had probably never been oiled.

Two words were spray-painted onto the door. For the second time in a couple of weeks, I wondered what the hell they meant.

NOBODY CARES.

Chapter Two

It looked like a particularly grisly suicide, except that the spray-paint can was nowhere around. I heard Charlie Clapper and his CSU team arrive and begin to unpack forensic equipment in the outer room. I stood aside as the photographer took his shots of the victim, then I yanked the electric cord out of the wall.

Charlie changed the fuse. 'Thank You, Jesus,' he said, as light flooded the god-awful place.

I was riffling through the victim's clothes, finding not a scrap of ID, when Claire Washburn, my closest friend and the Chief Medical Examiner for San Francisco, walked through the door.

'It's pretty nasty,' I told her as we went into the bathroom. Claire is a center of warmth in my life, more of a sister than my real one, Catherine. 'I've been having an impulse.'

'To do what?' Claire asked me mildly.

I swallowed hard, forcing down the gorge that kept rising in my throat. I'd gotten used to a lot of things but I would never get used to the murder of children.

'I just want to reach in and pull out the stopper,' I told her.

The victim looked even more stricken in the bright light. Claire crouched beside the tub, squeezing her size sixteen body into a size six space.

'Pulmonary edema,' she said of the pink foam in the dead boy's nasal and oral orifices. She traced the faint bruising on the lips, around the eyes. 'He was tuned up a bit before they threw the switch on him.'

I pointed to the vertical gash on his cheekbone. 'What do you make of that?'

'My guess? It's going to match the push-down lever on the toaster. Looks like they clocked this child with that Sunbeam *before* they chucked it into the tub.'

The boy's hand was resting on the bathtub's rim. Claire lifted it tenderly, turned it over. 'No rigor. Body's still warm and lividity is blanching. He's been dead less than twelve hours, probably less than six. No visible track-marks.' She ran her hands through the boy's matted hair, lifted his bruised top lip with her gloved fingers. 'He hadn't seen a dentist in a while. Could be a runaway.'

'Yeah,' I said. Then I must've gotten quiet for a minute or so.

'Whatcha thinking, honey?'

'That I've got another John Doe on my hands.'

I was remembering another teenage John Doe, a homeless kid who'd been murdered in a place like this when I was just getting started in Homicide. It was one of my worst cases ever and ten years later, the death still gnawed at me.

'I'll know more when I get this young man on my table,' Claire was saying when Jacobi stuck his head through the doorway again.

'The informant said the partial plate-number came off a Mercedes,' he said. 'A black one.'

A black Mercedes had been seen at the other electrocution murder. I grinned as I felt a surge of hope. Yes, I was making it personal. I was going to find the bastard who had killed these kids and I was going to put him away before he could do it again.

Chapter Three

A week had gone by since the nightmare at the Lorenzo Hotel. The Crime Lab was still sifting through the abundant detritus of Room 21 and our informant's three-digit partial license-plate number was either half wrong or a wild guess. As for me, I woke up every morning feeling pissed off and sad because this ugly case was nowhere.

The dead kids haunted me as I drove to Susie's for a get-together with the girls that evening. Susie's is a neighborhood café; a bright hot spot with walls sponge-painted in tropical colors, serving spicy but tasty Caribbean food.

Jill, Claire, Cindy and I had adopted this place as our sanctuary as well as our clubhouse. Our straight-shooting girl-talk, unhampered by rank or department lines, had often cut through weeks of bureaucratic b.s. Together, we'd broken cases wide open in this very spot.

I saw Claire and Cindy in 'our' booth at the back. Claire was laughing at something Cindy had said, which happens a lot because Claire has a great laugh and Cindy is a funny girl as well as a first-class investigative reporter for the *Chronicle*. Jill, of course, was gone.

'I want what you're having,' I said as I slid into the booth next to Claire. There was a pitcher of margaritas on the table and four glasses, two of them empty. I filled a glass and looked at my friends, feeling that almost magical connection that we'd forged because of all we'd gone through together.

'Looks like you need a transfusion,' Claire joked.

'I swear I do. Bring on the IV.' I took a gulp of the icy brew, snagged the newspaper that was beside Cindy's elbow and paged through until I found the story buried on page 17 of the Metro section, below the fold. INFO SOUGHT IN TENDERLOIN DISTRICT MURDERS.

'I guess it's a bigger story in my mind,' I said.

'Dead street people don't make page one,' Cindy said sympathetically.

'It's odd,' I told the girls. 'Actually, we have *too much* information. Seven thousand prints. Hair, fiber, a ton of useless DNA from a carpet that hadn't been hoovered since Nixon was a boy.' I stopped ranting long enough to pull the rubber band off my ponytail and shake out my hair. 'On the other hand, with all the potential snitches crawling through the Tenderloin District, all we have is one shitty lead.'

'It sucks, Linds,' said Cindy. 'Is the Chief on your ass?'

'Nope,' I said, tapping the tiny mention of the Tenderloin District Murders with my forefinger. 'As the killer says – nobody cares.'

'Ease up on yourself, honey,' Claire said. 'You'll get a bite into this thing. You always do.'

'Yeah, enough about all this. Jill would give me hell for whining.'

'She says "No problem",' Cindy cracked, pointing to Jill's empty seat. We lifted our glasses and clinked them together.

'To Jill,' we said in unison.

We filled Jill's glass and passed it around in remembrance of Jill Bernhardt, a spectacular Assistant District Attorney and our great friend, who'd been murdered only months ago. We missed her terribly and said so. In a while, our waitress, Loretta, brought a new pitcher of margaritas to replace the last.

'You're looking chirpy,' I said to Cindy, who jumped in with her news. She'd met a new guy, a hockey player who played for the Sharks in San Jose, and she was pretty pleased with herself. Claire and I started pumping her for details while the reggae band tuned up and soon we were all singing a Jimmy Cliff song, plinking our spoons against the glassware.

I was finally getting loose in Margarita-ville, when my Nextel rang. It was Jacobi.

'Meet me outside, Boxer. I'm a block away. We've got a lead on that Mercedes.'

What I should've said was 'Go without me, I'm off duty.' But it was *my* case and I had to go. I tossed some bills down on the table, blew kisses at the girls and bolted for the door. The killer was wrong about one thing. *Somebody cared.*

Chapter Four

I got in the passenger side door of our unmarked gray Crown Vic.

'Where to?' I asked Jacobi.

'The Tenderloin District,' he told me. 'A black Mercedes has been seen cruising around down there. Doesn't seem to fit in with the neighborhood.'

Inspector Warren Jacobi used to be my partner. He'd handled my promotion pretty well, all things considered; he has more than ten years on me, and seven more years in grade. We still partner up on special cases and even though he reports to me, I had to turn myself in.

'I had a few at Susie's.'

'Beers?'

'Margaritas.'

'How many is a few?' He swung his large head toward me.

'One and a half,' I said, not admitting to the third of the one I drank for Jill.

'You all right to come along?'

'Yeah, sure. I'm fine.'

'Don't think you're driving.'

'Did I ask?'

'There's a Thermos in back.'

'Coffee?'

'No, it's for you to take a piss in, if you've got to, because we don't have time for a pit-stop.'

I laughed and reached for the coffee. Jacobi was always good for a tasteless joke. As we crossed onto Sixth just south of Mission, I saw a car matching the description in a one-hour parking zone.

'Lookit, Warren. That's our baby.'

'Good catch, Boxer.'

Apart from the spike in my blood pressure, there was a whole lot of nothing happening on Sixth Street. It was a crumbling block of grimy storefronts and vacant SROs with blank plywood eyes. Aimless jay-walkers teetered and street sleepers snored under their piles of trash. The odd bum checked out the shiny black car.

'I hope to hell no one boosts that thing,' I said. 'Stands out like a Steinway in a junkyard.'

I called in our location and we took up our position a half-block away from the Mercedes. I punched the plate-number into our computer and this time gongs went off and it spit quarters. The car was registered to Dr Andrew Cabot of Telegraph Hill.

I called the Hall and asked Cappy to check out Dr Cabot on the NCIC database and call me back. Then Jacobi and I settled in for a long wait. Whoever Andrew Cabot was, he was definitely slumming. Normally, stakeouts are as fascinating as yesterday's oatmeal, but I was drumming the dash with my fingers. Where the hell was Andrew Cabot? What was he doing down here?

Twenty minutes later, a street-sweeping machine, a bright yellow, car-sized hulk, like an armadillo with flashing lights and honking back-up alerts, rolled right up onto the sidewalk, as it did every night. Derelicts rose up off the pavement to avoid the brushes. Papers swirled in the low light of the streetlamps.

The sweeper blocked our view for a few moments and when it had passed, Jacobi and I saw it at the same time: both the driver's side and the passenger side doors of the Mercedes were closing.

The car was on the move.

'Time to rock and roll,' said Jacobi.

We waited tense seconds as a maroon Camry got between us and our subject. I radioed Dispatch: 'We're following a black Mercedes, Queen Zebra Whiskey Two Six Charlie, heading north on Sixth toward Mission. Request units in the area – *aw, shit!*'

It was meant to be a quick pullover, but without warning or apparent cause, the driver of the Mercedes floored it, leaving Jacobi and me in the freshly washed dust.

Chapter Five

I watched in disbelief as the Mercedes' tail-lights became small red pinpoints, vanishing even further into the distance as the Camry backed carefully into a parking space, hemming us in.

I grabbed the mike and barked over the car's PA system, 'Clear the street! Move over now!'

'Fuck this,' said Jacobi. He flipped the switches that turned on the grill lights and the headlight strobes. And as our siren screamed into action, we tore past the Camry, clipping its tail-light.

'Good one, Warren.'

We blew across the intersection at Howard Street and I called in a Code 33 to keep the radio band free for the pursuit.

'We're going northbound on Sixth, south of Market in pursuit of a black Mercedes, attempting to pull it over. All units in the area, head into this vicinity . . .'

'Reason for the pursuit, Lieutenant?'

'Ongoing homicide investigation.'

Adrenaline flooded my body. We were going to land this baby and I prayed we wouldn't kill any bystanders in the process. Radio units sang out their locations as we crossed Mission against the light, doing at least sixty.

I pressed my foot against virtual brakes as Jacobi gunned our car across Market, the largest and busiest street in town, heavy now with buses, Muni trains and late commuter traffic.

'Hang a right!' I shouted to Jacobi.

The Mercedes veered onto Taylor, a three-way split in the road. We were two car lengths behind, but not close enough in the darkening night to get any sense of who was driving, who was riding shotgun.

We followed the car onto Ellis, heading west past the Hotel Coronado where the first electrocution murder had happened. This was the killer's turf, wasn't it? The bastard knew these streets as well as I did.

Cars hugged the curbs and we blew past cross streets at eighty, our siren blaring, speeding uphill at full throttle, going airborne for a few heart-stopping seconds before dropping onto the down-side curve of the incline; even so, we lost the Mercedes at Leavenworth as cars and pedestrians clogged the intersection.

I screamed into the mike again and thanked God when a radio car called in, 'We've got him in sight, Lieutenant. Black Mercedes heading west on Turk, going at seventy-five.' Another unit joined the chase at Hyde.

'I'm guessing he's headed toward Polk,' I said to Jacobi.

'My thoughts exactly.'

We deferred the main route to the squad cars, shot past Krim's and Kram's Palace of Fine Junk on the corner of Turk and picked up Polk heading north. There were about a dozen one-way alleys branching off Polk. I drilled each one of them with my eyes as we passed Willow, Ellis and Olive.

'That's him, dragging his butt,' I said, and pointed. The Mercedes wobbled on a blown right rear tire as it took the turn past the Mitchell Brothers' theater, then onto Larkin.

I grabbed the dash with both hands as Jacobi followed. The Mercedes lost control, caromed off a parked mini-van, flew up onto the pavement and charged a mailbox. Torn metal screamed as the mailbox punched the undercarriage of the car, which then came to rest with its nose pointing upwards at a forty-five degree angle, the driver's side canting down toward the gutter.

The hood popped and steam poured out as the radiator hose gave up the ghost. The stink of burned rubber and the candy-apple smell of anti-freeze permeated the air.

Jacobi halted our vehicle and we ran toward the Mercedes, guns in hand.

'Get your hands in the air!' I yelled. 'Do it now!'

I saw that both occupants were pinned by the airbags. As the airbags deflated I got my first look at their faces. They were white kids, maybe thirteen and fifteen, and they were terrified.

As Jacobi and I gripped our weapons with both hands and approached the Mercedes – the kids started bawling their hearts out.

Chapter Six

M y heart was booming almost audibly and now I was furious. Unless Dr Cabot was Doogie Howser's age, he wasn't in this car. These kids were idiots or speed freaks or car thieves – or maybe all three.

I kept my gun pointed at the driver's side window.

'Put your hands in the air. That's it. Touch the ceiling. *Both* of you.'

Tears were cascading down the driver's face and with a shock, I realized it was a girl. She had a short, pink-tipped haircut, no makeup, no face piercings; a *Seventeen* magazine version of punk that she hadn't quite pulled off. When she lifted her hands, I saw glass shards dusting her black T-shirt. Her name hung from a chain around her neck.

I admit I yelled at her. We'd just been through a chase that could have killed us all.

'What the *hell* did you think you were doing, Sara?'

'I'm sorrrry,' she wailed. 'It's just – I only have

a Learner's permit. What are you going to do to me?'

I was incredulous. 'You ran from the police because you don't have a driver's license? Are you insane?'

'He's going to kill us,' said the other kid, a lanky young boy hanging sideways from the over-the-shoulder seatbelt holding him into the passenger seat.

The boy had huge brown eyes and blond hair falling across them. His nose was bleeding; it was probably broken from the slam he'd taken from the airbag. Tears dribbled down his cheeks.

'Please don't tell,' he blubbered. 'Just say the car was stolen or something and let us go home. Please. Our dad's going to really kill us.'

'Why is that?' Jacobi asked sarcastically. 'He won't like the new hood ornament on his sixty-thousand-dollar car? Keep your hands where we can see them and get out real slow.'

'I can't. I'm stuh-uh-uck,' cried the boy. He wiped his nose with the back of his hand, smearing blood across his face. Then he threw up on the console.

Jacobi muttered, 'Aw, shit,' as our instincts to render aid took over.

We holstered our pistols. It took our combined strength to wrench open the ruined driver's side door. I reached in and shut off the ignition and after that, we eased the kids out of the vehicle and onto their feet.

'Let's see that Learner's permit, Sara,' I said. I

was wondering if her father was Dr Cabot and if the kids were afraid of him for good reason.

'It's here,' Sara said. 'In my wallet.'

Jacobi was calling for an ambulance when the young girl reached inside her jacket pocket and pulled out an object so unexpected and so chilling my blood froze.

I yelled, 'GUN!' a split second before she shot me.

Chapter Seven

Time seemed to slow, every second distinct from the one before it, but the truth is, everything happened in under a minute.

I flinched, turning sideways as I felt the bullet's hard punch to my left shoulder. Then another shot slammed into my thigh. Even as I struggled to understand, my legs buckled and I fell to the ground. I reached a hand out toward Jacobi and saw his face register shock.

I didn't lose consciousness. I saw the boy shoot Jacobi – *blam-blam-blam*. Then he walked over and kicked my partner in the head. I heard the girl say, 'C'mon, Sammy. Let's get out of here.'

I felt no pain, just rage. I was thinking as clearly as I had at any time in my life. They'd forgotten about me. I felt for my 9mm Glock, still at my waist, wrapped my hand around the grip and sat up.

'Drop your gun!' I shouted, pointing my weapon at Sara.

'Fuck you, bitch,' she yelled back. Her face was etched with fear as she leveled her .22 and squeezed

off three rounds. I heard shell casings ping against the sidewalk all around me.

It's notoriously hard to hit your target with a pistol, but I did what I was trained to do. I aimed for central mass, the center of her chest, and double tapped: *boom-boom*. Sara's face crumpled as she collapsed. I tried to get to my feet but only managed to rise to one knee.

'Drop it!' I screamed at the bloody-faced boy who was still holding a pistol in his hand. He pointed it at me.

'You shot my sister!'

I aimed, double-tapped again: *boom-boom*. The boy dropped his gun, his whole body going limp.

He cried out as he fell.

Chapter Eight

There was a terrible hushed silence on Larkin Street. Then sounds kicked in. A radio played rap in the middle distance. I heard the soft moans of the boy. I heard police sirens coming closer.

Jacobi wasn't moving at all. I called out to him, but he didn't answer. I unhooked my Nextel from my belt and to the best of my ability, I called in.

'Two officers down. Two civilians down. Need medical assistance. Send two ambulances. Now.'

The dispatcher was asking me questions: location, badge number, location again. 'Lieutenant, are you all right? Lindsay. Answer me.'

The sounds were fading in and out. I dropped the telephone and put my head down on the soft, soft pavement. I'd shot children. Children! I had seen their shocked faces as they went down. Oh, my God, what had I done?

I felt hot blood pooling under my neck and around my leg. I played the whole thing over in my mind, this time throwing the kids against the car. Cuffing them. Frisking them. Being smart. Being competent!

We'd been inexcusably stupid, and now we were all going to die. Mercifully, darkness closed over me and I shut my eyes.

PART TWO

Unscheduled Vacation Time

Chapter Nine

A man sat quietly in a nondescript gray car on Ocean Colony Road in the nicest section of Half Moon Bay, California. He wasn't the kind of man people would notice, even though he was out of place here. Even though he had no legitimate business surveilling the people who lived in the white colonial house with the pricey cars in the driveway.

The Watcher held a camera that was no bigger than a book of matches up to his eye. It was a wonderful device with a gig of memory and a 10x zoom.

He zoomed in and pressed the shutter, capturing the family moving behind the kitchen window, downing their wholesome multi-grain cereal, having morning chit-chat in their breakfast nook.

At 8:06 on the dot, Caitlin O'Malley opened the front door. She was wearing a school uniform, a purple knapsack and two watches, one on each wrist. Her long auburn hair positively shone.

The Watcher took Caitlin's picture as the teenager got into the passenger side of the black

Lexus SUV in the driveway and soon he heard the faint sounds of Rock FM.

Placing his camera on the dash, the Watcher took his blue notebook and a fine-tip pen from the center console and made notes in a careful, nearly calligraphic hand.

It was essential to get it all down. The Truth demanded it.

At 8:09 the front door opened again. Dr Ben O'Malley was wearing a lightweight gray wool suit and a red bow tie that cinched the collar of his starched white shirt. He turned to his wife, Lorelei, pecked her on the lips and then strode down the front path.

Everyone was right on time.

The tiny camera captured the images. *Zzzzt. Zzzzt. Zzzzzt.*

The doctor carried a bag of trash to the blue recycling bin at the curb. He sniffed the air and looked up and down the street, sweeping his eyes across the gray car and its occupant without pausing. Then he joined his daughter in the SUV. Moments later, Dr O'Malley backed out onto Ocean Colony Road, and headed north toward Cabrillo Highway.

The Watcher completed his notes, then returned the notebook, the pen and the camera to the console.

He had seen them now; the girl in her freshly pressed uniform and clean white knee-socks, lots of spirit showing in her pretty face. This so touched the Watcher that tears gathered in his eyes. She was so real, so different from her father, the doctor, in his bland, everyday-citizen's disguise.

But there was one thing he did like about Dr Ben O'Malley. He liked his surgical precision. The Watcher was counting on that.

He just hated to be surprised.

Chapter Ten

A voice in my head yelled, 'Hey! *Sara!*' I came awake with a jolt and reached for my gun, only to find that I couldn't move at all. A dark face loomed over me, lit from behind with a hazy white glow.

'The Sugar Plum Fairy,' I blurted.

'I've been called worse,' she laughed. It was Claire. I was on *her* table, and that meant I was a goner for sure.

'Claire? Can you hear me?'

'Loud and clear, baby.' She hugged me gently, wrapping me with a mother's embrace. 'Welcome back.'

'Where am I?'

'San Francisco General. Recovery room.'

The fog was lifting. I remembered the dark chill of Larkin Street. Those kids. *Jacobi was down!*

'Jacobi,' I said, reaching out to Claire with my eyes. 'Jacobi didn't make it.'

'He's in the ICU, honey. He's fighting hard.' Claire smiled at me. 'Look who's here, Lindsay. Just turn your head.'

It took tremendous effort, but I rolled my heavy head to the right, and his handsome face came into view. He hadn't shaved and his eyelids were weighted with fatigue and worry, but just seeing Joe Molinari made my heart sing like a flippin' canary.

'Joe. You're supposed to be in D.C.'

'I'm right here, sweetie. I came as soon as I heard.'

When he kissed me, I felt his tears on my cheeks. I tried to tell him that I felt all broken inside.

'Joe, she's dead. Oh God, it was a horrible screw-up.'

'Honey, the way I hear it, you had no other choice.'

Joe's rough cheek brushed mine.

'My pager number is right by the phone. Lindsay? Do you hear me? I'll be back in the morning,' he said.

'What, Joe? What did you say?'

'Try to get some sleep, Lindsay.'

'Sure, Joe. I will . . .'

Chapter Eleven

A nurse named Heather Grace, a saint if ever there was one, had secured a wheelchair for me. I sat in it beside Jacobi's bed as the late-afternoon light poured through the window in the ICU and pooled on the blue linoleum floor. Two bullets had tunneled through his torso. One had collapsed a lung, the other had punctured a kidney, and the kick he'd taken to the head had broken his nose and turned his face a brilliant shade of eggplant.

This was my third visit in as many days and though I'd done my best to cheer him, Jacobi's mood remained unrelentingly dark. I was watching him sleep when his swollen eyes flickered open to slits.

'Hey, Warren.'

'Hey, Slick.'

'How're you feeling?'

'Like the world's biggest horse's ass.' He coughed painfully, and I winced in sympathy.

'Take it easy, bud.'

'It sucks, Boxer.'

'I know.'

'I can't stop thinking about it. Dreaming about it.' He paused, touched the bandages over his nose. 'That kid popping me while I stood there holding my dick.'

'Um. I think it was your cell phone, Jacobi.'

He didn't laugh. That was bad.

'No excuse for it.'

'Our hearts were in the right place.'

'Hearts? Shit. Next time, less heart, more brains.'

He was right, of course. I was taking it all in, nodding, adding a few strokes in my own mind. Like, would I ever feel right with a gun in my hand again? Would I hesitate when I shouldn't? Shoot before thinking? I poured Jacobi a glass of water. Stuck in a striped straw.

'I blew it. I should've cuffed that kid—'

'Don't even start, Boxer. It's *we* shoulda – and you probably saved my life.'

There was a flash of movement in the doorway. Chief Anthony Tracchio's hair was slicked across his head, his off-duty clothes were plain and neat and he was gripping a box of candy. He looked like a teenager coming to pick up his first date. Well, not really.

'Jacobi. Boxer. Glad I caught you two together. How ya' doing – okay?'

Tracchio wasn't a bad guy, and he'd been good to me – still, ours was no love affair. He bounced a bit on his toes, then approached Jacobi's bed.

'I've got news.'

He had our full attention.

'The Cabot kids left prints at the Lorenzo.' A light danced around in his eyes. 'And Sam Cabot confessed.'

'Holy shit. Is this true?' Jacobi wheezed.

'On my mother's head. The kid told a nurse that he and his sis were playing a game with those runaways. They called it "a bullet or a bath".'

'The nurse will testify?' I asked.

'Yes, indeed. Swore to me herself.'

'"A bullet or a bath". Those little fuckers,' Jacobi snorted. 'A game.'

'Yeah, well, that game's over. We even found notebooks and collections of crime stories in the girl's bedroom at home. She was obsessed with homicides. Listen, you two get well, okay? Don't worry about nothin'. Oh, and this is from the Squad,' he said, handing me the Ghirardelli chocolates and a Get Well card with a lot of signatures. 'We're prouda ya both.'

We talked for another minute or so, passing along thanks to our friends at the Hall of justice. When he was gone, I reached out and took Jacobi's hand. Having almost died together had forged an intimacy between us that was deeper than friendship.

'Well, the kids were dirty,' I said.

'Yeah. Break out the champagne.'

I couldn't argue with him. That the Cabot kids were murderers didn't change the horror of the shooting. And it didn't change the notion I'd been harboring for days.

'I'll tell you something, Jacobi. I'm thinking of giving it up. Quitting the job.'

'C'mon. You're talking to *me*.'

'I'm serious.'

'You're not going to quit, Boxer.'

I straightened a fold in his blanket, then pushed the call button so a nurse would come and roll me back to my room.

'Sleep tight, partner.'

'I know: "Don't worry about nothin'".'

I leaned over and kissed his stubbly cheek for the first time ever. I know it hurt to do it, but Jacobi actually smiled.

Chapter Twelve

It was a day that had been ripped from the pages of a child's coloring book. Bright yellow sun. Birds tweeting and the flowery smell of summer everywhere. Even the pollarded trees on the hospital green had sprouted flamboyant hands of leaves since I'd last been outside three weeks before.

A lovely day, for sure, but somehow I couldn't reconcile life-as-usual with my creeping feeling that all was not well. Was it paranoia – or was another shoe about to drop?

My younger sister Cat's green Subaru Forester cruised around the elliptical driveway at the hospital entrance and I could see my nieces waving their hands and bouncing up and down on the seats. Once I was strapped into the passenger seat, my mood lifted. I even started singing 'What a day for a daydream . . .'

'Aunt Lindsay, I didn't know you could sing,' six-year-old Brigid piped up from the back seat.

'Sure I can. I played my guitar and sang my way through college, didn't I, Cat?'

'We used to call her Top Forty,' said my sister. 'She was like a human Juke box.'

'What's a joooot box?' asked Meredith, age two and a half.

We laughed and I explained, 'It's like a giant CD player that plays records,' and then I explained what records were, too.

I rolled down the window and let the breeze blow back my long yellow hair as we drove east on Twenty-second Street toward the rows of pretty pastel two- and three-story Victorian houses that stair-stepped up and across the ridgeline of Potrero Hill.

Cat asked me about my plans and I gave her a big wide-open shrug. I told her I was benched pending the IAB investigation of the shooting and that I had a whole pile of 'injured on duty' time I might put to good use. Clean out my closets. Sort out those shoeboxes full of old photos.

'Here's a better idea. Stay at our house and recuperate,' Cat said. 'We're off to Aspen in another week. Use the house, please! Penelope would love your company.'

'Who's Penelope?'

The little girls giggled behind me.

'Whooooooo's Penelope?'

'She's our friend,' they chorused.

'Let me think about it,' I said to my sister as we turned left onto Mississippi and pulled up to the blue Victorian apartment house I call home.

Cat was helping me out of the car when Cindy loped down the front steps with Sweet Martha running in front of her.

My euphoric doggy almost knocked me over, licking me and woofing so loudly I only hoped Cindy heard me thank her for taking care of my girl.

I waved goodbye to everyone and bumped up the stairs fantasizing about a hot soak in my shower and a long sleep in my own bed – when the doorbell rang.

'Okay, okay,' I grumbled. My guess? I was getting flowers.

I clumped down the stairs again and flung open the door. A young stranger wearing khakis and a Santa Clara sweatshirt stood at the threshold with an envelope in his hand. I didn't believe his cheese-eating smile for a second.

'Lindsay Boxer?'

'Nope. Wrong address,' I said perkily. 'I think she lives over on Kansas.'

The young man grinned – and I heard the clatter of that other shoe dropping.

Chapter Thirteen

'Kill,' I said to Martha. She looked up at me and wagged her tail. Trained border collies respond to many commands, but 'Kill' isn't one of them. I took the envelope from the kid who backed away with his hands in the air. I slammed the door shut with my cane.

Upstairs in my apartment, I took what was clearly a legal notice out to the glass-and-tubular steel table on my terrace, which had a staggering view of San Francisco Bay. Carefully, I eased my sorry butt into a chair. Martha settled her head onto my good thigh and I stroked her as I stared out across the hypnotic swells of glinting water.

The minutes ticked by and when I couldn't stand it any longer, I opened the envelope and unfolded the document.

Legalese jumped all around the Writ, Summons and Complaint as I tried to find the point of it. It wasn't that hard. Dr Andrew Cabot was suing me for 'wrongful death, excessive use of force and police misconduct'. He was asking for a preliminary hearing in a week's time in order to attach my apartment, my bank account and any worldly goods I might attempt to hide before the trial.

Cabot was suing me!

I felt hot and cold at the same time as a sense of profound injustice roared through me. I replayed the whole scene again. Yes, I'd made a mistake by trusting those kids, but excessive force? Police misconduct? Wrongful death?

Those murdering kids had guns.

They'd shot me and Jacobi while our weapons were holstered. I'd ordered them to drop their guns before I returned fire! Jacobi was my witness. This was a clear-cut case of self-defense. Crystal clear!

But I was still scared. No, actually I was petrified.

I could see the headlines now. The public would set up a howl; sweet-faced little kids gunned down by a cop. The press would lap it up. I would be pilloried on Court TV.

In a minute or so, I would have to call Tracchio, get legal representation, marshal my forces. But I couldn't do anything yet. I was frozen in my chair, paralyzed by a growing notion that I'd forgotten something important.

Something that could really hurt me.

Chapter Fourteen

I woke up in a sweat, having thrashed my Egyptian cotton sheets to a fine froth. I took a couple of Tylenol for the pain and a sky-blue Valium the shrink had given me, then I stared at the pattern the streetlights cast on the ceiling.

I rolled carefully onto my uninjured side and looked at the clock: 12:15. I'd only been asleep for an hour and I had the feeling I was in for a really long night.

'Martha. Here, girl.'

My pal jumped onto the bed and settled into the fetal hollow I made with my body. In a minute, her legs twitched as she herded sheep in her sleep while my brain continued to churn with Tracchio's new, neatly-hedged version of 'Don't worry about nothin'.'

To wit:

'You're gonna need two attorneys, Boxer. Mickey Sherman will represent you on behalf of the SFPD, but you'll need your own lawyer to defend you in case . . .

Well, in case you've done something outside the scope of your job.'

'Then what? I'm on my own?'

I was hoping the drugs would tumble my mind off the hard edge of consciousness into the comfort of slumber, but it didn't happen. Mentally, I ticked off the remains of the day; the meetings I'd set up with Sherman and *my* lawyer, a young woman called Ms Castellano. Molinari had recommended her highly – and it means something when you get a rave review from the deputy director of Homeland Security.

Once again I concluded that I was taking good care of myself, given the circumstances. But the coming week was going to be hell. I needed something to look forward to.

I hadn't been to Cat's house since she moved there right after her divorce two years ago, but the images of where she lived were unforgettable. Only forty minutes south of San Francisco, Half Moon Bay was a little bit of paradise. There was a crescent-shaped bay with a sandy beach, redwood forests, and a panoramic ocean view and it was warm enough in June to relax on Cat's sun-porch and bleach the ugly pictures from my brain.

I simply couldn't wait until morning. I called my sister at quarter to one. Her voice was husky with sleep.

'Lindsay, of course I meant it. Come whenever you like. You know where the keys are.'

I fixed my thoughts on Half Moon Bay, but every time I nodded off dreaming of paradise, I snapped awake, my heart racing like a cyclotron. Fact is, my looming court date had taken hold of my mind and I couldn't think about anything else.

Chapter Fifteen

Thunderclouds grazed the roof of the Civic Center Courthouse at 400 McAllister and a lashing rain soaked the streets. Having dispensed with my cane this morning, I leaned against Mickey Sherman, attorney for the city of San Francisco, as we climbed the slick courthouse steps. I was leaning on him in more ways than one.

We passed Dr Andrew Cabot and his lawyer, Mason Broyles, who were giving an interview to the press beneath a cluster of black umbrellas. The only blessing was that there were no cameras pointed at me.

I grabbed a quick look at Mason Broyles as we passed. He had hooded eyes, flowing black hair, and a wolfish curl to his lip. I heard him say something about 'Lieutenant Boxer's savagery' and I knew he was going to gut me if he could. As for Dr Cabot, grief had turned his face to a mask of stone.

Mickey pulled open one of the heavy steel and etched-glass doors and we entered the foyer of the courthouse. Mickey was a cool old hand, respected for his doggedness, street smarts and considerable charm. He loathed losing and rarely did.

'Look, Lindsay,' he said, furling his umbrella, 'he's grandstanding because we have a great case. Don't let him get to you. You have a lot of friends out there.'

I nodded, but I was thinking about how I'd put Sam Cabot in a wheelchair for life and his sister in the Cabot family plot for eternity. Their father didn't need my apartment or my pathetic little bank account. He wanted to destroy me. And he'd hired just the guy to do it.

Mickey and I took the back stairs and slipped into Courtroom C on the first floor. In a few minutes it was all going to happen inside this small, plain room with gray-painted walls and a window looking out onto an alley.

I'd stuck an SFPD pin in the lapel of my navy-blue suit so I'd look as official as possible without wearing a uniform. As I took a seat beside him, I reviewed Mickey's instructions. 'When Broyles questions you, don't give long explanations. "Yes, sir; no, sir." That's it. He's going to try to provoke you to show that you've got a quick temper and that's why you pulled the trigger.'

I had never thought of myself as an angry person, but I was angry now. It had been a good shoot. A good shoot! The DA had cleared me! And now I felt like a target again. As the rows of seats filled with spectators, I was conscious of the chatter building behind me.

That's the cop who shot the kids. That's her.

Suddenly there was a reassuring hand on my shoulder. I turned and my eyes watered when I saw Joe. I put my hand over his and at the same time my eyes caught those of my other lawyer, a young Japanese-American woman with the unlikely name of Yuki Castellano. We exchanged 'hellos' as she took her place beside Mickey.

The rumble in the courtroom cut out suddenly as the bailiff called out, 'All rise.'

We stood as Her Honor Rosa Algierri took the bench. Judge Algierri could dismiss the complaint and I could walk out of the courtroom, heal my body and soul, resume my life. Or she could send the case forward and I'd be facing a trial that could cost me everything I cared about.

'You okay, Lindsay?'

'Never better,' I said to Mickey.

He caught the sarcasm and touched my hand. A minute later, my heart started hammering as Mason Broyles rose to make his case against me.

Chapter Sixteen

Cabot's lawyer shot his cuffs and stood silently for so long you could've twanged the tension in the room like a guitar string. Someone in the gallery coughed nervously.

'The plaintiff calls Chief Medical Examiner, Dr Claire Washburn,' said Broyles at last, and my best friend took the stand for the plaintiffs.

I wanted to wave, smile, wink – something – but of course all I could do was watch. Broyles warmed up with a few easy lobs across the plate, but from then on, it was fast balls and knuckle curves all the way.

'On the evening of May tenth did you perform an autopsy on Sara Cabot?' Broyles asked.

'I did.'

'What can you tell us about her injuries?'

All eyes were fixed on Claire as she flipped through a leather-bound notepad before speaking again.

'I found two gunshot wounds to the chest, pretty close together. Gunshot wound A was a penetrating gunshot wound situated on the left upper/outer chest six inches below the left shoulder and two and a half inches left of the anterior midline.'

Claire's testimony was crucial, but still my mind drifted out of the courtroom and into the past. I saw myself standing in a dusky patch of streetlight on Larkin Street. I watched Sara take her gun out of her jacket and shoot me. I fell, rolled into a prone position.

'Drop your gun!'

'Fuck you, bitch.'

I fired my gun twice and Sara fell only yards from where I lay. I'd killed that girl and although I was innocent of the charges against me, my conscience was guilty, guilty, guilty.

I listened to Claire's testimony as she described the second shot, which had gone through Sara's sternum.

'It's what we call a K-five,' said Claire. 'It went through the pericardial sac, continued on through the heart and terminated in thoracic vertebra number four, where I retrieved a semi-jacketed, copper-colored, partially deformed, medium-sized projectile.'

'Is this consistent with an eight millimetre bullet?'

'It is.'

'Thank you, Dr Washburn. I'm finished with this witness, Your Honor.'

Mickey put his hands flat on the defense table and came to his feet.

'Dr Washburn, did Sara Cabot die instantly?'

'I'd say so. Within a heartbeat or two. Both of those gunshot wounds perforated the heart.'

'Uh-huh. And, Doctor, had the deceased recently fired a gun?'

'Yes. I saw some darkening at the base of her index finger that would be consistent with cylinder flare.'

'How do you know that that's gunshot residue?'

'I photographed that smudging, documented it and did a gunshot-wound residue test, which was submitted to the laboratory and came back positive.'

'Could the deceased have shot Lieutenant Boxer after she herself was shot?'

'I don't see how a dead girl could shoot anyone, Mr Sherman.'

Mickey nodded. 'Did you also note the trajectory of those gunshot wounds, Dr Washburn?'

'I did. They were fired upward at angles of forty-seven and forty-nine degrees.'

'So to be absolutely clear, Doctor: Sara Cabot shot Lieutenant Boxer first – and the Lieutenant returned fire upwards from where she lay on the ground?'

'In my opinion, yes, that's how it happened.'

'Would you call that "excessive force" or "wrongful death" or "police misconduct"?'

The judge sustained Broyles's outraged objection. Mickey thanked Claire and dismissed her. He was smiling as he came toward me. My muscles relaxed and I even returned Mickey's smile. But the hearing was just beginning.

I felt a shock of fear when I saw the look in

Mason Broyles's eyes. You could only describe it as anticipatory. He couldn't wait to get his next witness on the stand.

Chapter Seventeen

'Please state your name,' Broyles said to a petite brunette in her early thirties.

'Betty D'Angelo.'

Her dark eyes behind her large horn-rimmed glasses darted quickly over to me, then back to Broyles again. I looked at Mickey Sherman and shrugged. To the best of my knowledge, I'd never seen this woman before.

'And what is your position?'

'I'm a Registered Nurse at San Francisco General.'

'Were you on duty in the ER on the evening and night of May tenth?'

'I was.'

'Did you have occasion to take blood from the defendant, Lindsay Boxer?'

'Yes.'

'And why was blood drawn?'

'We were prepping her for surgery, for extraction of the bullets and so on. It was a life-threatening situation. She was losing a lot of blood.'

'Yeah, I know, I know,' Broyles said, batting away

her comment like a housefly. 'Tell us about the blood test.'

'It's normal procedure to take blood. We had to match her up for transfusions.'

'Ms D'Angelo, I'm looking at Lieutenant Boxer's medical report from that night. It's quite a voluminous report.' Broyles plopped a fat stack of paper on the witness-stand and stabbed at it with a forefinger. 'Is this your signature?'

'Yes.'

'I'd like you to look at this highlighted line right here.'

The witness tossed her head as if she smelled something bad. Emergency Room staff often feel part of the cop team and will try to protect us. I didn't get it, but this nurse plainly wanted to duck Broyles's questions.

'Can you tell me what this is?' Broyles asked the witness.

'This? You mean the ETOH?'

'That stands for ethyl alcohol content, is that right?'

'Yes. That's what it stands for.'

'What does .067 mean?'

'Ahh . . . That means the blood alcohol level was sixty-seven milligrams per deciliter.'

Broyles smiled and lowered his voice to a purr. 'In this case, it refers to the blood alcohol level in Lieutenant Boxer's system, doesn't it?'

'Well, yes, that's correct.'

'Ms D'Angelo, .067 – that's drunk, isn't that right?'

'We do refer to it as "under the influence," but—'

'Yes or no?'

'Yes.'

'I have nothing further,' said Broyles.

I felt like my head had been struck with a sledge-hammer. *My God, those fucking margaritas at Susie's.*

The blood drained from my face and I almost fainted.

Mickey turned to me, the expression on his face demanding, *'Why didn't you tell me?'*

I looked at my attorney, open-mouthed and absolutely sick with remorse.

I could hardly bear Mickey's look of incredulity as, armed with nothing but his wits, he leaped to his feet and approached the witness.

Chapter Eighteen

There were only twelve rows of seats in Courtroom C in the San Francisco Civic Center Courthouse, and no jury box. It would have been hard to find a courtroom more intimate than this one. I don't think anyone breathed during Mickey's walk to the witness-stand.

He greeted Ms D'Angelo, who looked relieved to be off the hot seat Mason Broyles had fired up for her.

'I only have a couple of questions,' he said. 'It's common practice to use ethyl alcohol swabs to clean the wounds, isn't it? Couldn't that alcohol have been confused with the blood alcohol?'

Betty D'Angelo looked like she wanted to cry. 'Well, um, we use betadine to swab the wounds. We don't use alcohol.'

Mickey brushed off the response and turned to the judge. He asked for a recess and it was granted. The reporters bolted for the doors and in the relative privacy, I apologized with all my heart.

'I feel like a real schmuck,' he said, not unkindly.

'I saw that medical report and I didn't notice the ETOH.'

'I just completely forgot until now,' I said. 'I must have blanked it out.'

I told Mickey that I had been off duty when Jacobi called me at Susie's. I listed what I had had to drink, and said that if I wasn't completely straight when I got into the car, the adrenaline rush of the chase that followed had been completely sobering.

'You usually have a couple of drinks with dinner?' Mickey asked me.

'Yes. A few times a week.'

'Well, there you go. Drinks at dinner were an ordinary occurrence for you and .067 is borderline anyway. Then comes a major trauma. You were shot. You were in pain. You coulda died. You killed someone – and that's what you've been obsessing about. Half of all shooting victims block out the incident entirely. You've done fine, considering what you've been through.'

I let out a sigh. 'What now?'

'Well, at least we know what they have. Maybe they'll put Sam Cabot on the stand, and if they give me a chance at that little bastard, we'll come out on top.'

The courtroom filled once more and Mickey went to work. A ballistics expert testified that the slugs taken from my body matched those fired from Sara Cabot's gun, and we had Jacobi's videotaped deposition from his hospital bed. He was my witness on the scene.

Although in obvious pain from his gut wound, Jacobi testified about the night of 10 May. First, he described the car crash.

'I was calling for an ambulance when I heard the shots,' he said. 'I turned and saw Lieutenant Boxer go down. Sara Cabot shot her twice and Boxer didn't have a gun in her hand. Then the boy shot me with a revolver.' Jacobi's hand gingerly spanned his taped torso. 'That's the last I remember before the lights went out.'

Jacobi's account was good, but it wouldn't be enough to overturn the margaritas.

Only one person could help me now. I was wearing her clothes, sitting in her chair. I was queasy and my wounds throbbed. I honestly didn't know if I could save myself or if I would make everything worse.

My lawyer turned his warm brown eyes on me. *Steady, Lindsay.*

I wobbled to my feet as I heard my name echo through the courtroom.

Mickey Sherman had called me to the stand.

Chapter Nineteen

I'd been a witness dozens of times during my career, but this was the first time I'd had to defend *myself*. All my years of protecting the public, and now I had a bull's-eye on my back. I was raging inside, but I couldn't let it show.

I got to my feet, swore to God on an old worn Bible, and placed my fate in the hands of my attorney.

Mickey cut straight to the chase. 'Lindsay, were you drunk on the night of May tenth?'

The judge broke in: 'Mr Sherman, please don't address your client by her first name.'

'Okay. Lieutenant, were you drunk that night?'

'No.'

'Okay, let's back up. Were you on duty that night?'

'No. My shift was over at five p.m.'

Mickey took me through the events of that night in excruciating detail and I told it all. I described the drinks I'd had at Susie's, and explained to the court about getting the call from Jacobi. I stated that I'd told Jacobi the truth when I'd said that I was 'good to go along that night.'

When Mickey asked why I'd responded to the call when I was off duty, I said, 'I'm a cop twenty-four hours a day. When my partner needs me, I'm there.'

'Did you locate the car in question?' Mickey asked me.

'We did.'

'And what happened then?'

'The car took off at high speed and we chased it. Eight minutes later, the car went out of control and crashed.'

'After the crash, when you saw that Sara and Sam Cabot were in medical distress, were you afraid of them?'

'No. They were kids. I figured they'd stolen the car or made some other bad decision. Happens every day.'

'So what did you do?'

'Inspector Jacobi and I put away our guns and tried to render aid.'

'At what point did you pull out your guns again?'

'After Inspector Jacobi and I had both been shot and after warning the suspects to drop their weapons.'

'Thank you, Lindsay. I have no further questions.'

I reviewed my testimony and gave myself a passing grade. I looked across the room and saw Joe smile and nod even as Mickey turned away from me.

'Your witness,' he said to Mason Broyles.

Chapter Twenty

A silence stretched between me and Broyles, who sat staring at me for so long I wanted to scream. It was an old interrogator's trick and he had perfected it. Voices rippled across the small gray room until the judge banged her gavel and jolted Broyles into action.

I looked straight into his eyes as he approached.

'Tell us, Lieutenant Boxer, what are the proper police procedures for a felony stop?'

'Approach with guns drawn, get the suspects out of their car, disarm them, cuff them, get the situation safely under control.'

'And is that what you did, Lieutenant?'

'We did approach with guns drawn, but the occupants couldn't get out of the car without assistance. We put our guns away in order to free them from the vehicle.'

'You violated police procedures, didn't you?'

'We had an obligation to render aid.'

'Yes, I know. You were trying to be kind to the

"kids". But you're admitting that you didn't follow police procedures, correct?'

'Look, I made a *mistake*,' I blurted. 'But those kids were bleeding and vomiting. The car could've caught fire—'

'Your Honor?'

'Please limit your answers to the question, Lieutenant Boxer.'

I sat back hard in the chair. I'd seen Broyles operate many times before in the courtroom and recognized his genius for finding his opponent's pressure point.

He'd just fingered mine.

I was still blaming myself for not cuffing those kids, and Jacobi, with more than twenty years on the force, had been suckered, too. But, Christ, you can only do what you can do.

'I'll rephrase that,' Broyles said offhandedly. 'Do you always try to follow police procedures?'

'Yes.'

'So, what's the police policy about being intoxicated on the job?'

'*Objection!*' Mickey shouted, leaping to his feet. 'There's evidence that the witness had been drinking, but there's no evidence that she was *intoxicated*.'

Broyles smirked and turned his back to me. 'I have nothing further, Your Honor.'

I felt huge wet circles under my arms. I stepped down from the witness-stand, forgetting about my leg injury until the pain called it sharply to my attention. I limped back to my seat, feeling worse than I had before.

I turned to Mickey, who smiled his encouragement, but I knew the smile was fake.

His brow was corrugated with worry.

Chapter Twenty-One

I was shaken by the way Mason Broyles had flipped the events of 10 May and placed the blame on me. He was good at his job, that slime, and it took all my strength to park my face in neutral and sit calmly as Broyles made his closing argument.

'Your Honor,' he said, 'Sara Cabot is dead because Lindsay Boxer killed her. And Sam Cabot, age thirteen, is in a wheelchair for life. The defendant admits that she didn't follow proper police procedures. Granted, there may have been some misdoing on the part of my clients, but we don't expect juveniles to exercise good judgment. Police officers, however, are trained to deal with all manner of crises and the defendant couldn't handle a crisis, because she was drunk.

'Simply put, if Lieutenant Boxer had properly performed the duties of her job, this tragedy wouldn't have occurred and we wouldn't be here today.'

Broyles's speech outraged me, but I had to admit

he was persuasive, and had I been sitting in the gallery instead of the dock, I might have seen it his way. By the time Mickey stood to mount his closing argument, my blood was pounding so hard in my ears it was as though a rock band were jamming inside my head.

'Your Honor, Lieutenant Lindsay Boxer didn't put loaded guns into the hands of Sara and Samuel Cabot,' Mickey said, his voice ringing with indignation. 'They did that themselves. They shot unarmed police officers without provocation and my client returned fire in pure self-defense. The only thing she's guilty of is being too kind to citizens who showed her no kindness in return.

'In all fairness, Your Honor, this suit should be dismissed and this fine officer allowed to return to her duties without blame or blemish to her distinguished service record.'

Mickey finished his summation sooner than I had expected. A gap opened behind his last ringing words and my fear poured in. As he sat down beside me, the courtroom filled with slight mouse-like stirrings; papers rustling, the clicking of laptop keys, bodies shifting in their chairs.

I gripped Mickey's hand under the table and I even prayed. *Dear God, let her dismiss the charges, please.*

The judge pushed her glasses up onto the bridge of her nose, but I couldn't read her face. When she spoke, she did so concisely and in a weary tone.

'I believe the defendant did everything she could to salvage a situation gone horribly wrong,' said

Judge Algierri. 'But the alcohol bothers me. A life has been lost. Sara Cabot is dead. There's enough evidence here to merit sending this case to a jury.'

Chapter Twenty-Two

I went rigid with shock as the trial date was set for a few weeks into the future. Everyone stood as the judge left the courtroom, and then the mob closed in around me. I saw blue uniforms at the edge of the throng, eyes not quite meeting mine, and then clumps of microphones were pushed up to my face. I still held Mickey's hand.

We should have gotten a dismissal.

We should have won.

Mickey helped me to my feet and I followed him as he cut through the crowd. Joe's hand was on the small of my back as the three of us and Yuki Castellano exited the courtroom and made for the stairs. We stopped in the ground-floor stairwell.

'When you walk outside, hold your head up,' Mickey advised me. 'When they scream, "Why did you kill that girl?" just walk slowly to the car. Don't smile, don't smirk, and don't let the media beat you. You did nothing wrong. Go home and don't answer your phone. I'll stop by your house later.'

The rain had ceased by the time we stepped out

of the courthouse into the dull, late afternoon. I shouldn't have been shocked to see that hundreds of people had gathered outside the courthouse to see the cop who'd shot and killed a teenage girl.

Mickey and Yuki split away from us to address the press, and I knew that Mickey's thoughts were turning now to how he was going to defend the SFPD and the City of San Francisco.

Joe and I walked through the jostling, yelling crowd toward the alley where the car was waiting. I heard a chant, *'Child killer, child killer,'* and questions were lobbed at me like stones.

'What were you thinking, Lieutenant?'

'How did you feel when you shot those kids?'

I knew the faces of the television reporters – Carlos Vega, Sandra Dunne, Kate Morley, all of whom had interviewed me when I'd been a witness for the prosecution. I did my best to ignore them now and to look past the rolling cameras and the jouncing placards reading *Guilty of Police Brutality*.

I kept my eyes focused just ahead and my steps matching Joe's until we reached the black sedan.

As soon as the doors thunked closed, the driver put the car into reverse and backed out fast onto Polk Street. Then he wheeled the car around and pointed it toward Potrero Hill.

'He murdered me in there,' I said to Joe once we were under way.

'The judge saw you, saw the kind of person you are. It's too bad she felt she had to do what she did.'

'Cops are watching me, Joe – cops who work for

me and who expect me to do the right thing. I'm supposed to keep their respect after this?'

'Lindsay, the right-minded people in this city are rooting for you. You're a good person, damn it, and a fine cop.'

Joe's words got to me in a way that Mason Broyles's vicious barbs had not. I put my head on his nice blue shirt and let the pent-up tears come as he held and comforted me.

'I'm okay,' I said at last. I mopped up with the hanky he offered me. 'It's my hay fever. A high pollen count always makes me weep.'

Molinari laughed and gave me a good hug as the car climbed homeward. We crossed Twentieth Street and the staggered rows of pastel Victorian houses came into view.

'I'd quit my job right now,' I said, 'but that would only make it look like I'm guilty.'

'Those murdering kids, Lindsay. No jury's going to find in their favor. There's just no way.'

'Promise?'

Joe squeezed me again, but he didn't answer. I knew that he believed in me completely, but he wouldn't make a promise that he couldn't keep.

'You going back right now?' I asked at last.

'I wish I didn't have to. But yeah, I need to go.'

Joe's work for the government rarely allowed him to break away to be with me.

'Someday I'll have a life,' he said tenderly.

'Yeah, me too.'

True? Or a dumb fantasy? I put my head back on Joe's shoulder. We held hands and savored what could have been our last moments together for weeks, not speaking again until we kissed and murmured goodbyes at my doorstep.

Upstairs, in the quiet of my apartment, I realized how emotionally depleted I was. My muscles ached from holding myself together, and there was no relief in sight. Instead of freeing me from this assault on my reputation and my belief in myself, the hearing had only been a dress rehearsal for another trial.

I felt like a tiring swimmer, way out past the breakers. I got into my big, soft bed with Martha, pulled the blankets up to my chin and let sleep roll over me like a thick fog.

Chapter Twenty-Three

A shaft of early-morning sunlight split the clouds as I tossed a last suitcase into the back of the car, strapped in and backed the Explorer out of my driveway. I was hot to get out of town and so was Martha, who had her head out of the passenger-side window and was already creating quite a breeze with her wagging tail.

The stop-and-go rush-hour traffic was typical for a weekday, so I pointed the Explorer in a southerly direction and used the time to replay my last brief talk with Chief Tracchio.

'If it were me, I'd get the hell out of here, Boxer,' he'd told me. 'You're on restricted duty, so call it vacation time and get some rest.'

I understood what he wasn't saying. While my case was pending, I was an embarrassment to the Department.

Get lost?

Yes, sir, Chief. No problem, sir.

Agitated thoughts bounced around inside my

skull about the preliminary hearing and my fears about the upcoming trial.

Then I thought about my sister Cat putting out the welcome mat and how lucky that was for me.

Within twenty minutes I was heading southbound on Highway 1, the open road cutting through thirty-foot tall boulders. The crashing waves of the Pacific pounded the rocky incline to my right, and great green mountains rose high on my left.

'Hey, Boo,' I said, calling my dog by her pet name. 'This is what's called a vacation. Can you say va-ca-tion?'

Martha turned her sweet face and gave me a loving, brown-eyed look, then put her nose back into the wind and resumed her joyous surveillance of the coastal route. She'd gotten with the program, and now I had to do the same.

I'd brought along a few things to help me do just that – about a half-dozen books I'd been wanting to read, my screwball comedy videos, and my guitar, an old Seagull acoustic that I'd strummed sporadically for twenty years.

As sunshine brightened the road, I found my mood lightening. It was a stunning day and it was all mine. I turned on the radio and fiddled with the dial until I found a station in the thick of a rock and roll revival.

The disk jockey was practically reading my mind, spinning hits of the seventies and eighties, sending me back to my childhood and to my college days and memories of a hundred nights with my all-girl band jamming in bars and coffee houses.

It was June once again, and school was out – maybe for good.

I turned up the volume.

The music took me over and my lungs filled as I sang LA dude rock and other hits of the times. I crooned 'Hotel California' and Fleetwood Mac's 'You Make Loving Fun' and when Springsteen bellowed 'Born to Run', I was pounding the steering-wheel, feeling the body and soul of the song out to the ends of my hair.

I even egged Martha on, getting her to howl along with Jackson Browne's 'Running on Empty'.

And that's when it dawned on me.

I really *was* running on empty. The little blinking gas light was frantically signaling that my tank was dry.

Chapter Twenty-Four

I coasted into a filling station right inside the limits of Half Moon Bay. It was an indie that had somehow avoided takeover by the oil conglomerates, a rustic place with a galvanized steel canopy over the tanks and a hand-lettered sign over the office door: *Man in the Moon Garage.*

A sandy-haired guy, looking to be in his late twenties, wiped his hands on a rag and approached as I got out of the car to work a cramp out of my bum leg.

We had a brief exchange about octane, then I headed toward the soda machine in front of the office. Around the side yard I saw a lot full of sticker weeds, teetering towers of worn-out tires and a few beached old junkers. I'd just lifted a cold can of Diet Coke to my lips when I noticed a car in the shadows of the garage that made my heart do a little dance.

It was a bronze-colored 1981 Pontiac Bonneville, the twin of the car my Uncle Dougie had owned when I was in high school. I wandered over and peered into the passenger compartment, then I looked under the open hood. The battery was encrusted and mice had eaten the spark-plug wires, but to my eyes, the innards looked clean.

I had an idea.

As I handed my credit card to the gas-station attendant, I pointed a thumb back over my shoulder and asked, 'Is that old Bonneville for sale?'

'She's a beauty, isn't she?' He grinned at me from under the bill of his cap. He balanced a clipboard against a denim thigh, ran the slider over my card, then turned the sales slip around for me to sign.

'My uncle bought a car like that the year it came out.'

'No kidding? It's a classic, all right.'

'Does it run?'

'It will. I'm working on it now. The tranny's in good shape. Needs a new starter motor, alternator, a little this and a little that.'

'Actually, I'd like to fool around with the engine myself. Kind of a project, you know?'

The gas-station guy grinned again and seemed pleased by the idea. He told me to make him an offer and I put up four fingers. He said, 'You wish. That car's worth a thousand if it's worth a nickel.'

I held up the flat of my hand, five fingers waggling in the breeze.

'Five hundred bucks is my limit for a pig in a poke,' I said.

The kid thought about it for a long moment, making me realize how much I wanted that car. I was about to up the ante when he said, 'Okay, but it's "as is", you understand. No guarantees.'

'You've got the manual?'

'It's in the glove box. And I'll throw in a socket wrench and a couple of screwdrivers.'

'Deal,' I said.

We high-fived, low-fived, bopped our fists and shook on it.

'I'm Keith Howard, by the way.'

'And I'm Lindsay Boxer.'

'So, where am I delivering this heap, Lindsay?'

It was my turn to grin. Caveat emptor, indeed. I gave Keith my sister's address and directions on how to get there.

'Go up the hill then turn onto Miramontes and then onto Sea View. It's a blue house on the right, second one in from the end of the road.'

Keith nodded. 'I'll drop it by day after tomorrow, if that's okay.'

'Excellent,' I said, climbing back into the Explorer. Keith cocked his head and flashed me a flirtatious look.

'Don't I know you from somewhere, Lindsay?'

'No,' I said, laughing. 'But nice try.' The gas-station guy was coming on to me! I was old enough to be his big sister.

The kid laughed along with me.

'Well, anyway, Lindsay. Call me anytime if you need me to bring over an engine hoist or whatever.'

'Okay, I'll do that,' I said, meaning just the opposite. But I was still smiling as I honked the horn goodbye.

Chapter Twenty-Five

Sea View Avenue was a link in a looping chain of cul-de-sacs, separated from the curving arms of the Bay by a quarter-mile stretch of dune grass. I opened the car door, and as Martha bounded out, I was almost blown away by the heady scent of rockroses and the fresh ocean breeze.

I stood for a minute, taking in Cat's cheery house with its dormers and porches and sunflowers growing against the fence in the front yard, before taking the keys from the niche above the lintel and opening the door into my sister's life.

Inside, Cat's home was a comfy hodge-podge of overstuffed furniture, crammed bookshelves and gorgeous views of the Bay from every room. I felt my entire body relax, and the idea of retiring from the force rose up in me again.

I could live in a place like this.

I could get used to waking up in the morning thinking about life instead of death.

Couldn't I?

I opened the sliders to the back deck and saw a

playhouse out in the yard. It was painted dusky blue like the house itself and was fenced all around with white pickets. I made my way down the back steps right behind Martha, who was running with her head down low.

I suspected that I was about to meet Penelope.

Chapter Twenty-Six

Penelope was a large Vietnamese pot-bellied pig, all black and whiskery. She waddled over to me, huffing and snoodling, so I leaned over the fence and patted her head.

'Hi, Gorgeous,' I said.

Hi, Lindsay.

There was a note tacked to Penelope's little bungalow, so I entered the pen to get a better look at *The Pig House Rules*, as 'written' by Penelope.

Dear Lindsay,

This note is all about me.

> *1) I'd like a cup of pig chow twice a day and a clean bowl of water.*

> *2) I also like cherry tomatoes, Saltines with peanut butter and peaches.*

3) Please, come out and talk to me every day. I like riddles and the theme song to SpongeBob SquarePants.

4) In case of emergency, my vet is Dr Monghil in town and my pig sitters are Carolee and Allison Brown. Allison is one of my best friends. Their numbers are by the kitchen phone.

5) Don't let me into the house, okay? I've been warned.

6) If you scratch me under the chin, you can have three wishes. Anything you want in the whole wide world.

The note was signed with big Xs and a pointy little hoof-print. *The Pig House Rules*, indeed! Cat, you funny girl.

I catered to Penelope's immediate needs, then changed into clean jeans and a lavender sweatshirt and took Martha and the Seagull out to the front porch. As I ran through some chords, the fragrance of roses and the salty ocean tang sent my mind drifting back to the first time I'd come to Half Moon Bay.

It had been just about this time of year. The same beachy smell had been in the air and I was working my first homicide case. The victim was a young man we'd found savagely murdered in his room in the back of a sleazy transient hotel in the Tenderloin.

He had been wearing only a T-shirt and one white tube sock. His red hair was combed, his blue eyes were wide open and his throat had been slashed in a gaping grin stretching from ear to ear, nearly decapitating him. When we turned him over, I saw that the skin on his buttocks had been flayed to ribbons with some kind of lash.

We'd tagged the young man John Doe #24, and at the time I fully believed that I'd find his killer. John Doe's T-shirt had come from The Distillery, a tourist restaurant situated in Moss Beach, just north of Half Moon Bay.

It was our only real clue – and although I'd combed this little town and the neighboring communities, the lead had gone nowhere.

Ten years later, John Doe #24 was still unidentified, unclaimed, unavenged by the justice system, but he would never be just another cold case file to me. It was like a wound that ached when it rained.

Chapter Twenty-Seven

I was about to drive into town for dinner when the late-evening newspaper landed with a *whomp* on the lawn.

I picked it up, shook out the folds, and felt the headline reach out and hook me: POLICE RELEASE PRIME SUSPECT IN CRESCENT HEIGHTS SLAYINGS. I read the article all the way through.

> When Jake and Alice Daltry were found slain in their house in Crescent Heights on 5 May, Police Chief Peter Stark announced that Antonio Ruiz had confessed to the crime. According to the Chief today, the confession didn't jibe with the facts. 'Mr Ruiz has been cleared of the charges against him,' said Stark.
>
> Witnesses say Ruiz, 34, a maintenance worker for California Electric and Gas, couldn't have been in the Daltrys' house on the day of the murders because he was working his shift in the plant in full view of his co-workers.

Mr and Mrs Daltry had their throats slashed. Police will not confirm that the husband and wife were tortured before they were killed.

The article went on to say that Ruiz, who'd done some handiwork for the Daltrys, claimed that his confession had been coerced. And Chief Stark was quoted again, stating that the police were 'investigating other leads and suspects'.

I felt a reflexive, visceral pull. 'Investigating other leads and suspects' was code for 'We've got squat' and the cop in me wanted to know everything; the how, the why, and especially the who. I already knew the where.

Crescent Heights was one of the communities along Highway 1. It was on the outskirts of Half Moon Bay – only five or six miles from where I was standing.

Chapter Twenty-Eight

Get in and out in under five minutes. Absolutely no more than five.

The Watcher noted the exact time as he stepped out of his gray panel van onto Ocean Colony Road. He was dressed as a meter man this morning; dun-colored coveralls with a red-and-white patch over the right breast pocket. He pulled down the bill of his cap. Patted his pockets, feeling his folding knife in one, his camera in the other. Picked up his clip-board and a tube of caulk, tucked them under his arm.

His breathing quickened as he took the narrow footpath alongside the O'Malleys' house. Then he stooped at one of the basement window wells, stretched latex gloves over his hands and used a glass cutter and a suction cup to remove a 24 x 20 inch pane of glass.

He froze, waiting out the yipping of a neighbor's dog, then slipped feet-first down into the basement.

He was in. Not a problem.

The basement stairs led up through an unlocked

door to a kitchen filled with deluxe appliances and a ridiculous excess of gadgets. The Watcher noted the alarm code posted by the phone. Committed it to memory.

Thanks, Doc. You dummy.

He took out his small, excellent camera, preset to shoot in bursts of three consecutive shots, and pointed it around all sides of the room. *Zzzt-zzzt-zzzt. Zzzt-zzzt-zzzt.*

The Watcher bounded up the stairs and found a bedroom door wide open. He stood for a moment in the doorway, taking in all the girly things: the four-poster bed, ruffles in lavender-blue and creamy pink. Posters of Creed and endangered wildlife.

Caitlin, Caitlin . . . what a sweet girl you are.

He pointed the camera at her vanity table, *zzzt-zzzt-zzzt*, capturing images of lipsticks and perfume bottles, the open box of tampons. He sniffed the girly scents, ran his thumb across her hairbrush, pocketed a long strand of red-gold hair from the bristles.

Leaving the girl's room, the Watcher entered the adjacent master bedroom. It was draped in rich colors, redolent with the smell of potpourri.

There was a super-sized plasma screen TV at the foot of the bed. The Watcher pulled open the night table, rifled through it and found a half-dozen packets of photographs wrapped in rubber bands.

He undid one of the packets and fanned the photos out like a deck of cards. Then he returned the packet and closed the drawer. He took a slow pan around the room with his camera whirring.

That's when he noticed the little glass eye, smaller than a shirt button, glittering from the closet door.

He felt a thrill of fear. Was he being taped?

He pulled open the closet door and found the video recorder on a shelf at the back wall. The on-off button was in the off position.

The machine wasn't recording.

The Watcher's fear lifted. He was elated now. He panned his camera, capturing each room on the first floor, every niche and surface before heading down to his basement exit. He'd been inside for four minutes and a few seconds.

Now, outside the house, he ran a line of caulking along the window glass and pressed it back into place. The caulk would hold – until he was ready to enter the house again – *and torture and kill them.*

Chapter Twenty-Nine

I opened Cat's front door and Martha yanked on her lead, pulling me into shocking sunshine. The beach was a short walk away and we were headed toward it when a black dog zoomed out of my peripheral vision and lunged at Martha – who pulled free of my grasp and bolted!

My scream was cut short when something rammed me hard from behind. I fell and something, *someone*, piled on top of me. *What the hell?*

I tore free of the tangle of flesh and metal and stood up, ready to swing.

Damn! Some idiot had run me over with his bicycle. The guy struggled to his feet. He was twenty-something, with thinning hair and pink-framed glasses hanging from one ear.

'So-*phieeeee!*' he yelled in the direction of the two dogs now barreling toward the water's edge. 'Sophie, NO!'

The black dog braked and looked back at the cyclist, who adjusted his glasses and turned a worried look toward me.

'I'm so s-s-sorry. You okay?' he asked. I felt him grappling with his stutter.

'I'll let you know in a minute,' I said, fuming. I limped down the street to see Martha trotting toward me, ears back, looking whipped, poor thing.

I ran my hands over her, checking for bites, hardly listening as the cyclist explained that 'Sophie' was just a puppy and didn't mean any harm.

'Look,' he said, 'I'll g-g-get my car and drive you to the hospital.'

'What? No, I'm okay.' And Martha was fine, too. But I was still pissed. I wanted to blast the guy, but, hey, accidents happen, right?

'What about your leg?'

'Don't worry about it.'

'If you're sure . . . ?'

The bike guy leashed Sophie and introduced himself. 'Bob Hinton,' he said. 'If you need a good lawyer, here's my card. And I'm *really* sorry.'

'Lindsay Boxer,' I said, taking his card. 'And I *do* need a good lawyer. Some guy with a baby Rottie ran over me with his Cannondale.'

The guy smiled nervously. 'I've never seen you around here before.'

'My sister Catherine lives there.' I pointed to the pretty blue house. Then, since we were headed the same way, we all trooped off together along the sandy footpath that bisected the dune grass.

I told Hinton that I was staying at my sister's house while taking a few weeks off from my job with the SFPD.

'A cop, huh? You've come to the right place. All those murders that have happened around here.'

I went hot and cold at the same time. My cheeks flamed, but my insides turned to ice. I didn't want to *think* about murders around here. I wanted to detox. Take my R & R. And I certainly didn't want to talk any more with this blind-siding lawyer, although he seemed nice enough.

'Listen, I've gotta go,' I said. I tightened Martha's lead so that she was beside me and walked quickly on. 'Take care,' I shot over my shoulder. 'And try to watch where you're going.'

I clambered down the sandy cliff to the beach, distancing myself from Bob Hinton as quickly as possible.

Out of sight. Out of mind.

Chapter Thirty

The sea was too cold for swimming in, but I sat cross-legged near the water's edge and stared out at the horizon where the aqua-blue Bay met the great rolling Pacific.

Martha was running along the curve of the beach, the sand spraying out behind her feet, and I was enjoying the warmth of the sun on my face when I felt something hard jab the back of my neck.

I froze.

I didn't even take a breath.

'*You shot that girl,*' a voice said. 'You shouldn't have done that.'

At first I didn't recognize the voice. My mind spun, searching for a name, an explanation, the right words to say. I reached my arm behind me so that I could grab the gun and I saw his face for a split-second.

I saw the hatred in his eyes. I saw his fear.

'*Don't you move!*' the boy shouted, jabbing the gun muzzle hard against my vertebrae. Sweat trickled down my sides. *'You killed my sister. You killed her for nothing!'*

I remembered the empty look on Sara Cabot's face when she fell.

'I'm so sorry,' I said.

'No, you're not, but you will be. And guess what? Nobody cares.'

You're not supposed to hear the bullet that gets you, but that must be a myth. The booming report of the shot that drilled through my spine sounded like a bomb.

I slumped over, paralyzed. I couldn't speak, and I couldn't stop the flow of blood pulsing out of my body, ebbing into the cold water of the Bay.

But how had it come to this? There was a *reason* that just eluded my grasp. Something I should have done.

Slap the cuffs on them. I should have done that.

That's what I was thinking when my eyes flew open.

I was lying on my side, my fists full of sand. Martha was looking down at me, breathing on my face.

Somebody cared.

I sat up and reached my arms around her, buried my face in her neck.

The dream's sticky sense clung to me. I didn't need a PhD in psychology to know what it meant. I was churning in the violence of last month.

Stuck in it up to my eyeballs.

'Everything's fine,' I told Martha.

Lying my face off to my little dog.

Chapter Thirty-One

While Martha herded shore birds, I sent my mind skywards and pretended that I was drifting effortlessly, up there with the wheeling gulls. I was ruminating on both my recent past and my uncertain future when I leveled my gaze and saw him.

My heart lurched. His smile was bright, but his deep blue eyes were scrunched against the glare.

'Hi, Gorgeous,' he said.

'Oh my God, look what the tide brought in.'

'No tide in the Bay, Lindsay.' I laughed and let him help me to my feet. We kissed, and I felt this sensational heat searing my insides.

'How'd you manage to get the day off?' I finally asked, squeezing him hard.

'You don't understand. This *is* work. I'm scouring the coastline for terrorist infiltration,' he cracked. 'Ports and shorelines, that's what I do.'

'And here I thought your job was to pick out the day's color alert.'

'That too,' he said. He flapped his tie at me. 'See? Yellow.'

I liked that Joe could josh about his job, because it would have been too depressing otherwise. Our shoreline was extremely porous and Joe saw the holes.

'Don't tease,' he said, then we kissed again. 'This is hard work.'

I laughed. 'All work, no play makes Joe a dull guy.'

'Hey, I've got something for you,' he said, as we walked together along the jetty. He pulled a packet of tissue paper out of his pocket and handed it to me. 'I wrapped it myself.'

I grinned. The packet was sealed with Scotch tape and Joe had penned a string of Xs and Os where a ribbon would've been. I ripped open the tissue and poured a bright silver chain and a medallion into my palm.

'It's supposed to keep you safe,' Joe said.

'Sweetie, it's Kokopelli. How did you know?' I held the little disk level with my eyes.

'The Hopi pottery in your apartment kinda gave me a clue.'

'I love it. What's more, I *need* it,' I said, turning my back to him so he could fasten the long silver chain around my neck.

Joe swept the hair off my nape and kissed me just there. His lips, the roughness of his cheek against that tender spot, sent a thrill through me. I gasped, then turned into his arms again. I liked it there a lot.

I kissed him softly, and the kiss turned deeper and more urgent. I finally pulled away from him. 'Let's get you out of those clothes,' I said.

Chapter Thirty-Two

Cat's guest bedroom was peach and gauzy with a double bed next to the window. Joe's jacket flew onto the chair, followed by his blue denim shirt and yellow tie.

I lifted my arms and he gently pulled my skimpy halter top over my head. I took his hands and pressed his palms to my breasts and the warmth of his touch made me feel almost weightless. I was panting by the time my shorts hit the floor.

I watched from the bed as Joe finished undressing and climbed into bed beside me. God, he was a good-looking boy. Then I went into his arms.

'I have something else for you, Lindsay,' Joe said. What he had was quite apparent. I laughed into the crook of his neck.

'Not just that,' Joe told me. 'This.'

I opened my eyes and saw that he was pointing to small letters clumsily written on his chest with a ball-point pen. He'd written my name over his heart.

Lindsay.
'You're funny,' I said with a smile.
'No, I'm romantic,' said Joe.

Chapter Thirty-Three

It wasn't *just* about sex with Joe. He was too real and too good a person for me to think of him simply as a hunk and a real good time. But I paid a terrible price for feeling more. At times like this, when our jobs permitted, we had an indescribable intimacy. Then morning came and Joe jetted back to Washington, and I didn't know when I'd see him – or if it would ever feel this good – again.

It's been said that love finds you when you're ready.

Was I ready?

The last time I had loved a man so much, he'd died a terrible death.

And what about Joe?

He'd been scalded by a divorce. Could he ever really trust again?

Right now, as I was lying in his arms, my heart was divided between taking down all of the walls – and protecting myself against the wrenching pain of our imminent separation.

'Where are you, Linds?'

'Right here. I'm here.'

I held Joe tightly, forcing myself back into the moment. We kissed and touched until being apart was unbearable and we joined together again, a perfect fit. I moaned and told Joe how good he felt – how good he was.

'I love you, Linds,' he murmured.

I was saying his name and telling him that I loved him when waves of pleasure overtook me and I allowed all of my scared, undermining thoughts to go away.

We held each other for a long time afterwards, just catching our breath, getting a grip on our spinning world, when the doorbell rang.

'Shit,' I said. 'Pretend it's not happening.'

'Gotta get the door,' said Joe softly. 'It could be for me.'

Chapter Thirty-Four

I climbed over Joe's body, threw his shirt on over my cut-offs and went to the door. An attractive fifty-ish woman was standing on the front porch with an expectant smile on her face. She was too hip in her tennis dress and Lilly Pulitzer sweater to be a Jehovah's Witness, and she looked too sunny to be a Federal Agent.

She introduced herself as Carolee Brown.

'I live down on Cabrillo Highway about a mile north of here. That blue Victorian with a lot of chain-link fencing.'

'Sure. I know the place. A school, isn't it?'

'Yes, that's the one.'

I didn't mean to be snappish, but I felt awkward standing there with my beard-roughened face and love-smushed hair.

'What can I do for you, Ms Brown?'

'It's Dr Brown, actually, but please call me Carolee. Lindsay, right? My daughter and I help your sister out with Penelope. This is for you.' She handed me a platter covered in aluminum foil.

'Oh, Cat did mention you. I'm sorry. I'd invite you in, but . . .'

'Don't even think about it. I wasn't paying a visit, just being the Cookie Lady. Welcome to Half Moon Bay.'

I thanked Carolee and we exchanged a few more words before she said goodbye and got into her car. I stooped to pick up the morning paper, glancing at the front page on the way back to the bedroom. Sunny today, NASDAQ down 10 points, Crescent Heights murder investigation still going nowhere. It was nearly impossible to believe that people had been murdered in this lovely place.

I told Joe about the slayings, then peeled the dome of aluminum foil off the platter.

'Chocolate chip,' I announced. 'From the Cookie Lady.'

'The Cookie Lady. Like the Easter Bunny?'

'I guess. Something like that.'

Joe was staring at me with that dreamy look of his.

'You look great in that. My shirt.'

'Thanks, big fella.'

'You look even better out of it.'

I grinned and put down the platter. Then I slowly unbuttoned Joe's nice blue shirt and let it fall from my shoulders.

Chapter Thirty-Five

'I used to have a pig like this one,' Joe said as we leaned over the pigpen fence that evening.

'Come on! You're from Queens.'

'There are backyards in Queens, Linds. Our pig's name was Alphonse Pignole and we fed him pasta and sautéed escarole topped off with a hit of Cinzano. Which he loved.'

'You're making this up!'

'Nope.'

'What happened to him?'

'Ate him at one of our famous Molinari Family pig roasts. With apple sauce.'

Joe saw the look of disbelief on my face.

'Okay, that part was a lie. When I went to college, Al got a great home in upstate New York. Let me show you something.'

He reached for a rake that was leaning against the pig house and Penelope began grunting and woofling as soon as she saw it.

Joe grunted and woofled right back.

'Pig Latin,' he said, grinning over his shoulder.

He reached the rake over the fence and scratched Penelope's back with it. She dropped to her knees and with a pleasurable groan rolled over onto her back and stuck her legs in the air.

'Your talents know no bounds,' I said. 'By the way, I think you're entitled to three wishes.'

Chapter Thirty-Six

The waning sun was streaking the sky as Joe, Martha and I had our dinner out on the deck facing the Bay. I'd used my mom's barbecue sauce recipe on the chicken, and we followed it up with a pint each of Cherry Garcia and Chunky Monkey.

We sat nestled together for hours, listening to the crickets, and music on the radio, watching the candle flames do the mambo in the soft, sultry breeze.

Later, we slept in snatches, waking up to reach for each other, to laugh together, to make love. We ate chocolate chip cookies, swapped memories of our dreams, and fell back to sleep, our limbs entwined.

At dawn, Joe's cell phone brought the rest of the world crashing back. Joe said, 'Yes, sir. Will do,' and snapped the phone shut.

He opened his arms and folded me back in. I reached up and kissed his neck.

'So. When is the car coming for you?'

'Couple of minutes.'

Joe didn't exaggerate. I had 120 seconds to watch him dress in the dark room, one lone ray of light slipping beneath the window shades to show me how sad he looked as he left me.

'Don't get up,' Joe said as I pushed off the covers. He drew them back up to my chin. He kissed me about eleven times; my lips, cheeks, eyes.

'By the way, I got my three wishes,' he said.

'Which were?'

'Not telling, but one of them was the Cherry Garcia.'

I laughed. I kissed him.

'Love you, Lindsay.'

'Love you, too, Joe.'

'I'll call you.'

I didn't ask when.

Chapter Thirty-Seven

The three of them gathered at the Coffee Bean early that morning, settling into deck chairs on the stone terrace, a wall of fog obscuring their view of the Bay. They were alone out there, conversing intensely, discussing murder.

The one called the Truth, wearing a black leather jacket and blue jeans, turned to the others and said, 'Okay. Run it by me again.'

The Watcher studiously read from his notebook, citing the times, the habits, his conclusions about the O'Malleys.

The Seeker didn't need to be sold. The family was his discovery and he was glad the Watcher's investigation had confirmed his instincts. He began to whistle the old blues standard, 'Crossroads' – until the Truth shot him a look.

The Truth had a slight build but a weighty presence.

'You make good points,' said the Truth. 'But I'm not convinced.'

The Watcher became agitated. He pulled at the

collar of his crew-neck sweater, riffled through the photographs. He stabbed the close-ups with his finger, circled details with his pen.

'It's a good beginning,' said the Seeker, coming to the Watcher's defense.

The Truth waved a hand, a dismissive gesture. 'Don't jerk me around. Get me the goods.' Then, 'Let's order.'

The waitress, named Maddie, pranced out onto the terrace in skinny hip huggers and a tank top that exposed a smooth expanse of tummy.

'That's what I call a "belly-blinker",' said the Seeker, his charm overshadowed by the hunger in his eyes.

Maddie gave him a wan smile, before refilling their coffee mugs. Then she pulled out her order pad and took the Truth's order; scrambled eggs, bacon and a freshly baked cinnamon bun.

The Seeker and the Watcher ordered, too, but unlike the Truth, they only picked at their food when it came. They continued to speak in muted voices.

Working the angles.

Trying it on.

The Truth stared into the fog, listening intently as a plan finally came together.

Chapter Thirty-Eight

The day unfurled like a yellow beach blanket. It was a terrible shame that Joe wasn't here to share it with me.

I whistled Martha into the car and we headed into town for provisions. As we sped along Cabillo Highway I saw the sign: Bayside School, Department of Child Welfare, State of California.

The big blue Victorian house loomed large on my right side. On an impulse, I pulled the car into the parking area.

I sat for a long moment taking in the house, the playground, the tall chainlink fence. Then I locked the car and walked up a gravel pathway to a heavy oak door.

A very overweight black woman, probably in her mid-thirties, answered the bell.

'Hi,' I said. 'I'm looking for Dr Brown.'

'Come on in. She's in the teachers' lounge. I'm Maya Abboud. I'm one of the teachers here.'

'What kind of school is this?' I asked as I followed

her through dark, narrow hallways and up two flights of stairs.

'The State stashes runaways here, mostly. These kids are the lucky ones.'

We passed small classrooms, a TV lounge, and dozens of children from very small ones to adolescents. It was a far cry from *Oliver Twist*, but the fact that all of these children were essentially homeless was sad and troubling.

Ms Abboud left me at the threshold of a bright, many-windowed room and inside it was Carolee Brown. She jumped to her feet and came toward me.

'Lindsay. Good to see you.'

'I was passing by and, well, I wanted to apologize for being abrupt yesterday.'

'Oh, stop. I surprised you and you didn't know me from a tuna-fish sandwich. I'm glad you're here. There's someone I want you to meet.'

I told Carolee that I couldn't stay long but she assured me it would just take a minute.

I followed her outside to the playground and saw that we were headed toward a pretty, dark-haired girl of about eight, sitting at a table under a shade tree, playing with her Power Rangers.

'This is my daughter, Allison,' said Carolee. 'Ali, this is Brigid and Meredith's aunt Lindsay. She's a *police lieutenant*.'

The little girl's eyes got very bright as she turned them on me.

'I know exactly who you are. You're taking care of Penelope.'

'I sure am, Ali, but it's just for a few weeks.'

'Penelope is so cool, isn't she? She can read minds.'

The little girl chattered on about her pig friend as she and her mom walked me to the parking area.

'It's *really* cool that you're a policewoman,' Allison said, grabbing my hand.

'It is?'

'Sure. Because it means you're good at fixing things.'

I was wondering what the little girl meant, when she squeezed my fingers excitedly, then sprinted to my car. Martha wagged her tail and barked until I let her out. Then she danced around Allison and covered her with sloppy kisses.

We eventually separated child and dog, and Carolee and I made plans to get together soon. As I waved goodbye through the open window, I thought, *I've made a new friend.*

Chapter Thirty-Nine

The Watcher nervously stroked the steering-wheel as he waited for Lorelei O'Malley to leave the house. It was bad news that he had to go in again.

At last, the silly-ass woman exited her house in her shopping outfit *du jour* and locked the door behind her. She gunned her little red Mercedes down Ocean Colony Road without looking back.

The Watcher got out of his car. He was wearing a blue sports jacket and slacks, dark sunglasses – what a field supervisor from the telephone company might wear. He walked quickly toward the house.

As he had before, the Watcher stooped at the basement window well and pulled on gloves. Then, slicing through the caulking with the blade of his hunting knife, he removed the pane of glass and dropped into the basement.

He moved swiftly through the house, up the stairs to the O'Malleys' bedroom. Once there, he opened the closet, pushed aside a raft of dresses and examined the video camera on the shelf attached to the back wall.

The Watcher took the tape out of the camera and slipped it into a pocket. He took another tape at random from a messy stack of tapes on the same shelf, resisting the impulse to tidy the rest. Then he took a packet of photos from the nightstand drawer.

He'd only been in the house for two minutes and twenty seconds when he heard the front door *slam*.

His mouth went dry. In all his days of watching this house, no one had ever come back after leaving for the morning. The Watcher went to the closet and crouched beneath a shimmying curtain of skirts. He reached up and closed the door.

The carpet dampened the sound of footsteps and the Watcher was startled when the doorknob turned. He had no time to think. The closet door opened, the clothing parted – and the Watcher was revealed, crouching like a thief.

Lorelei O'Malley gasped out loud and clutched at her breasts, then her face darkened.

'I know you,' she said. 'What are you doing here?'

The knife was already in his hand. Lorelei saw it and let out a piercing scream. The Watcher felt he had no choice. He lunged forward, the long blade popping buttons off her blue silk dress as it slid into her belly.

Lorelei twisted, trying to escape the knife, but the Watcher held her tightly in what could have passed for a lover's embrace.

111

'Oh. GOD. Why are you doing this?' she moaned, her eyes rolling back, her voice fading to a sigh.

Pressing his hand against the small of her back, the Watcher sliced the blade up through the soft tissues of Lorelei's abdominal cavity, severing her aorta. The blood didn't spray; it poured from the woman's body like water from a bucket until her knees gave and she fell onto the shoes lining the closet floor.

The Watcher knelt and touched two fingers to her carotid artery. Her eyelids flickered faintly. She would be dead in seconds.

He had just enough time to do what needed to be done. He pushed up her blue skirt, took off his belt and whipped Lorelei O'Malley's buttocks until she was dead in her clothes closet.

Chapter Forty

It could only get worse, and it did. The Watcher sat in the van in a parking lot on Kelly Street across from the two-story house the doctor used as his office.

He flicked his eyes over to the Seeker, who looked dazed and confused in the seat beside him. Then he surveyed the parking lot again. He nervously noted the shoppers, the few cars entering and leaving.

When Dr Ben O'Malley stepped outside, the Watcher jostled the Seeker. They locked eyes. 'Get ready.'

Then the Watcher got out of the van. He sprinted toward the doctor, overtaking him before he reached his SUV.

'Doc, Doc, thank God! I need help.'

'What is it, son?' the doctor asked, looking both startled and annoyed.

'It's my friend. Something's happened. I don't know if it's a seizure or a heart attack or what!'

'Where is he?'

'Over there,' he said, pointing to the panel van fifty feet away. 'Hurry, okay? Please?'

The Watcher jogged ahead, looking back to make sure that the doctor was following. When he reached the van, he wrenched open the passenger-side door, stepping aside so that O'Malley could see the Seeker slumped across the front seat.

The doctor peered into the interior, reached in and lifted one of the Seeker's eyelids. He jerked in surprise as he felt the sharp point of a blade piercing the nape of his neck.

'Get in,' said the Watcher.

'Don't say a word,' said the Seeker, charming, disarming, unflappable. 'Or we'll kill your whole family.'

Chapter Forty-One

The Watcher heard the doctor's bound body bump and roll in the back of the van as they climbed the steep road.

'What about here?' he asked the Seeker. He checked the rear-view mirror, then turned off the roadside into a niche between clumps of trees. He applied the brakes.

The Seeker leaped out of the van, hauled back on the sliding door and propped the doctor into a sitting position.

'Okay, Doc, time to go,' he said, ripping the duct tape from his mouth. 'Any last words? Or forever hold your peas.'

'What do you want me to *say*?' Dr O'Malley gasped. 'Just tell me. Do you want money? I can get money for you. Drugs? Anything you want.'

'That's really stupid, Doc,' said the Seeker. 'Even for you.'

'Don't do this. Help me,' he pleaded. 'Help me, please.'

'*Help me, please,*' mocked the Watcher.

'What did I do to you?' Dr O'Malley sobbed.

A rough shove sent the doctor out of the van and into the grit on the side of the road.

'It's easier than you think,' the Seeker said kindly, leaning close to the doctor's ear. 'Just fill your mind with things you love ... and say good-bye.'

The doctor never saw the rock that caved the back of his skull. The Seeker opened his knife and lifted the doctor's head by a handful of salt-and-pepper hair. As neatly as if he were slicing a melon, he slit the man's throat.

Then the Watcher used his belt as a lash, striking hard, leaving brownish stripes on the bright white skin of O'Malley's buttocks.

'Feel that?' he said, panting over the dying man.

The Seeker wiped his prints off the knife using the doctor's shirt-tail. Then he hurled the knife and the rock far down the hillside where they were swallowed by trees, brush, and tall rasping grasses.

Together the two men lifted the doctor's body by his arms and legs and carried him to the cliff-side edge of the road. They swung the limp body and on the count of three, launched it over the side. They listened as the body crashed into the under-brush, tumbling downhill to a place so remote it would lie hidden, they hoped, until coyotes dragged off the worthless carcass.

Chapter Forty-Two

I was on the front porch picking out notes on my Seagull, when a Godawful clanking mangled my concentration. It was a tow-truck, of all things, rattling along the peaceful curves of Sea View Avenue. I scowled until I noticed that it was towing a 1981 Bonneville.

My 1981 Bonneville.

The driver waved when he saw me.

'Hey, lady. I've got a special delivery for you.'

Ah. The Man in the Moon. The gas-station guy. I grinned as Keith worked the gears that let the car down. When it was on all fours, he got out of the cab and came toward me with a little swagger in his walk.

'So what makes you think you can make this jalopy go?' he asked, taking a seat on the step.

'I've tinkered around with a few engines,' I told him. 'Patrol cars, mostly.'

'You're a mechanic?' He whistled through his teeth. 'Holy shit. I knew there was something neat about you.'

'Not exactly a mechanic. I'm a cop.'

'You lie.'

'I don't lie,' I said, laughing off the kid's moon-eyed attention.

He stretched a muscular arm toward me and with a cursory 'Do you mind?' snatched up my guitar.

Help yourself, buddy.

The kid put the Seagull in his lap, strummed some chords, then belted out a few lines of a country sob song of the 'My baby's left me all alone' variety. He put so much ham into it, I could only laugh at his performance.

Keith took a mock bow then handed the guitar back to me.

'So what's your specialty?' he asked.

'Acoustic rock. The Blues. I'm working on a song right now – fooling around with some pieces and parts.'

'Here's an idea. Why don't we talk about it over dinner? I know this fish place in Moss Beach,' he said.

'Thanks, Keith. That's a nice idea, but I'm already taken.' I reached up and clutched the Kokopelli Joe had given me.

'I don't mind telling you that you're breaking my heart.'

'Awww. You'll survive.'

'No, it's true. I'm smitten. Beautiful, a mechanic in her spare time. What more could a guy ask for?'

'Come on, Keith,' I said, patting his arm. 'Show me around my new car.'

I stepped down from the porch, ran my hand over the Bonneville's fender, opened the driver's door and settled in. The car had a roomy, comfy feel and the dash was full of whizz-bang dials and gizmos, just as I remembered.

'It's a good choice, Lindsay,' Keith said, leaning on the roof of the car. 'I wouldn't sell you a junker. My back-up toolbox is in the trunk, but call if you have any problems.'

'Will do.'

He flashed a sheepish smile, took off his cap, shook out his sandy hair, repositioned his cap and said, 'Well, take care, okay?'

I waved as he drove away. Then I put the key into my new baby's ignition and turned it.

The engine didn't start. It didn't even cough, buzz or whine.

It was as dead as a flat frog in the middle of the road.

Chapter Forty-Three

I made a shopping list of the parts I'd need, and then spent the rest of the day bringing up the Bonneville's shine with a tube of compound I found in Keith's tool kit. I was supremely happy buffing dull brown into a high bronze gleam.

I was still admiring my work when the evening paper came sailing out the window of a passing car. I back-pedalled quickly and plucked it out of the air, earning a 'Nice catch!' from the paper guy.

I snapped open the thin local *Gazette* and the bold black headline grabbed me: LOCAL DOCTOR'S WIFE STABBED TO DEATH AT HOME. DOCTOR MISSING.

I stood rooted to the lawn and read:

> *Lorelei O'Malley, wife of Dr Ben O'Malley, was found slain in her home on Ocean Colony Road this afternoon, apparently the victim of a burglary gone wrong. The victim's stepdaughter, Caitlin, 15, found her stepmother's body in the bedroom closet when she returned home from school. Dr*

O'Malley, a respected general practitioner and long-time member of the community, is missing.

This afternoon, Chief Peter Stark asked the crowd outside the police station to be calm but vigilant.

'There appear to be similarities in the recent homicides,' said Stark. 'But I can't comment further because it would jeopardize the overall investigation. What I can do is give you my word that this police force will not rest until the murderer is caught.'

In answer to questions from reporters, Chief Stark said, 'Dr O'Malley was last seen at around noon. He was on his way out to lunch, but did not return to his office or call in. He's not a suspect at this time.'

I rolled up the paper and stared blankly at the pretty pastel and shingled houses on Sea View Avenue. My instincts were screaming. I was a cop without a case, a cop without a job. I didn't want to read about homicides. I wanted first-hand information.

I put away the materials I'd been using to polish the car, then I went inside and had the phone company set up a conference call.

I was suddenly lonely for the girls.

Chapter Forty-Four

The operator connected me with Claire first and her mellow voice warmed me.

'Hi, Doll. Sleeping in? Getting some color in your cheeks?'

'I'm trying, Butterfly, but my brain is like a hamster on a wheel.'

'Don't waste this downtime, Lindsay, please. God, what I wouldn't do for some time off.'

Cindy joined the conference call, her youthful voice ringing with the usual excitement. 'It's not the same without you, Linds. Sucks.'

'I wish you guys were *here*,' I told my friends. 'It's all blue sky and yellow sand. And hey, Joe came and spent the night.'

Cindy had some news about her second date with the hockey player, prompting whistles, and I came back with the story of Keith, the sandy-haired gas-station guy.

'He's in his twenties, I think – Brad Pitt type. He actually put the moves on me.'

Claire said, 'You two really make me feel like the boring old married woman.'

'I want to be as bored as you are with Edmund,' said Cindy. 'That's for *sure*.'

The laughing and teasing made me feel as if we were gathered around a dimly-lit table at Susie's.

And, as we always did at Susie's, we talked shop.

'So, what about these murders I've been hearing about?' Claire asked.

'Aw, Jeez. The town is freaking out. A young couple were killed a few weeks ago – and a woman was murdered about a mile from here this morning.'

'It was on the wire,' Cindy said. 'A bloody scene.'

'Yeah. It's starting to look like a killer on a spree, and you know it's irking me that I can't *do* anything. I want to comb the crime scene. I hate not being in the loop.'

'Well, you'll be interested in this little tidbit,' Claire said. 'I got this off the Medical Examiners' list serve. That couple who were murdered in Crescent Heights a few weeks ago? They were *whipped*.'

I think I blanked out for a moment as my mind flew to John Doe #24. *He'd been slashed and whipped.*

'They were whipped? Claire, you're sure about that?'

'Absolutely sure. Back and buttocks.'

Just then, a beep came over the line and the name on the Caller ID was like the past slamming into the present. I said, 'Hold on, guys,' and I pressed the flash button.

'Lindsay, it's Yuki Castellano. Got time to talk?'

It was good that I was still on the phone with Claire and Cindy. I needed some time to shift gears into talking to my lawyer about the shooting on Larkin Street. Yuki said she'd call back in the morning, and I got on the line with the girls again, but my mind was scrambling.

For the past few days, I'd gotten away from everything – *except the upcoming trial of my life.*

Chapter Forty-Five

The Watcher walked along the path through the dune grass under a slender crescent moon. He was wearing a wool cap and black sweats and had his micro-camera with the 10x zoom in hand.

He used it to watch a couple making out at the end of the beach, then he turned the lens toward the houses 100 yards away on the outer loop of Sea View Avenue.

He narrowed his focus to one particular house: a blue Cape Cod with a lot of windows and a double set of sliders leading out to the deck. He could see Lieutenant Lindsay Boxer walking around in the living room.

Her hair was pinned up off her neck and she was wearing a thin white T-shirt. Twirling a chain around her neck as she talked on the phone. He could see the outline of her breasts under that shirt.

Full, but perky.

Nice tits, Lieutenant, sir.

The Watcher knew exactly who Lindsay was, what kind of work she did, and why she *said* she was in Half Moon Bay. But he wanted to know a lot more.

He wondered who she was talking to on the phone. Maybe the dark-haired guy who'd stayed over last night and had left in a black government-issue town car. He wondered about that guy; who he was and if he was coming back.

And he wondered where Lindsay kept her gun.

The Watcher took some pictures of Boxer, smiling, frowning, taking down her hair. Holding the phone between her shoulder and her chin, reaching, breasts moving as she did so, to put up her hair again.

As he watched, the dog crossed the room and lay down near the sliders, staring out through them – almost as if she were looking directly at him.

The Watcher walked a ways down the beach, toward the smooching lovers, then cut across the dune grass to a parking area where he'd left his car. Once inside, he took his notebook out of the glove box and turned to the tab with Lindsay's name written in meticulous script.

Lieutenant Lindsay Boxer.

There was just enough glow from the streetlights to add to his notes.

He wrote: *Wounded. Alone. Armed and dangerous.*

PART THREE

Back in the Saddle Again

Chapter Forty-Six

The sun was only a blush on the dawn sky when a loud ringing jarred me out of sleep. I fumbled for the phone, nailed it on the fourth ring.

'Lindsay, it's Yuki. I hope I didn't wake you. I'm in the car and this is my only free minute, but I can tell you everything fast.'

Yuki was passionate and smart, and I knew this about her – she *always* spoke at ninety miles an hour.

'Okay. I'm ready,' I said, flopping back into the bed.

'Sam Cabot is out of the hospital. I deposed him yesterday,' Yuki said, her voice a rhythmic rat-tat-tat. 'He recanted his confession of the hotel murders, but that's the DA's problem. As for the action against you, he says you fired first, missed him, and that he and Sara returned fire in self-defense. Then you gunned them down. Crock of shit. We know it and they know it, but this is America. He can say whatever he wants.'

My sigh came out as a kind of strangled groan.

Yuki kept on talking. 'Our only problem is that he's such a heart-breaker, that pathological little crud. Paralyzed, propped up in that chair with his neck in a brace, quivering lower lip. Looks like a cherub who's been blindsided—'

'—by a vicious, gun-happy chick cop,' I interrupted.

'I was going to say, "blindsided by a sixteen-wheeler", but whatever.' She laughed. 'Let's get together and strategize. Can we make a plan?'

My calendar was so sparkling clean it was practically virginal. Yuki, on the other hand, had booked depositions, meetings and trials almost every hour for the next three weeks. Still, we picked a date a few days before the trial.

'Right now the media are churning up the waters,' Yuki continued. 'We leaked to the press that you're staying with friends in New York so they won't hound you. Lindsay? Are you there?'

'Yep. I'm here,' I said, eyes fixed on the ceiling fan, ears ringing.

'I'd suggest that you relax if you can. Keep a low profile. Leave the rest to me.'

Right.

I showered, dressed in linen slacks and a pink T-shirt and took a mug of coffee out to the back yard. I had a question for Penelope as I scooped breakfast into her trough: '*How much chow can a big pig chow if a big pig chows pig chow?*'

City girl talking to a pig. Who woulda thunk it?

I considered Yuki's advice as the sea breeze wafted across the deck. *Relax and keep a low profile.*

It made good sense except that I was in the clutches of a monster desire to *do* something. I wanted to shake things up, bang heads, right wrongs.

I really couldn't help myself.

I whistled to Martha and started up the Explorer. Then we headed out toward a certain house in Crescent Heights – the scene of a double homicide.

Chapter Forty-Seven

'Bad dog,' I said to Martha. 'You can't keep out of trouble, can you?'

Martha turned her melting brown eyes on me, wagged her tail, then resumed her surveillance of the boulder-sculpted highway.

As I drove south on Highway 1, I was bristling with excitement. Three miles down the road, I turned off at Crescent Heights, an idiosyncratic collection of houses freckling the face of the hill at the tip of Half Moon Bay.

I pointed the Explorer up the gravelly one-laner, feeling my way along until the scene of the crime nearly jumped out at me. I pulled over and turned off the engine.

The yellow, clapboard-sided house was a charmer with three gabled dormers, an overgrown flower garden and a whirligig of a lumberjack sawing wood attached to the post-and-rail fence. The name DALTRY was painted on the handmade mailbox and a half-mile of yellow plastic tape was still wrapped around this, the American dream.

Crime scene. Do not enter by order of the Police.

I tried to imagine that two people had been brutally murdered in this homey little cottage – but the images didn't fit together. Murder should never happen in a place like this.

What had drawn a killer to this particular house? Was it a targeted hit – or had the killer just happened on this home-sweet-home by chance?

'Stay, girl,' I told Martha as I got out of the car.

The murder had occurred more than five weeks ago, and by now the police had relinquished the crime scene. Anyone who wanted to snoop could do so, as long as they didn't break into the house – and I saw signs of snoopers everywhere; foot-prints in the flower beds, cigarette butts on the pavement, soda cans on the lawn.

I stepped through the open gate, ducked under the tape and walked around the house, slowly frisking the scene with my eyes.

There was an abandoned basketball under the shrubbery, and a single child's sneaker on the back steps, still wet from last night's dew. I noticed that one of the basement windows had been removed from its frame and was leaning against a wall of the house: the probable point of entry.

The longer I stayed at the Daltry house, the harder my heart pounded. I was creeping around a crime scene instead of taking charge of it, and that made me feel weird and bad; as though this crime was none of my business and I shouldn't be here. At the same time, I felt driven by what Claire had told me on the phone last night.

The Daltrys of Crescent Heights weren't the first murder victims to be whipped. Who else had been savaged this way? Did these killings connect with my unsolved case, John Doe #24?

Relax and keep a low profile, Yuki had said. I actually laughed out loud. Then I got into the Explorer, patted my furry sidekick's flank, and bumped down the gravelly road to the highway.

We would be back in the center of Half Moon Bay in ten minutes. I wanted to see the O'Malley house.

Chapter Forty-Eight

Ocean Colony Road was lined with patrol cars on both sides of the street. The insignias on the car doors told me that the local cops were finally getting the help they badly needed. They'd called in the State Police.

As I drove past, I saw that a uniformed officer was guarding the front door of the house and another cop was interviewing the UPS man.

Detectives and Crime Scene techs entered and left the house at irregular intervals. A media tent had been set up on a neighbor's lawn and a local reporter was going live from Half Moon Bay.

I parked my car down the block and walked toward the house, blending in with a clump of bystanders who were watching the police process the scene from the sidewalk across the street. It was a good enough vantage point and as I stood there, I sifted through my impressions, hoping for a nugget of insight.

To start with, the houses of the victims were as different as chalk and cheese. Crescent Heights was a blue-collar community with Highway 1 whizzing between the unpretentious homes and their view of the Bay. Ocean Colony backed up onto a private golf course. The O'Malley house and the others around it fairly glistened with all of the nicest things money could buy. What did the two homes and the people who'd lived in them have in common?

I studied the O'Malleys' spiffy colonial with its slate roof and boxwood topiaries in pots by the door, and once again ran through the preliminary questions. What had drawn a killer here? Was it a personal hit – or a random killing of opportunity?

I turned my eyes up to the blue shuttered windows on the first floor where Lorelei O'Malley had been stabbed to death in her bedroom.

Had she been whipped, too?

I was concentrating so intently, I must have attracted attention to myself. A young uniformed cop with a florid face and an excitable manner was headed toward me.

'Miss? Miss? I'd like to ask you some questions.'

Damn. If I had to show my badge, this cop would run me through the database. Pass the news along. *Lieutenant Lindsay Boxer, SFPD, was at the scene of the crime.* In twenty minutes the media would be ringing the doorbell and camping out on Cat's lawn.

I assumed my most innocent expression.

'Just passing through, Officer. I'm leaving now.' I flipped a little wave, turned around and walked quickly to the Explorer.

Nuts. I saw him do it.

That cop wrote down my plate-number as I drove past.

Chapter Forty-Nine

The quaint little watering-hole was named after a soaring sea bird, The Cormorant, an elegant facsimile of which hung from the ceiling over the bar.

The place had a raw bar, six kinds of beer on tap, loud music, and a full Friday-night crowd. I looked around until I spotted Carolee Brown at a table near the bar. She was dressed in slacks and a hot pink pullover. A gold crucifix glinted discreetly at her throat.

The Cookie Lady on her night off.

Carolee saw me a split second after I saw her, and she smiled broadly, gesturing for me to join her. I shimmied my way through the crowd and hugged her lightly as she stood to greet me.

We ordered Pete's Wicked Ale and linguini with clams and as women sometimes do, we got personal within minutes. Carolee had been briefed by my sister, Cat, and knew about the shooting that had left me twisting slowly in the California legal system.

'I misjudged the situation because they were kids,' I told Carolee now. 'After they shot my partner and me, I had to bring them down.'

'It really sucks, Lindsay.'

'Doesn't it ever? Killing a kid. I never thought I could do such a thing.'

'They *forced* you to do it.'

'They were murderers, Carolee. They'd killed a couple of other kids and when we apprehended them, they saw only one way out. But you'd think kids with all the advantages these two had wouldn't be so whacked.'

'Yeah, I know. But judging from the hundreds of kids who've come through my school, believe me, psychologically damaged kids come from everywhere,' Carolee said.

When Carolee spoke of damaged children, something slammed into my brain. I saw myself as a kid, flying across my bedroom, careening into my bureau. *Don't talk back to me, Missy.* My father swaying in the doorway, King of the Hill. *I was a damaged child, myself.*

I struggled to drag myself back to The Cormorant.

'So what are you, Lindsay?' Carolee was saying. 'Single? Divorced?'

'Divorced – from a guy I think of as the brother I never had,' I said, relieved that she'd changed the subject. 'But I could be talked into hooking up again.'

'Now I remember,' Carolee said with a smile. 'If I'm not mistaken, you had company when I came around with my cookies.'

I grinned at the memory of answering the door dressed in Joe's shirt. I opened my mouth to tell Carolee about Joe – when my attention was drawn to the movement behind her.

I'd been aware of three guys drinking steadily at the bar. Suddenly, two of them left. The remaining guy was strikingly handsome: dark wavy hair, a symmetrical face, rimless glasses, pressed pants and a Ralph Lauren polo shirt.

The bartender rubbed the bar with a rag, and I heard him ask, 'Ready for another?'

'Actually, I'd like some of that pint-sized brunette. And I might go for that tall blonde as a chaser.'

Although this remark was accompanied by a pleasant smile, I felt that there was something wrong about this guy. He *looked* like an ex-jock JP Morgan banker, but he sounded more like a salesman living on his draw.

My jaw tensed as he swiveled on his barstool – and turned his gaze on me.

Chapter Fifty

I noted the guy's stats automatically: white male, maybe six two, a fit 190lbs, forty to forty-two years old, no distinguishing marks except for a healing wound between the thumb and forefinger of his right hand. As if he'd been cut with a knife.

He got down off his bar stool and came toward us.

I said quietly to Carolee, 'This is my fault. I looked at him.' I did my best to head the guy off, making a big show of turning my face toward Carolee, but he kept coming.

'How are you two ladies tonight? You're both so pretty, I just had to say hello.'

'Thanks,' said Carolee. 'Nice of you to say.' Then she turned her back on him.

'I'm Dennis Agnew,' he said, pressing on. 'Sure, you don't know me, but listen, we can change all that. Why don't you girls offer me a seat? Dinner's on me.'

'Thanks anyway, Dennis,' I said, 'but we're

having a nice time on our own. You know – girls' night out.'

A frown suddenly crossed the guy's face, like the lights dimming during a brown-out. A fraction of a second later, his cockiness surged back, as did his beautiful smile.

'You couldn't be having *such* a good time. Come on. Even if you're the kind of girls who don't like guys, it's okay with me. It's just dinner.'

Dennis Agnew was a crazy blend of smooth and crude, but whatever he was up to, I'd had enough of it.

'Hey, Dennis,' I said, fishing my badge out of my handbag and flashing it at him. 'I'm a police officer and this conversation is private. Okay?'

I could see the pulse beating in his temple as he tried to strike a face-saving pose.

'You really shouldn't make snap judgments, *Officer*. Especially about people you don't know.'

Agnew walked back to the bar, put down some bills and gave us a final look.

'You take care, now. I'll be seeing you around.'

Then he stiff-armed the door that led out to the parking lot.

'Nice work, Lindsay.' Carolee made a cocked gun of her hand and blew imaginary smoke off the end of her finger.

'What a *creep*,' I said. 'Did you see the look on his face? Like he couldn't believe we were blowing him off. Who does he think he is? George Clooney?'

'Yeah,' said my new friend. 'His mom and his

mirror have been telling him that he's irresistible for his whole life.'

Too funny! We laughed hard, clinked glasses. It was great to be with Carolee, I felt that I'd known her for years. Because of her, I stopped thinking about Dennis Agnew, killers and corpses, and even my looming court date.

I lifted my hand and ordered another round of Pete's Wicked.

Chapter Fifty-One

The Seeker stashed his new knife under the front seat of his car, then got out and opened the door to the convenience store. He was instantly refreshed by the air conditioning, the soothing sight of the tall, frosty coolers filled with soda and beer.

He was especially gratified to see a small, dark-haired woman wearing an expensive Fila tracksuit in line at the check-out counter.

Her name was Annemarie Sarducci, and the Seeker knew that she had just finished her nightly run. She'd buy her bottle of imported spring water, then walk home and have dinner with her family in their home overlooking the Bay.

The Seeker already knew a great deal about Annemarie: that she was vain about her figure – size 3, 112 pounds – that she was screwing her personal trainer, that her son was dealing drugs to his classmates, and that she was insanely jealous of her sister, Juliette, who had a long-running role in a daytime soap filmed down in Los Angeles.

He also knew that she authored a blog under the

screen name Twisted Rose. He'd probably been her most attentive reader for months. He'd even signed her 'guest book' with his own screen name.

I like the way you think. THE SEEKER.

The Seeker filled a paper cup with strong black coffee from the urn in the corner of the store, then joined the line behind Mrs Sarducci. He jostled her a little, brushed her breast as though it were an accident.

'I'm *sorry*. Oh. Hey there, Annemarie,' he said.

'Yeah. Hi,' she answered, dismissing him with a bored glance and a nod. She handed a five to the sallow young girl behind the cash register, accepted her change for the bottled water and left without saying goodbye.

The Seeker watched Annemarie leave the store wiggling her little ass, because it was her habit to do so. In a couple of hours he'd be reading her online diary, all the kinky things she didn't want people in her real life to know.

See you later, Twisted Rose.

Chapter Fifty-Two

When Carolee called and asked me to keep Allison for a few hours, I wanted to plead, *'Please, don't ask me to babysit.'* But Carolee got to me before the words left my mouth.

'Ali misses that pig,' she said. 'If you'll let her visit Penelope, she'll amuse herself and I can get my molar fixed. I'd really appreciate it, Lindsay.'

A half-hour later, Allison bounced out of her mom's mini-van and ran up to the front door. Her dark, glossy hair was in two bunches, one on either side of her head, and everything she wore, including her sneakers, was pink.

'Hi there, Ali.'

'I brought apples,' she said, pushing past me into the house. 'Wait'll you see.'

'Uh-huh,' I said, faking some enthusiasm.

As soon as I opened the back door, Penelope trotted over to the fence and began grunting a noisy string of squeals and woofles – and Allison squealed and woofled back. Just about the time I thought the neighbors would call the animal warden, Allison grinned at me and said, 'That's what we call Pig-ese.'

'So I've been told,' I said, smiling back at her.

'It's a real language,' Allison insisted. She raked the pig's back and Penelope rolled over, assuming her ecstatic, feet-in-the-air stupor. 'When Penelope was a piglet, she lived in a big house near the sea with pigs from all over the world,' Ali told me. 'She used to sit up all night and talk Pig-ese with the other pigs and during the day she gave pedicures, called pigatures.'

'Is that right?'

'Pigs are a lot smarter than people think,' Ali confided. 'Penelope knows lots of things. More than people would ever realize.'

'I simply had no idea,' I said.

'Look,' Ali continued. 'You feed her the apples. I have to paint her nails.'

'Really?'

'It's what she wants,' Ali nodded, assuring me that it was okay to let the pig onto the back deck. I did what I was told. I held Granny Smith apples so that Penelope could chomp them while Allison chattered to us both and painted the pig's cloven hooves with pearly pink nail polish.

'All done, Penny,' Ali beamed proudly. 'Just let them dry. So,' she said to me. 'What can Martha do?'

'Well, as a matter of fact, border collies also have a language. Martha is trained to herd sheep on command.'

'Show me!'

'Do you see any sheep around here?'

'You're silly.'

'Yes, I am. But you know what I love most about Martha? She keeps me company and she warns me about bad guys or even about things that go bump in the night.'

'And you have a gun, right?' Ali asked with an almost cagey look on her sweet face.

'Yup. I have a gun.'

'Wow. A gun *and* a dog. You rock, Lindsay. You might be the coolest person I know.'

I finally threw back my head and laughed. Ali was such a cute and imaginative child. I was shocked at how much I liked her and how fast! I'd come to Half Moon Bay to rethink my whole life. Now I was being visited by a vivid fantasy of me, Joe, a home, a little girl.

I was turning this shocking thought around in my mind when Carolee came into the backyard with a lopsided Novocaine smile. I couldn't believe two hours had gone by and I was so, so sorry to see Ali go.

'Come back soon,' I said, hugging her goodbye. 'Ali, come back any time.'

Chapter Fifty-Three

I stood on the street waving until Carolee's mini-van disappeared around the loop in Sea View Avenue. But when it was gone, a thought that had been circling the periphery of my consciousness parked in my forebrain.

I took my laptop to the living room, settled into a puffy chair and booted up the NCIC database. Within minutes I learned that Dr Ben O'Malley, age forty-eight, had been cited for speeding a few times, and arrested on a DWI five years before. He had been married and widowed twice.

Wife number one was Sandra, the mother of their daughter, Caitlin. She'd hanged herself inside their two-car garage in 1994. The second Mrs O'Malley, Lorelei née Breen, murdered yesterday at age thirty-nine, had been arrested for shoplifting in 1998. Fined and released.

I did the same drill on Alice and Jake Daltry and reams of information scrolled onto my screen. Jake and Alice had been married for eight years and had left twin boys, aged six, when they were slaughtered in their yellow house in Crescent Heights. I pictured that cute place with its sliver of Bay view, the abandoned basketball, and the child's sneaker.

Then I focused back on the screen.

Jake had been a bad boy before he married Alice. I clicked down through his rap sheet; soliciting a prostitute and forging his father's signature on his Social Security checks – for which he'd served six months – but for the last eight years he'd been clean and had a full-time job working in a pizzeria in town.

Wife, Alice, thirty-two, had no record. She'd never even run a red light or backed into a car at the supermarket.

Still, she was dead.

So what did this add up to?

I phoned Claire, and she picked up on the first ring. We got right into it.

'Claire, can you dig around for me? I'm looking for some kind of link between the O'Malley murder and those of Alice and Jake Daltry.'

'Sure, Lindsay. I'll reach out to a few of my colleagues around the state. See what I can find.'

'And could you also look into Sandra O'Malley? Died in 1994, hanged herself.'

We talked for a few more minutes, about Claire's husband, Edmund, and a sapphire ring he'd given her for their anniversary. And we talked about a little girl named Ali who could channel pigs.

When I hung up the phone, I felt as if I were breathing air of a richer kind. I was about to close down my computer when something caught my eye. When Lorelei O'Malley went to trial for boosting a twenty-dollar pair of earrings, a local lawyer by the name of Robert Hinton had represented her.

I knew Bob Hinton.

His card was still in the pocket of my shorts from the morning he mowed me down with his ten-speed.

And as I remembered it, the guy owed me a favor.

Chapter Fifty-Four

Bob Hinton's office was a shoebox of space on Main Street, nestled between Starbucks and a bank. Taking the chance that he might be in on a Saturday, I pushed open the glass door and saw Bob sitting behind a large wooden desk, his balding scalp bent over the *San Francisco Examiner*.

At the sight of me, he jerked his head up and his arm flew out, knocking over his coffee and spilling it across his newspaper. I saw the picture on the front page just before it became a coffee-sodden mess. It was a close-up of a fair-haired boy in a wheelchair.

Sam Cabot. My own little nightmare.

'Sorry, Bob, I didn't mean to startle you like that.'

'You have nothing to be s-s-sorry for,' Bob said. He adjusted his pink-framed glasses and pulled some paper napkins out of his desk drawer to blot the spill. 'Have a seat. Please.'

'Thank you. I will.'

Bob asked me how I was getting along in Half Moon Bay and I told him I was managing to keep busy.

'I was just reading about you, Lieutenant,' he said, mopping the front page of the paper with a wad of napkins.

'There are no secrets in a nano-second world,' I said with a smile. Then I told Bob that I'd become interested in the homicides that were going on a few miles from my door and wondered what he could tell me.

'I knew Lorelei O'Malley,' he said. 'Represented her on a case. Got her off with a wrist slap,' he said with a self-deprecating shrug. 'I know Ben only slightly. People are saying he must have had something to do with Lorelei's death, but I can't see him killing Caitlin's stepmother. The child was so traumatized by her real mother's suicide.'

'Cops always look at the spouse first.'

'Sure. I know. I've got friends on the force. I grew up in Half Moon Bay,' he explained, 'and I started practicing here right after law school. I like being a small fish in a small pond.'

'You're too modest, Bob.' I waved my hand, indicating the photos hanging on the walls of Bob shaking hands with the state governor and other dignitaries. There were also some neatly framed parchment awards.

'Oh, those,' Bob said, shrugging again. 'Well, I do some *pro bono* work as a *guardian ad litem* for abused or neglected kids. You know, representing them in court, making sure that their rights are protected.'

'Very commendable,' I said. I was starting to warm up to this very likeable guy, and I noticed that he was getting more comfortable with me. He hadn't stuttered since the coffee incident.

Bob leaned back in his chair and pointed to a photo of an award ceremony in the Town Hall: Bob shaking hands with someone who was handing him a plaque.

'See this guy?' he asked, indicating a dapper man sitting with a line of others on the stage. 'Ray Whittaker. He and his wife Molly lived in LA but they summered here. Murdered in their beds a couple of years ago. Lindsay, do you know that all these people were whipped and slashed to death?'

'I'd heard,' I said. I zoned out for a minute as my brain grappled with the fact of yet another set of murders a couple of years ago. *What did the whippings mean? How long had the killer been working?*

When I tuned back in, Bob was still talking about the Whittakers.

'. . . folksy, real nice people. He was a photographer and she was a bit player in Hollywood. It makes no sense. These were *all* good people, and it's tragic that their kids end up in foster homes or with relatives they hardly know. I worry about the kids.' He shook his head and sighed. 'I try to leave this kind of stuff at the office at the end of the day, but it never really works.'

'I know what you mean,' I said. 'If you've got a few minutes, I'll tell you a story that I've been bringing home from the office for the past ten years.'

Chapter Fifty-Five

Bob got up and walked over to a Mr Coffee sitting on a filing cabinet. He poured us each a cup of coffee.

'I've got all the time in the world,' he said. 'I don't like chain coffee house prices.' He smiled over at me. 'That whole yuppie-on-the-go scene.'

Over tepid coffee with powdered milk, I told Bob about my first homicide case.

'We found him in a squalid hotel in the Mission District. I'd seen corpses before, but I was unprepared for this, Bob. He was young – somewhere between seventeen and twenty-one – and when I walked into the room I found him lying spread-eagled on his back, decomposing in a congealed pool of his own blood. Flies were all over him. A shimmering blanket of flies.'

My throat closed up as the images came flooding back; it was as clear as if I were standing in that hotel room right now thinking, *Oh God, get me out of here.* I sipped at the terrible coffee until I could speak again.

'He was wearing only two items of clothing; an ordinary Hanes tube sock, which was identical to hundreds of thousands that were sold all across the country that year, and a T-shirt from The Distillery. You know the place?'

Bob nodded. 'I'll bet every tourist passing through Half Moon Bay since 1930 has eaten there.'

'Yeah. Hell of a clue.'

'How did he die?'

'Throat slashed with a knife. And there were stripes, like lashmarks, across his buttocks. Sound familiar?'

Bob nodded again. He was listening intently, so I continued. I told him that we'd canvassed the city and Half Moon Bay for weeks.

'No one knew the victim, Bob. His prints weren't on file, and the room he died in was so dirty, it was a classic case of instant cross-contamination. We were utterly clueless.

'No one ever came forward to claim the body. It's not so uncommon; we already had twenty-three unclaimed John Does that year. But I still remember the innocence of his young face. He had blue eyes,' I said. 'Light red hair. And now all these years later, more murders are happening, with the same signature.'

'You know what feels really weird, Lindsay? To think that this killer could be someone who lives in this town—'

The phone rang, cutting Bob off mid-sentence.

'Robert Hinton,' he said.

In the next instant, the color drained from his

face. There was silence, punctuated by Bob saying, 'Uh-huh, uh-huh.' Then he said, 'Okay, thanks for letting me know,' and hung up the phone.

'That was a friend of mine who works at the *Gazette*,' he explained. 'Ben O'Malley's body was found by some kids hiking in the woods.'

Chapter Fifty-Six

Jake Daltry's parents lived in a housing development in Palo Alto, a thirty-minute drive southeast of Half Moon Bay. I parked the Explorer on the street in front of their cream-colored raised ranch, one of a dozen like it on Brighton Street.

A portly, unkempt man with gray flyaway hair, wearing a flannel shirt and blue drawstring pants, answered the door.

'Mr Richard Daltry?'

'We don't want any,' he said, and slammed the door. *I've come back from bigger slams than that, buster.* I took out my badge and rang the bell again. This time a small woman with hennaed hair and gray roots, wearing a bunny-print housedress, opened the door.

'What can I do for you?'

'I'm Lieutenant Lindsay Boxer, SFPD,' I said, showing her my badge. 'I'm investigating a homicide case that's been in our cold case files.'

'And what's that got to do with us?'

'I think there may be similarities between my old case and the deaths of Jake and Alice Daltry.'

'I'm Agnes, Jake's mother,' she said, opening the door. 'Please forgive my husband. We've been under a terrible strain. The press is just awful.'

I followed the elderly woman into a house that smelled of Lemon Pledge and a kitchen that didn't seem to have changed since John Hinckley shot Ronald Reagan. We sat at a red Formica table and I could see the backyard through the window. Two little boys played with trucks in a sandbox.

'My poor grandsons,' said Mrs Daltry. 'Why did this happen?'

Agnes Daltry's heartbreak was written on her deeply lined face, her stooped shoulders. I could see how much she needed someone to talk to who hadn't heard it all before.

'Tell me what happened,' I urged her. 'Tell me everything you know.'

'Jake was a wild child,' she said. 'Not bad, you understand, but headstrong. When he met Alice, he grew up overnight. They were so much in love and wanted children so badly. When the boys were born, Jake vowed to be a man they could respect. He loved those boys and, Lieutenant, he lived up to that promise. He was such a good man and he and Alice had such a good marriage – oh.'

She put her hand over her heart, and shook her head miserably. She couldn't go on and she hadn't talked about the murders yet, at all.

Agnes looked down at the table as her husband came through the kitchen. He glared at me, took a beer out of the refrigerator, slammed the door shut and left the room.

'Richard is still angry at me,' she said.

'Why is that, Agnes?'

'I did a bad thing.'

I was almost desperate to know. I put my hand on her bare arm and at my touch, tears rose in her eyes.

'Tell me,' I said softly. She grabbed tissues out of a box and pressed them to her eyes.

'I was going to pick up the boys at school,' she said. 'I stopped off at Jake and Alice's house first to see if they needed milk or juice. Jake was naked, lying dead in the foyer. Alice was on the stairs.'

I stared at Agnes, urging her on with my eyes.

'I cleaned up the blood,' Agnes said with a sigh. She looked at me as if she expected to be whipped herself. 'I dressed them. I didn't want anyone to see them that way.'

'You destroyed the crime scene,' I said.

'I didn't want the boys to see all that blood.'

Chapter Fifty-Seven

I wouldn't have done this a month ago. I would've been too busy thinking about the job I had to do. I stood and I opened my arms to Agnes Daltry.

She put her head against my shoulder and cried as though she would never stop. I understood now. Agnes wasn't getting the comfort she needed from her husband. Her shoulders shook so hard, I could feel her pain as if I knew her; as if I had loved her family as much as she did.

Agnes's grief moved me so much that I was thrown back into the loneliness of losing people I had loved; my mom, Chris, Jill.

I heard the distant sound of the doorbell. I was still holding Agnes when her husband came back into the kitchen.

'Someone's here to see *you*,' he said, his anger coming off his body like a sour smell.

'To see me?'

The man waiting in the living room was a study in dung brown; brown sports jacket and pants, brown-striped tie. He had brown hair, a thick brown moustache and hard brown eyes.

But his face was red. He looked furious.

'Lieutenant Boxer? I'm Peter Stark, Chief of Police, Half Moon Bay. You need to come with me.'

Chapter Fifty-Eight

I parked the Explorer in the 'guest' spot outside the gray-shingled barracks-style police station. Chief Stark got out of his vehicle and crunched across the gravel toward the building, without once looking back to see if I was following him.

So much for professional courtesy.

The first thing I noticed inside the Chief's office was the framed motto behind his desk: *Do the right thing and do it well*. Then I took in the mess; piles of papers over every surface, old fax and copy machines, cockeyed, dusty photos on the wall of Stark posing with dead animals. Half a cheese sandwich on a file cabinet.

The Chief took off his jacket, exposing a massive chest and monster-sized arms. He hung the jacket on a hook behind the door.

'Sit down, Lieutenant. I keep hearing about you,' he said, riffling through a stack of phone messages. He hadn't given me eye-contact since the Daltry house. I took a motorcycle helmet off a side chair, put it on the floor and sat down.

'What the hell do you think you're doing?' he asked.

'Sorry?'

'What the hell gives you the right to come into my backyard and start poking around?' he said, drilling me with his eyes. 'You're on restricted duty, aren't you, Lieutenant?'

'With all due respect, Chief, I don't get your point.'

'Don't screw with me, Boxer. Your rep as a loose cannon precedes you. Maybe you shot those kids without cause—'

'Hey, look—'

'—maybe you got scared, lost your nerve, whatever, and that would make you a dangerous cop. *Get that?*'

I got the message all right. The guy outranked me and a report from him saying that I had violated police procedures or disobeyed direct orders could hurt me. Still, I kept my expression neutral.

'I think these recent murders link up with an old homicide of mine,' I said. 'The killer's signature looks the same. We might be able to help each other.'

'Don't use the "we" word with me, Boxer. You're benched. Don't mess with my crime scenes. Leave my witnesses alone. Take some walks. Read a book. Get a grip. Whatever. Just stay out of my hair.'

When I spoke again, my voice was so taut an aerialist could've cart-wheeled across it to the other side of the room.

'You know, Chief, in your place, all I'd be thinking about is this psychopath wandering your streets. Thinking, *How can I shut him down for good?* I might even *welcome* a decorated Homicide Inspector who wanted to help out. But I guess we think differently.'

My little speech set the Chief back a blink or two, and so I seized the opportunity to get out with my dignity.

'You know how to reach me,' I said, and marched out of the police station.

I could almost hear my lawyer whispering in my ear, *Relax. Keep a low profile.* Nuts, Yuki. Why not advise me to take up the harp?

I revved the engine and peeled out of the parking lot.

Chapter Fifty-Nine

I was driving along Main Street, muttering under my breath, thinking up several new things I wish I'd said to the Chief, when I noticed that my gas gauge light was practically screaming, *'Lindsay! You're out of gas!'*

I pulled into the *Man in the Moon*, ran the Explorer over the air bell and when Keith didn't appear, I walked across the asphalt apron, into the depths of his shop.

The Doors' 'Riders on the Storm' billowed out when I opened the door to the repair bay.

On the wall to my right was a calendar featuring Miss June wearing nothing but a wave in her hair. Above her was a splendid sight; rare and beautiful hood ornaments from Bentleys, Jags, and Maseratis, mounted on lacquered blocks of wood, like trophies. Curled inside a tire was a fat orange tabby cat having a snooze.

I admired the red Porsche parked in the bay and addressed Keith's jeans and work boots in the pit below.

'Nice ride,' I said.

Keith ducked out from under the car, a smile already lighting his grease-streaked face.

'Isn't it, though?' He climbed out of the pit, wiped his hands on a rag, and turned down the music. 'So, Lindsay. You having trouble with that Bonneville?'

'Not at all. I replaced the alternator and the plugs. Engine purrs like this guy.'

'This is Hairball,' Keith told me, scratching the cat under the chin. 'My attack cat. He rode in on the carburettor of a pick-up truck a couple of years ago.'

'Youch.'

'All the way from Encino. Burned his paws, but he's good as new now, aren't you, buddy?'

Keith asked if I needed gas and I said that I did. We walked together into the soft afternoon sunshine.

'I caught you on TV last night,' Keith told me as fuel gurgled into the Explorer's capacious tank.

'You did not.'

'No, I did. Your attorney was on the news and they showed a picture of you in your blues,' he said, grinning at me. 'You really *are* a cop.'

'You didn't believe me?'

The kid shrugged winningly. 'I pretty much believed you. But it was okay either way, Lindsay. Either you were a cop or you just had a great line.'

I hooted and Keith's face crinkled in laughter. After a bit, I told him about the Cabot case – just the overview, minus the grief and the gore. Keith was supportive and a damned sight more fun to talk to than Chief Stark. Hell, I was even enjoying his attention. Brad Pitt, right?

He unlatched the Explorer's hood, pulled out the dipstick and gave me a direct look with his bright blue eyes. I stared into them long enough to notice that his irises were rimmed with navy blue and flecked with brown, as if there were little drifts of gold dust in them.

'You need oil,' I heard him say. I felt my face color.

'Sure. Okay.'

Keith punched open a can of Castrol and poured it into the engine. As he did, he put his other hand in the back pocket of his jeans, adopting a posture of studied nonchalance.

'So, satisfy my curiosity,' he said. 'Tell me about your boyfriend.'

Chapter Sixty

I wrenched myself out of whatever the heck was going on between us and told Keith about Joe; what a great guy he was, how funny, how kind and how smart. 'He works in D.C.; Homeland Security.'

'I'm impressed,' said Keith.

I saw the kid swallow before he asked, 'Are you in love with the guy?'

I nodded, picturing Joe's face, thinking how much I missed him.

'Lucky guy, that Manicotti.'

'Molinari,' I said, grinning.

'Lucky, whatever his name is,' Keith said, closing the hood. Just then, a black sedan with rental car plates pulled up to the garage.

'Damn,' Keith muttered. 'Here comes "Mr Porsche" and his car's not ready.'

As I handed Keith my MasterCard, 'Mr Porsche' stepped out of his rent-a-car and into my peripheral vision.

'Hey, Keith,' he called out. 'How's it coming, my man?'

Wait a minute. *I knew him.* He looked older in broad daylight, but it was that obnoxious guy who'd hit on me and Carolee in The Cormorant. *Dennis Agnew.*

'Just give me five minutes,' Keith called back.

Before I could ask him about that creep, Keith was heading toward the office and Agnew was walking straight toward me. When he got within spitting distance, he stopped, put his hand heavily on the hood of my car and shot me a look that hit me right between the eyes.

He followed up the look with a slow, insinuating smile. 'Slumming, Officer? Or do you just like young meat?' I was honing a retort when Keith came up from behind.

'You calling me "meat"?' Keith said, aligning his body with mine. He matched Agnew's sarcastic smile with a sunny one of his own. 'I guess I should consider the source, you dirty old man.'

It was a grin-off, both men holding their ground. A long blistering moment passed.

Then, Agnew took his hand off my hood.

'C'mon, Meat. I want to see my car.'

Keith winked at me, got me to sign the slip and handed me back my card.

'Stay in touch, Lindsay. OK?'

'Sure thing. You, too.'

I got into my car and started up the engine, but I just sat for a while watching Agnew follow Keith into the repair shop. The guy was wrong, but how wrong, and in what way, I just didn't know.

Chapter Sixty-One

I'd slept badly. Wild, fractured dreams had awoken me repeatedly. Now I leaned over the bathroom sink and brushed my teeth with a goofy vengeance.

I was edgy and I was furious, and I knew why.

By threatening me, Chief Stark had effectively stopped me from investigating leads that might finally solve the John Doe #24 homicide. If I was right, Doe's killer was still active in Half Moon Bay.

I banged glass and crockery around in the kitchen, feeding Martha, making coffee, eating my Wheaties.

I was half-watching *The Today Show* on the small kitchen TV when a red banner flashed on the screen. *LIVE. Breaking News.*

A somber young woman, a local TV reporter, stood in front of a redwood house, the crime-scene tape stretched behind her cordoning off the house from the street. Her voice rose over the sounds of a crowd visible at the edges of the frame.

'At seven thirty this morning Annemarie and

Joseph Sarducci were found dead in their home at 825 Marina Road. Their slashed and partially nude bodies were found by their thirteen-year-old son Anthony, who was unharmed. We spoke with Police Chief Peter Stark just minutes ago.'

The scene cut away to a shot of Stark facing reporters outside the station house. The crowd jostled for position. There were network call-letters on some of the microphones. This was a siege.

I turned up the sound.

'Chief Stark. Is it true that the Sarduccis were slaughtered like animals?'

'Chief! Over here! Did Tony Sarducci find them? Did the kid find his parents?'

'Hey, Pete. Do you have a suspect?'

I watched transfixed as Stark negotiated the balancing act of his life. Either tell the truth or lie and pay for it later, but keep the public calm and don't give the killer any information he can use. I'd seen the same look on the face of Chief Moose when the D.C. Sniper was at large.

'Look, I can't say more than this,' Stark said. 'Two more people have died, but I can't tell you anything of an evidentiary nature. We're on it. And we'll inform the public as soon as we have something substantive to report.'

I grabbed a chair, pulled it right up to the screen and sat down hard. Even though I'd seen so many murdered people, this case got me to the core. I didn't think I could have a reaction like this. I was so outraged at the killer's audacity I was shaking.

I joined the throng outside the police station by proxy. I found myself talking at a 13-inch Sony and Chief Stark's shrunken image.

'Who is doing this, Chief?

'Who the hell is murdering all of these people?'

PART FOUR

Trials and Tribulation

Chapter Sixty-Two

They were carrying the bodies out of the house just as I arrived. I parked between two black-and-whites on the lawn and looked up at a stunning glass and redwood contemporary.

The gaping crowd parted as paramedics bumped down the steps with the stretchers, then slid the two body bags into the open maw at the back of the EMS van. Although I didn't know Annemarie and Joseph Sarducci, I was swamped by unspeakable sadness.

I edged my way through the mob and up to the front door, where a uniformed officer was on security detail, at ease, with his hands behind his back.

I could tell he was a pro because he gave me both a warm smile and a cold eye. I took a chance and badged him.

'The Chief's inside, Lieutenant.'

I rang the bell.

The first bar of Vivaldi's *Four Seasons* chimed. Chief Stark opened the door, and when he saw that it was me, his jaw tightened.

'What are you fucking doing here?' he said, biting down on his words. I put my heart into my reply, because it was true.

'I want to help, damn it. May I come in?'

We stared at each other across the threshold until finally Chief Stark blinked.

'Anyone ever tell you that you're a *persistent* pain in the ass?' he said, stepping aside so that I could enter.

'Yes. And thanks.'

'Don't thank me. I called a friend of mine on the SFPD. Charlie Clapper says you're a good cop. He's right about half the time. Don't make me sorry.'

'You honestly think you could feel sorrier than you do right now?'

I walked past Stark through the foyer and into the living room with its wall of windows facing the water below. The furnishings were of a spare Scandinavian variety; clean lines, flat woven carpets, abstract art, and although the Sarduccis were dead, I could feel their presence in the things they'd left behind.

Even as I mentally catalogued everything I could see, I noticed what was missing. There were no cones, tags or markers on the ground floor. *So where had the killer entered?*

I turned to the Chief. 'Mind running the scene for me?'

'Bastard broke in through the skylight upstairs,' said Stark.

Chapter Sixty-Three

The master bedroom felt not just cold, but hollowed-out, as if the room itself were suffering from the terrible loss.

Windows were open and the vertical blinds clacked in the breeze, like the rattling bones of the dead. The rumpled, ice-blue bed linens were spattered with arterial blood, and the sight of that made the room feel even colder.

A half-dozen CSU techs bagged knick-knacks from the nightstand, vacuumed the carpet, brushed surfaces for prints. Except for the blood, the room seemed oddly undisturbed.

I borrowed some surgical gloves, then leaned in close to look at the studio shot of the Sarduccis that was propped on the bureau. Annemarie was pretty and petite. Joe had a 'gentle giant' look, his arms proudly surrounding his wife and son.

Why would someone want this couple dead?

'Annemarie's throat was slashed,' Stark said, his voice breaking into my thoughts. 'Just about cut her head off.'

He indicated the blood-drenched carpet beside the bed. 'She fell there. Joe wasn't in bed when it happened.'

Stark pointed out that Annemarie's blood spatter radiated out straight across the bed, and that the stain pattern was uninterrupted.

'No signs of a struggle,' said the Chief. 'Joey bought it in the bathroom.'

I followed Stark across the blond carpet to a white marble bath. Bright blood was concentrated on one side of the room, a lateral swath sprayed against the wall at about knee-level. It dripped down the wall and joined the congealing lake of blood on the floor. I could see the outline of Joe's body where he had fallen.

I crouched to get a better look.

'The intruder must've found the lady alone in bed,' said the Chief, running me through his hypothetical. 'Maybe he puts his hand over her mouth, asks, "Where's your husband?" Or maybe he hears the toilet flush. He offs Annemarie quick. Then he surprises Joe in the can. Joe hears the door open and says, "Honey?" He looks up now. "Wait. Who are you? What do you want?"'

'This blood's from his neck wound,' I said, indicating the swath low on the wall. 'The killer had to get Joe down on all fours so he could control him. Joe was the bigger man.'

'Yeah,' Stark said wearily. 'Looks like he got him down, stood behind him, pulled Joe's head back by the hair, and . . .' The Chief drew his finger across his throat.

I asked questions and the Chief answered: nothing had been stolen. The boy hadn't heard a sound. Friends and neighbors had come forward to say that the Sarduccis were happy, didn't have an enemy in the world.

'Just like the Daltrys,' Chief Stark said. 'Same story with the O'Malleys. No weapons, no clues, nothing funny with their finances, no apparent motive. The victims didn't know each other.' The Chief's face kind of crumpled in on itself. He was vulnerable for a split-second and I could see the pain.

'All the victims had in common was that they were married,' he said. 'So, where does that go? Eighty percent of the people in Half Moon Bay are married. The whole goddamned town is terrified. Me included.'

The Chief finished his speech. He looked away, stuffed the back of his shirt into his pants, patted down his hair. Collected himself so he didn't look as desperate as he must have felt. Then he looked me in the eye.

'So what are your thoughts, Lieutenant? Wow me, why don't you?'

Chapter Sixty-Four

I hadn't seen the bodies and the labs from this savage double homicide wouldn't start trickling in for days. Still, I ignored the Chief's sarcasm and told him what my gut had already told me.

'There were two killers,' I said.

Stark's head jerked back. He practically spat, *'Bullshit.'*

'Look,' I said. 'There was no sign of a struggle, right? Why didn't Joe try to overpower his assailant? He was big. He was a *bear*. Try it this way,' I went on. 'Joe was taken out of the room at knifepoint – and he cooperated because he *had* to. *Killer number two was still in the bedroom with Annemarie.'*

The Chief's eyes darted around, looking at the scene from a new angle, imagining it the way I saw it.

'I'd like to see the kid's room,' I said.

When I stepped across the threshold, I could see from his stuff that Anthony Sarducci was a smart kid. He had good books, terrariums full of healthy creepy-crawlers and a high-powered computer on his desk. But what got me most interested were the indentations in the carpet where the desk chair normally stood. *The chair had been moved. Why was that?*

I swung my head around and saw it, just inside the doorway.

I thought about that cop standing sentry outside the Sarducci house and made a mental leap.

The child had heard nothing.

But what would have happened if he had?

I pointed out the chair to the Chief.

'Anyone move this chair?' I asked.

'No one's been inside this room.'

'I changed my mind,' I told him. 'There weren't two intruders here. There were three. Two to do the killings. One to manage the boy if he woke up. He sat right over there in that chair.'

The Chief turned stiffly, walked down the hall and returned with a young female CSU tech. She waited by the door with her roll of tape until we had stepped out of the room. Then she cordoned it off.

'I don't want to believe this, Lieutenant. It was bad enough when we were dealing with one psycho.'

I held his gaze. Then, for just a second, he smiled.

'Don't quote me, now,' he said, 'but I think I just said "we".'

Chapter Sixty-Five

It was late in the afternoon when I left the Sarducci house. I drove southeast along Cabrillo, my mind buzzing with the details of the crime and my conversation with the Chief. When he confirmed that the Sarduccis, like the other double murder victims, had been whipped, I told him that I'd had a brush with these murderers myself.

I told him about John Doe #24.

All the dots between the Half Moon Bay murders and my John Doe hadn't been connected yet, but I was pretty sure I was right. Ten years on Homicide had taught me that though MOs might change over time, signatures always stayed the same. Whipping and slashing in combination was a rare, possibly unique signature.

The light was red as I approached the intersection just a few blocks from the Sarduccis'. As I braked, I glanced into the rear-view mirror and saw a red sports car coming up behind me very fast. I expected the car to stop, *but it didn't even slow down*.

I could not believe what I saw next. My eyes

were pinned to the rear-view mirror, watching as the car kept coming toward me on a collision course.

I leaned on my horn, but the car just got bigger in my rear-view. What the hell was going on? Was the driver on his freaking cell phone? Did he see me?

Adrenaline shot through me and time splintered into fragments. I stepped on the gas and jerked the wheel to avoid the collision, driving off the road and onto a front lawn, taking out a garden cart before coming to rest at the base of a Douglas fir.

I immediately jerked the Explorer into reverse, tearing up the lawn before getting back onto the roadway. Then I took off after the fast-disappearing maniac who'd almost driven through my back seat. Who hadn't stopped to check on the wreck he almost caused. The asshole could have killed me.

I kept the red car in sight, getting close enough to recognize its elegant shape. The car was a Porsche.

My face got hot as my fear and anger came together. I gunned my engine, following the Porsche as it wove through traffic, crossing the double yellow line repeatedly.

The last time I'd seen that car, Keith had been fixing the oil pan.

It was Dennis Agnew's car.

A dozen miles flew by. I was still on the Porsche's tail when we went up and over the hills into San Mateo and south on El Camino Real, a seedy thoroughfare bordering the Cal-train tracks. Then, without signaling, the Porsche hooked a sharp right into a strip mall entrance.

I followed, squealing into the turn, coming to a stop in a nearly desolate parking lot. I turned off the engine and, as my racing heart slowed to a canter, I looked around.

The mini-mall was a downmarket collection of retail shops – auto parts, a Dollar Store, a liquor store. Down at the far end of the lot was a square cement-block building with a red neon sign in the window: *Playmate Pen. XXX Live Girls.*

Parked in front of the poster-plastered storefront was Dennis Agnew's car.

I locked the Explorer and walked the twenty yards to the porn shop. I opened the door and went inside.

Chapter Sixty-Six

The Playmate Pen was an ugly place lit by harsh overhead lights and flashing neon. To my left were racks of party toys; dildos and ticklers in garish colors, and molded body parts in lifelike plastic. To my right were soda and snack machines – refreshment for all those film lovers trapped inside tiny video booths with their brains hooked into their fantasies, hands firmly on their joysticks.

I felt eyes tracking me as I walked the narrow aisles lined with videos. I was the only female wandering loose in the place and I guess I stood out more in my slacks and blazer than if I'd been stark naked.

I was about to approach the clerk in front when I felt a dark presence at my elbow.

'Lindsay?'

I started – but Dennis Agnew looked thrilled to see me.

'To what do I owe the honor, Lieutenant?'

I was caught in a maze of stacks and racks of chicks-and-dicks, but like a steer in the chute of a slaughterhouse, I could see that the only way out was straight ahead.

Agnew's office was a brightly lit, windowless cubicle. He took the chair behind a wood-grain Formica desk and indicated where I should sit – a black leather sofa that had seen better days.

'I'll stand. This isn't going to take long,' I said, but as I stood there in the doorway, I had to look around the room.

Every wall was hung with framed photos signed to *Randy Long* from g-stringed lovelies, porn film publicity stills of overheated couplings featuring Randy Long and his partners. I also saw a few flash-bulb snapshots of Agnew posing with grinning guys in suits.

Bells started clanging as I matched the mugs of young up-and-coming wise guys to the mobsters they'd later become. At least two of the suits were now dead.

It took me another couple of seconds to realize that Dennis Agnew and the younger, long-haired Randy Long in the photos were one and the same. *Agnew had been a freaking porn star.*

Chapter Sixty-Seven

'So, Lieutenant, what can I do you for?' Dennis Agnew said, smiling, making neat stacks of his papers, corraling a loose pile of cock rings and pouring them like coins from one hand to another, then onto the desktop.

'I don't know what you're trying to pull,' I said, 'but where I come from, running a car off the road is a crime.'

'Seriously, Lindsay. You don't mind if I call you Lindsay?' Agnew folded his hands and gave me one of his bleached-beyond-white smiles. 'I don't know what you're talking about.'

'That's crap. Twenty minutes ago you ran me off the road. People could've been killed. *I* could've been killed.'

'Oh, no. Couldn't have been me,' Agnew said, furrowing his brow and shaking his head. 'I think I would've noticed that. No, I think you've come here because you want to see me.'

It was infuriating. Not just that Agnew was a

creep with a fast car who didn't give a shit, but his mocking attitude really fried me.

'See these girls?' he said, hooking a thumb toward his 'wall of fame'. 'You know why they do these flicks? Their self-esteem is so low they think by debasing themselves with men, they'll actually feel more powerful. Isn't that ridiculous? And look at you, debasing yourself by coming here. Does it make *you* feel powerful?'

I was choking on this load of crap, sputtering, 'You arrogant horse's ass,' when I heard a voice saying, 'Whoa! Please tell me you're applying for a job here.'

A small man with a cheap green jacket buttoned over his beer belly appeared in the office doorway. He leaned against the door jamb, an arm's length from where I stood, running his eyes over me. It was a look that just about skeeved me out of my skin.

'Rick Monte, this is Lieutenant Lindsay Boxer. She's a Homicide cop from San Francisco,' Agnew said. 'She's on vacation – or so she says.'

'Enjoying your time off, Lieutenant?' Rick asked my bust-line.

'I'm loving it, but I could make this an official visit at any time.' As soon as I said those words, I felt a jolt straight to the heart.

What was I doing?

I was on restricted duty and out of my jurisdiction. I'd chased a citizen in my own car. I had no back-up, and if either of these jerk-offs phoned in a complaint, I'd be up on disciplinary action.

It was the last thing I needed before my trial.

'If I didn't know better, I'd think you were upset,' Dennis said in his oily voice. 'I haven't done anything to harm you, you know.'

'Next time you see me,' I said through clenched teeth, 'turn and walk the other way.'

'Oh. Pardon me. I must have it wrong. I thought it was *you* who followed *me*.'

I was hot to fire off a comeback, but this time I stifled it. He was right. He hadn't actually done anything to me. He hadn't even called me a name.

I left Agnew's office, kicking myself for showing up on this lowlife's turf.

I had pointed my nose toward the front of the shop, intent on putting this horrid little scene behind me, when my way was blocked by a brawny young guy with blond streaks in his mullet and tattooed flames shooting out of his T-shirt collar.

'Out of my way, Hot Stuff,' I said, trying to squeeze past him.

The guy held out his arms while standing like a boulder in the middle of the store. He smiled, daring me.

'Come on, Mama. Come to Rocco,' he said.

'It's all right, Rocco,' Agnew said. 'This lady is my guest. I'll walk you out, Lindsay.'

I reached for the door, but Agnew leaned against it, boxing me in. He was so close all I could see was his face; every pore, every capillary in his bloodshot eyes. He pressed a video cassette into my hands.

The cover advertised Randy Long's epic performance in *A Long Hard Night*.

'Take a look when you have a chance. I put my phone number on the back.'

I pushed away from Agnew and the video clattered to the floor.

'Move it,' I said.

He stepped back, just clearing the door enough so that I could open it. Agnew had a grin on his face and his hand on his crotch as I left.

Chapter Sixty-Eight

I woke up the next morning thinking about Dennis Agnew, that slime. I took my coffee out to the porch and before it had cooled enough to drink, I was taking my agitation out on a rattle in the Bonneville's engine.

I had a feeler gauge in my hand and was fiddling with the valves when a car rolled up and parked in the driveway.

Doors slammed.

'Lindsay? Helllooo.'

'I think she's been swallowed by that big gold boat.'

I ducked out from under the hood, wiped my greasy hands on a chamois and reached out my arms to Cindy and Claire, grabbing them both in one giant hug. We squealed and jumped around and Martha, who'd been sleeping on the porch, joined in.

'We were in the neighborhood,' said Claire when we broke from our clinch. 'Thought we'd stop by and see how much trouble you've gotten into. So what's this, Lindsay? I thought all these gas gluttons had been crushed and outlawed.'

'Don't be talking bad about my baby,' I said with a laugh.

'It runs?'

'No sirree, Butterfly. She flies.'

The girls handed me a beribboned spa basket from Nordstrom's full of great, mood-altering bath and body stuff, and after a unanimous show of hands, we piled into the Bonneville for a ride.

I buzzed down the electric windows and as the car's big whitewalls softened the road, the zephyr coming off the Bay mussed and tousled our hair. We rounded the loops of Cat's neighborhood and were headed up the mountain, when Claire showed me an envelope.

'Almost forgot. Jacobi sent this.'

I glanced at the 8 x 11 inch manila envelope in her hand. The night before, I'd called Jacobi and asked him to get me anything he could find on Dennis Agnew, aka Randy Long.

I filled Cindy and Claire in on my first accidental meeting with Agnew at The Cormorant bar, the set-to at Keith's garage, and the near-rear-ender. Then I described my skeevy tour of the Playmate Pen in minute detail.

'He said *that* to you!' Cindy exclaimed after I quoted Agnew on 'women debase themselves with men so they can feel powerful'. Her cheeks pinked; she was pissed off right up to her eyelashes. 'Now there's someone who should be crushed and outlawed.'

I laughed and told her, 'Agnew had this wall of fame, like something you'd see in Tony Soprano's office in the Bada-Bing. All these signed photos from porn queens and wise guys. Unreal. Claire, will you open that, please?'

Claire took three pages from the envelope. They were stapled together and annotated with a Post-it note from Jacobi.

'Read it out loud, if you don't mind,' Cindy said, leaning over the back of the front seat.

'There's some minor league stuff – DWI, assault, domestic violence, a drug bust and some time at Folsom. But here ya go, Linds. Says he was charged with first-degree murder five years ago. Case dismissed.'

I reached over and peeled off Jacobi's handwritten note: *The vic was Agnew's girlfriend. His lawyer was Ralph Brancusi.*

I didn't have to say more. We all knew Brancusi was a high-profile defense attorney. Only the wealthy could afford him.

Brancusi was also the lawyer of choice for the mob.

Chapter Sixty-Nine

When we got back to Cat's house, there was a patrol car in the driveway and Chief Stark was walking toward us. He looked as grim as ever, brow scrunched up, with a haunted look in his eyes that was actually contagious.

'What is it, Chief? What's happened now?' I asked.

'The ME's about to start the posts on the Sarduccis,' he said, squinting into the sun. 'This is your formal invitation.'

I felt a surge of excitement that I masked out of consideration for the Chief. I introduced Cindy and Claire.

'Dr Washburn is the CME in San Francisco,' I said. 'Okay for her to come along?'

'Sure, why not?' the Chief grunted. 'Take all the help I can get. I'm learning, right?'

Cindy looked at the three of us and saw that she wasn't being included in the invitation. Hell, she was the press.

'I get it,' she said, good-naturedly. 'Look, I'll hang

out here, no problem. I've got my laptop and a deadline. Plus, I'm a leper.'

Claire and I got back into the Bonneville and followed the Chief's car out to the highway.

'This is great,' I said, my enthusiasm brimming over. 'He's letting me into the case.'

'What am I doing?' Claire said, shaking her head. 'Aiding and abetting your completely ill-advised involvement when we both know you should be out on the porch with a gin and tonic, your butt in a chair and your legs propped up on the railing.'

I laughed. 'Admit it,' I said. 'You're hooked too. You can't turn away from this thing, either.'

'You're nuts,' she grumbled. Then she looked over at me. My grin set hers off.

'You kill me, Lindsay. You really do. But it's your ass, baby.'

Ten minutes later, we followed Stark's car off the highway into Moss Beach.

Chapter Seventy

The morgue was in the basement of the Seton Medical Center. It was a white-tiled room smelling as pristine and fresh as the frozen food section in a supermarket. A cooler hummed gently in the background.

I nodded at two evidence techies who were grousing about some bureaucratic scheduling screw-up as they folded the victims' garments into brown paper bags.

I was drawn to the autopsy tables in the middle of the room where the ME's young assistant was running a sponge and hose over the Sarduccis' bodies. He turned off the water and stepped aside as I approached.

Joseph and Annemarie lay naked and exposed under the bright lights. Their glistening bodies were unmarked except for ugly slash wounds across their necks, their faces as unlined in death as those of children.

Claire called my name, breaking my silent communion with the dead.

I turned and she introduced me to a man in blue scrubs and a plastic apron, with a net over his gray hair. He had a slight, stooped build and a lopsided smile, as if he had Bell's palsy or had suffered a stroke.

'Lindsay, this is Dr Bill Ramos, forensic pathologist. Bill, this is Lieutenant Lindsay Boxer, Homicide from SFPD. There may be a link between these murders and a cold case of hers.'

I was shaking Ramos's hand when Chief Stark came over.

'Doc, tell her what you told me on the phone.'

Ramos said, 'Why don't I show you?' He spoke to his assistant. 'Hey, Samir, I want to take a look at the female's back, so give me a half turn. Let's put her on the side.'

Samir crossed Annemarie's ankles, left over right, and the doctor reached over and took her left wrist. Then, the two of them pulled the corpse so that it rested on one side.

I peered at seven yellowish marks crossing over one another on the dead woman's buttocks, each about three-quarters of an inch in width, approximately three inches long.

'Tremendous force in these blows,' said Ramos. 'Still, you can barely make them out. Samir, let's turn Mr Sarducci now.'

The doctor and his assistant pulled the male onto his side, his head lolling back pathetically as they did so.

'Now, see,' the doctor said, 'here it is again. Multiple faint rectangular patterns – pressure-type abrasions. They aren't the red-brown color you'd see if the section had been struck while he was still alive, and they're not the yellow parchment-like abrasions you'd get if the blows were administered post-mortem.'

The doctor looked up to make sure I understood.

'Punch me in the face, then shoot me twice in the chest. There won't be enough blood pressure for me to get a rip-roaring bruise on my face, but there'll be *something* there if my heart pumps for a moment.'

The doctor took a scalpel to one of the marks on the male's back, cutting through unmarked tissue and the pale strapmark. 'You can see this light brownish color under the abrasions, what's called a "well circumscribed focal accumulation of blood".

'In plain English,' Ramos continued, 'and wouldn't you agree, Dr Washburn? The deep slash across the carotid artery and the vagus nerves stopped the heart almost instantly, but not instantaneously. This man had one last heartbeat when he was whipped.

'These blows were administered cum-mortem: just before or at the time of death. In the mind of the killer, the victim could still feel the lash.'

'Looks like it was personal,' said Stark.

'Oh, yes. I'd say the killers hated their victims.'

There was a hush in the room as the doctor's words sank in.

'The marks on Joe are narrower than the marks on Annemarie,' Claire noted.

'Yes,' Ramos agreed again. 'Different implements.'

'Like a belt,' I said. 'Could these whippings have been made by *two* different belts?'

'I can't say positively, but it's certainly *very likely*,' said Ramos.

Claire looked not only focused, but sad.

'What are you thinking?' I asked her.

'I hate to say it, Lindsay, but this really takes me back. The marks look like what I remember seeing on your John Doe.'

Chapter Seventy-One

It was after midnight when the Watcher headed inland from the beach. He climbed the sandy cliff, then stuck to the quarter-mile of path that cut through the thistles and thick dune grasses and ran east from the cliffs. The Watcher could finally make out the serpentine bayside road.

He was honing in on one particular house when he stumbled over a log in the path. He reached out to break his fall and went down hard, splaying out on his belly, hands scraping packed sand and saw grass.

The Watcher got quickly to his knees, slapping his breast jacket-pocket – his camera had flown.

'Fuck fuck fuck!' he yelled in frustration.

He crawled on all fours, patting the sand, feeling the sweat on his upper lip dry in the cool air.

Desperation clutched at him as the minutes leached away. At last, he found his precious camera, so small – lens-down in the sand.

He blew on the camera to dislodge the grit, pointed it at the houses and peered into the viewfinder. He saw through a haze of fine scratches across the plastic lens.

This was bad.

Cursing under his breath, the Watcher checked the time – 12:14 a.m. – and set out toward the house where Lindsay was staying.

Now that his zoom lens was useless, he would have to get closer, and on foot.

The Watcher stepped over the guard rail at the end of the field and stood square on the sidewalk with a streetlight blazing down on his head.

Two houses in from the end of the road, Cat Boxer's house glowed with lamplight.

He ducked into shadows and approached the house obliquely by cutting through side yards, crouching at last in the lee of the privet hedge bordering the Boxer living room.

With heart pounding, he stood and peered through the picture window.

The gang were all there: Lindsay in her SFPD T-shirt; Claire, the black ME from the city, in a gold caftan, and Cindy, her blond hair bunched on top of her head, a chenille robe covering all but the legs of her pink pajamas and her feet.

The women were talking intensely, sometimes laughing loudly, then getting serious again. If only he could make out what the hell they were saying.

The Watcher ran through the facts, recent events, the circumstances. *The chair in the kid's room.* It didn't connect any of them to anything, but it was a mistake that he'd made.

Was it safe to go forward?

There was so much more to do.

The Watcher felt the accumulating effects of stress on his body. His hands were shaking and his chest burned with acid. He couldn't stay here any longer, *he just could not.*

He looked around, making sure no one was walking a dog or taking out the garbage, then he stepped from behind the hedge and briefly into the streetlight. He jumped the guard rail and started along the darkened path to the beach.

A decision had to be made about Lindsay Boxer.

A tough one.

The woman was a cop.

Chapter Seventy-Two

I woke early in the morning with a thought that surfaced in my mind like a porpoise breaking from beneath the waves.

I let Martha out back, put coffee on to perk and booted up my laptop.

I remembered that Bob Hinton had said that two other people had been killed in Half Moon Bay two years before; Ray and Molly Whittaker. They were summer people, Hinton had said. Ray was a photographer, Molly a bit player, an extra in Hollywood.

I went online to the NCIC database and looked them up. I was still in shock when I went into the bedrooms to rouse the girls.

When they were dressed and had coffee and scones in front of them, I told them what I'd learned about Ray and Molly Whittaker.

'They were pornographers, both of them. Ray was behind the camera and Molly performed with kids. Boys, girls, it didn't seem to matter,' I said.

'They were busted for it and acquitted. Their lawyer? *It was Brancusi, again.*'

The girls knew me too well. They got on my case, warning me to be careful, reminding me that for all intents and purposes I was a civilian and that even though it seemed logical to check out a possible connection between the Whittakers and Dennis Agnew, I was out of my territory, no one had my back and I was heading for big trouble.

I must have said, 'I know, I know,' a half-dozen times, and as we said good-bye in the driveway I made a lot of promises to be a good girl.

'You should think about coming home, Lindsay,' said Claire finally, holding my face in her hands.

'Right,' I said. 'I'll definitely think about it.'

They both hugged me as though they would never see me again, and frankly, that got to me. As Claire's car pulled out of the driveway, Cindy leaned out the window.

'I'll call you tonight. Think about what we said. *Think*, Lindsay.'

I blew kisses and went inside the house. I found my handbag hanging from a doorknob and rooted around inside it until I felt my phone, my badge and my gun.

A minute later I started up the Explorer.

It was a short drive into town, with my mind churning right up to the second I pulled my car into a parking spot outside the police barracks.

I found the Chief in his office, staring at his computer, coffee mug in hand, a box of sugared donuts on the side chair.

'Those things will kill you,' I said. He moved the donuts so that I could sit down.

'If you ask me, death by donuts is a fine way to go. What's on your mind, Lieutenant?'

'This,' I said. I unfurled Dennis Agnew's rap sheet and slapped it down on top of the messy pile of papers on the Chief's desk. 'Ray and Molly Whittaker were whipped, weren't they?'

'Yup, they were the first.'

'Did you like anyone for their murders?'

The Chief nodded. 'Couldn't prove it then, can't prove it now, but we've been watching this guy for a long time.'

He picked up Agnew's rap sheet and handed it back to me. 'We know all about Dennis Agnew. He's our prime suspect.'

Chapter Seventy-Three

I was on the porch at sunset, noodling a little tune on my guitar when headlights at the bottom of the road crawled slowly up the street and stopped outside Cat's house.

I was already moving toward the car as the driver got out of the front seat and opened the rear passenger-side door.

'I get it,' I said, my face glowing enough to light up the dusk. 'You just happened to be in the neighborhood.'

'Exactly,' Joe said, reaching an arm around my waist. 'Thought I'd surprise you.'

I put my hand on the front of his crisp white shirt.

'Claire called you.'

'*And* Cindy.' Joe laughed a little sheepishly. 'Let me take you out to dinner.'

'Hmm. What if I make dinner here?'

'Deal.'

Joe tapped the roof and the sedan took off.

'C'mere,' he said, folding me in his arms, kissing

me, shocking me once again that a kiss could spark such a conflagration. I had one moderately sane thought as the heat surged through my body: *Here we go again. Another drive-by romantic interlude on the rollercoaster affair of my life.*

Joe cupped my face in his hands and kissed me again, and my heart surrendered its feeble protestation. We entered the house and I kicked the door shut behind us.

I stood on tiptoes with my arms around Joe's neck and let him walk me backwards through the house, until I was on my back in bed and Joe was taking off my clothes. He started with my shoes and kissed everything he exposed on his way up to my lips.

Dear God, he melted everything but my Kokopelli.

I gasped and reached for him, but he was gone.

I opened my eyes and watched him undress. He was gorgeous. Fit, tanned, hard. And all for me.

I smiled with sheer delight. Five minutes ago, I'd been looking forward to a *Law & Order* marathon. Now this! I opened my arms and Joe covered my body with his.

'Hey,' he said. 'I've missed you so much.'

'Shut up,' I said. I bit his lower lip, not too hard, then opened my mouth to his and wrapped my limbs around him.

When we emerged from the bedroom an hour later, barefoot and disheveled, it was pitch black outside. Martha thumped her tail, plainly meaning, *Feed me*, which I did.

Then I made a luscious tricolor salad with a

mustard vinaigrette and thinly shaved parmesan, and I put some pasta on to boil while Joe stirred basil, oregano and garlic into tomato sauce. Soon a divine aroma filled the air.

We ate at the kitchen table, exchanging our headlines of the past week. Joe's headlines were a lot like CNN's. Horrifying car bombs, airport infiltrations, and political dust-ups that I didn't need to have top-secret clearance to hear about. As we washed the dishes together, I told Joe the briefest, least inflammatory version of my encounters with Agnew.

His jaw clenched as I laid it out for him.

'Pretend I didn't tell you,' I said, kissing his brow as I refilled his glass with wine.

'Pretend I'm not mad at you for putting yourself in that kind of danger.'

Jeez, had everyone forgotten that I was a cop? And a smart one, by the way. First female Lieutenant in San Francisco and so on and so forth.

'How do you feel about Cary Grant?' I asked him. 'How does Katharine Hepburn grab you?'

We cuddled together on the sofa and watched *Bringing Up Baby*, one of my favorite screwball comedies. I cracked up as I always did at the scene where Cary Grant crawls around after a terrier with a dinosaur bone in its mouth and Joe laughed along with me, holding me in his arms.

'If you ever catch me doing that with Martha, don't ask.'

I laughed.

'I love you so much, Lindsay.'

'I love you so much, too.'

Later that night, I fell asleep inside the curve of Joe's body, thinking, *This is so right. I just can't get enough of this man.*

Chapter Seventy-Four

Joe cooked bacon and scrambled eggs in the dazzling light pouring through the kitchen windows. I filled mugs with coffee and Joe read the squint in my eyes for the unspoken question that it was.

'I'm here until I get the call. If you want, I'll help you brainstorm the murders.'

We got into the Explorer with Joe at the wheel and Martha on my lap. I filled Joe in on the Sarduccis as we slowly cruised past their glass house beside the Bay.

Then we headed up to Crescent Heights, taking the snaking dirt road to the door of the Daltrys' abandoned little house.

If ever a house looked devastated by murder, this was it. The front lawn had gone to seed, boards had been hammered over the windows and the doors, and scraps of crime-scene tape fluttered like little yellow birds in the bushes.

'Very different socio-economic class from the Sarduccis,' said Joe.

'Yeah. I don't think these murders have anything to do with money.'

We pointed the Explorer down the mountain and within a few minutes we entered Ocean Colony, the golf-course-bordered community where the O'Malleys had lived and died. I pointed out the white colonial with blue shutters as we neared it. There was a *For Sale* sign in the front yard and a Lincoln in the driveway.

We parked at the curb and saw a blonde woman in a pink Lilly Pulitzer dress exit the house and lock the front door. When she saw us, her face stretched into a heavily lipsticked smile.

'Hello,' she said. 'I'm Emily Harris, Pacific Homes Real Estate. I'm sorry, the Open House is *Sunday*. I can't show you the home now because I have an appointment in town . . .'

My face must have shown disappointment and I saw Ms Harris size us up as likely prospects.

'Listen. Replace the key in the lock box on your way out. Okay?'

We got out of the car and I linked my arm through Joe's. Looking every bit the married couple shopping for our new home, Joe and I climbed the front steps and unlocked the O'Malleys' front door.

Chapter Seventy-Five

The inside of the house had been sanitized, spiffed up and repainted – whatever it took to get top dollar for a very challenging property. I lingered in the center hall then followed Joe up the winding staircase.

When I got to the master bedroom, I found him staring at the closet door.

'There was a small hole here at eye-level – see, Linds? It was patched.' He dented the still malleable Spackle with his fingernail.

'A peephole?'

'A peephole in a closet,' said Joe. 'That's odd, don't you think? Unless the O'Malleys were making home movies.'

My mind whirled for a moment as I grappled with a possible connection between homemade porn and the Randy Long variety. Had the cops seen the camera set-up?

And if they had, so what?

There was nothing illegal about consenting adults at play.

I stepped inside the newly painted closet, batted the wire coat hangers aside, then grabbed them to stop their jangling.

That's when I saw another patch of Spackle visible under the fresh paint.

I prodded it with a finger and felt my heart start to hammer. *There was another peephole at the back of the closet and it went right through the wall.*

I took one of the hangers off the rod and straightened it into a long wire, which I inserted into the hole.

'Joe, could you go find where this comes out?'

The wire felt like a living thing as I waited for the tug that finally came from the other end. Joe returned seconds later. 'It goes through to another bedroom. You should see this, Lindsay.'

The room next door was still partly furnished with a ruffled four-poster, matching vanity, and an ornate full-length mirror affixed to the wall. Joe pointed out the hole disguised as a floral detail in the mirror's carved wooden frame.

'Shit, Joe. This is their daughter's room. Were those bastards spying on Caitlin? Were they filming her?'

I stared out the car window as Joe drove us back to Cat's house. I couldn't stop thinking about that second peephole. What kind of people had the O'Malleys been? Why would they have trained a camera on that child?

Had it been some kind of nanny-cam in the past?

Or was it something far more sinister?

My mind did pretzel loops around that peephole as I tried on every possibility. But it all came back to one question: *Did any of this tie in with the murders?*

Chapter Seventy-Six

It was only noon when we got back to Cat's house. Joe and I went into my nieces' bedroom so that we could use their wall-sized cork board to plot out what we knew about the murders.

I found marking pens and construction paper and pulled up two small red plastic stools to sit on.

'So what do we know?' Joe asked, tacking yellow paper across the board.

'Circumstantial evidence suggests three killers. The ME says it looks to him like various knives and belts were used, backing up my theory that there were multiple perps, but there's really nothing else. Not a hair, not a fiber, not a print, not a speck of DNA. It's like working a case in the 1940s. CSI wouldn't help crack this one.'

'What do you see as a pattern? Talk it out for me.'

'It's not coming in clear,' I said, moving my hands over a make-believe crystal ball. 'Stark told me that the victims were all married. Then he says, "That doesn't mean anything. Eighty percent of the population here is married."'

Joe printed the victims' names on the sheets of paper.

'Keep going,' he said.

'All of the couples had children except the Whittakers. The Whittakers made kiddie porn and Caitlin O'Malley may have been a victim. That's pure speculation. The porn angle makes me think there may be some connection to the local porn guys, and through them to organized crime – speculation again. And lastly, my John Doe doesn't seem to match the victim profile.'

'Maybe the first murder was an impulse,' said Joe, 'and the later murders were premeditated.'

'Hmm,' I said, letting my gaze drift to the windowsill where sweet potatoes grew in water glasses, sending out tendrils and fresh green leaves along the ledge. 'That makes sense. Maybe my John Doe was killed in a crime of passion. If so, the killer or killers didn't feel the urge again for quite a long time. Same signature. But what's the connection?'

'I don't know yet. Try boiling it down for me.'

'We've got eight related murders within a ten-mile radius. All the victims had their throats slit, except for Lorelei O'Malley, who was gutted. All eight plus John Doe were whipped. Motive unknown. And there's a prime suspect who's an ex-porn stud and a Teflon-coated sleazeball.'

'I'll make some calls,' Joe said.

Chapter Seventy-Seven

When Joe got off the phone with the FBI, I picked up the marking pen and Joe summarized his notes.

'*None* of the victims raised any red flags; no felonies, no changed names, no connections with Dennis Agnew. As for the Playmate Pen guys, Ricardo Montefiore aka Rick Monte has been convicted of pandering, lewd public behavior and assault – and that's it for him.

'Rocco Benuto, the bouncer at your porn shop, is a lightweight. One count of possession and one count of breaking and entering a convenience store in New Jersey when he was nineteen. Unarmed.'

'Hardly the typical profile of a serial killer.'

Joe nodded, then continued. 'All three come up as "known associates" of various low-to-mid-level mobsters. They attended a few wise-guy parties, provided girls. As for Dennis Agnew, you already know about the murder charge in 2000 that was dismissed.'

'Ralph Brancusi was the lawyer who got him off.'

Joe nodded again. 'The victim was a porn starlet from Urbana, Illinois. She was in her twenties, a heroin addict, busted a few times for prostitution. And she was one of Agnew's girlfriends before she disappeared for good.'

'Disappeared? As in, no body was found?'

'Sorry, Lindsay. No body.'

'So we don't know if her throat was slit.'

'No.'

I put my chin in my hands. It was frustrating to be so close to the very heart of this horror show, and yet have not one decent lead to run with.

But one pattern *was* clear. The murders were coming closer together. My John Doe had been killed ten years ago, the Whittakers eight years later, the Daltrys a month and a half ago. Now, two double homicides had taken place in one week.

Joe sat down on the little stool next to mine. He took my hand and we stared at the notes tacked to the cork board.

When I spoke, my voice seemed to echo in the girls' small room. 'They're ratcheting up their timetable, Joe. Right now, they're planning to do it again.'

'You know this for a fact?' Joe said.

'I do. I can feel it.'

Chapter Seventy-Eight

I awoke to the jarring sound of the bedside phone. I grabbed it on the second ring, noticing that Joe was gone and that there was a note on the chair where his clothes had been.

'Joe?'

'It's Yuki, Lindsay. Did I wake you?'

'No, I'm up,' I lied.

We talked for five minutes at Yuki's trademark warp speed and after we hung up, there was no falling back to sleep. I read Joe's sweet good-bye note, then I pulled on some sweats, put a leash on Martha and together we jogged to the beach.

A cleansing breeze whipped in off the Bay as Martha and I headed north. We hadn't gotten very far when I heard someone calling my name. A small figure up ahead came running toward me.

'Lindseee, Lindseee!'

'Allison! Hey, girl.'

The dark-eyed little girl hugged me hard around the waist, then dropped to the sand to embrace Martha.

'Ali, you're not here alone?'

'We're having an outing,' she said, pointing to a clump of people and umbrellas a ways up the beach. As we got closer, I heard kids singing 'Yolee-yolee-yolee', the theme song from *Survivor*, and I saw Carolee coming toward me.

We exchanged hugs and then Carolee introduced me to 'her kids'.

'What kind of mutt is that?' an eleven or twelve year old with a sandy mop of rasta hair asked me.

'She's no mutt. Sweet Martha is a border collie.'

'She doesn't look like Lassie,' said a little girl with strawberry curls and a healing black eye.

'Nope. Border collies are a different breed. They come from England and Scotland and they have a very serious job,' I said. 'They herd sheep and cattle.'

I had their attention now, and Martha looked up at me as if she knew that I was talking about her.

'Border collies have to learn commands from their owners, of course, but they're very smart dogs who not only love to work, they feel that the animals in the herd are *theirs* – and that they are responsible for them.'

'Do the commands! Show how she does it, Lindsay,' Ali begged me. I grinned at her.

'Who wants to be a sheep?' I asked.

A lot of the kids snickered but four of them, including Ali, volunteered. I told the 'sheep' to scatter and run down the beach and then I unleashed Martha.

'Martha. Walk up,' I called to her and she ran

toward the little group of five. They squealed and tried to evade her but they couldn't outdo Martha. She was fast and agile, and with her head down, eyes focused on them, she barked at their heels and the kids kept together and streamed forward in pretty tight formation.

'Come-bye,' I shouted and Martha herded the kids clockwise toward the Bay. 'Away,' I called out and Martha looped them back around toward the cliff, the children giggling gleefully.

'That'll do,' I called out, as my little black-and-white doggy kept the kids in a clump by running circles around their legs, shepherding them, breathless and giddy, back to the blankets.

'Stand, Martha,' I said. 'Good job. Excellent, sweetie.'

Martha barked in self-congratulation beside me. The kids clapped and whistled and Carolee handed out cups of orange juice and toasted us. When the attention had gone off me and Martha, I huddled with Carolee and told her about my conversation with Yuki.

'I need a favor,' I said.

'Anything,' said Carolee Brown. And then she felt compelled to say, 'Lindsay, you would be a *great* mom.'

Chapter Seventy-Nine

Minutes after saying good-bye to Carolee and the kids, Martha and I climbed the cliff and crossed the grassy field toward Miramontes Street. My feet had just touched the sidewalk when I saw a man maybe 100 yards away pointing a smallish camera in my direction.

He was so far away, all I could see was the glint of the lens, his orange sweatshirt and a baseball cap pulled down low over his eyes. And he didn't let me get any closer. Once he saw that I had noticed him, he turned and walked quickly away.

Maybe the guy was just taking pictures of the view, or maybe the tabloid press had found me at last, or maybe that pinging in my chest was just paranoia, but I felt kind of uneasy as I headed home.

Someone was watching me.

Someone who didn't want me to see him.

Back at Cat's, I stripped my bed and packed my things. Then I fed Penelope and changed her water.

'Good news, Penny,' I told the Wonderpig.

'Carolee and Allison promised that they'll come over later. I see apples in your future, babe.'

I put Joe's sweet goodbye-for-now note into my handbag and after a thorough look around, made for the front door.

'Home we go,' I said to Martha.

We scrambled up into the Explorer and headed back to San Francisco.

Chapter Eighty

At 7:00 p.m. that night, I opened the door to Indigo, a brand new restaurant on McAllister, two blocks from the courthouse, which ought to have taken my appetite away. I passed through the wood-paneled bar into the high-ceilinged restaurant proper. There, the maitre d' checked me off his list and escorted me to a blue velvet banquette where Yuki was leafing through a sheaf of papers.

Yuki stood to hug me and as I hugged her back, I realized how very glad I was to see my lawyer.

'How's it going, Lindsay?'

'Just fabulous, except for the part when I remember that my trial starts Monday.'

'We're going to win,' she said. 'So you can stop worrying about that.'

'Silly me for fretting,' I said.

I cracked a smile, but I was more shaken than I wanted her to know. Mickey Sherman had convinced the powers-that-be that we would all be best served if I were represented by a woman attorney and that Yuki Castellano was 'a great gal for the job'.

I wished I felt as sure.

Although I was catching her at the end of a long work day, Yuki looked fresh and upbeat. But most of all, she looked *young*. I reflexively clutched my Kokopelli as my twenty-eight-year-old attorney and I ordered dinner.

'So, what have I missed since I skipped town?' I asked Yuki. I pushed chef Larry Piaskowy's pan-seared sea bass with a parsnip purée to the far side of my plate and nibbled at the fennel salad with pine nuts, and a carrot-tarragon vinaigrette.

'I'm glad that you were outta here, Lindsay, because the sharks have been in a feeding frenzy,' Yuki said. I noticed that her eyes made direct contact with mine, but her hands never stopped moving.

'Editorials and TV coverage of the outraged parents have been running 24/7 . . . Did you catch *Saturday Night Live*?'

'Never watch it.'

'Well, just so you know, there was a skit. You've been dubbed "Dirty Harriet".'

'That must've been a riot,' I said, pulling a face. 'I guess someone made my day.'

'It's going to get worse,' said Yuki, tugging at a lock of her shoulder-length hair. 'Judge Achacoso okayed live TV coverage in the courtroom. And I just got the plaintiff's witness list. Sam Cabot's going to testify.'

'Well, that's okay, isn't it? Sam confessed to doing those electrocution murders. We can use that!'

"'Fraid not, Lindsay. His lawyers filed a motion to suppress because his parents weren't there when he blurted out his confession to that ER nurse. Look,' Yuki said, grabbing my hands, no doubt responding to the way my face had frozen in shock. 'We don't know what Sam's going to say – I'll take him apart, you can count on that. But we can't impeach him with his confession. It's your word against his – and he's thirteen and you're a drunken cop.'

'And so you're telling me, "Don't worry" because?'

'Because the truth will out. Juries are composed of human beings, most of whom have had a drink in their lives. I think they're going to find that you're entitled and probably even *expected* to have a few drinks now and then.'

She looked me in the eye.

'You tried to help those kids, Lindsay. And that ain't no crime.'

Chapter Eighty-One

'Don't forget that you're on trial from the minute you arrive at the courthouse,' Yuki said as we walked together through the cool and darkening night. We entered the Opera Plaza Garage on Van Ness and took the elevator down to where Yuki had parked her taupe, two-door Acura.

Soon we were driving east on Golden Gate Avenue toward my favorite watering hole, although I was sticking to Cokes tonight. Just to be safe.

'Come in a really plain car, not a cop car or a new SUV or anything like that.'

'I have a four-year-old Explorer. With a ding in the door. How's that?'

'There you go.' Yuki laughed. 'Perfect. And what you wore to the prelim was good. Dark suit, SFPD lapel pin, no other jewelry. When the press climbs all over you, you can smile politely, but don't answer any of their questions.'

'Leave all that stuff to you.'

'Bingo,' she said, as we pulled up to Susie's Bar.

A surge of happiness warmed me as we stepped inside Susie's. The calypso band had put the dinner crowd into a fine mood, and Susie herself, wearing a hot-pink sarong, was doing the limbo in the center of the dance floor. My two best friends waved us over to 'our' booth at the back.

I said, 'Claire Washburn, Yuki Castellano; Yuki, Cindy Thomas,' and the girls stretched out their hands and shook hers in turn. But I could see from the strained look on their faces that my buds were as worried about my upcoming ordeal as I was.

When Claire took Yuki's hand, she said, 'I'm Lindsay's friend – and I don't have to tell you, I'm also a witness for the plaintiffs.'

Cindy, looking quite grave, said, 'I work for the *Chronicle* and I'll be yelling rude questions outside the courthouse tomorrow.'

'And chopping her into bite-sized chunks if that's the way the story goes,' said Yuki.

'Absolutely.'

'I'm going to take good care of her, you guys,' Yuki said. 'We're going to have a real nasty fight on our hands, to be sure, but we're going to win.'

As if we'd known in advance we were going to do it, we clasped our combined eight hands across the center of the table.

'Fight, team, fight,' I said.

It felt good to laugh and I was glad when Yuki took off her suit jacket and Claire poured margaritas for everyone but me.

'My first one of these,' Yuki said dubiously.

'It's about time, Counselor. But drink it nice and

slow, okay? Now,' said Claire. 'Tell us all about yourself. Start at the beginning.'

'Okay, I know, what gives with the funny name?' Yuki said, licking salt from her upper lip. 'First, you should know, the Japanese and the Italians are like polar opposites. Their food, for instance: raw squid and rice meets scungilli marinara over linguine.' Yuki laughed, a lovely sound, like the ringing of bells.

'When my petite, demure Japanese mom met my burly, passionate Italian-American dad at an exchange student mixer, it was pure magnetism,' she told us in her funny, rapid-fire delivery. 'My daddy-to-be said "Let's get married while we're still in love", which they *did* about three weeks after they met. And I arrived nine months after that.'

Yuki explained that there was a lot of prejudice against 'half-breeds' in still-conservative Japan, and that her family moved to California when she was only six. But she remembered well what it felt like to be tormented in school because she was of mixed race.

'I wanted to become a lawyer from the time I was old enough to know what Perry Mason did on TV,' she said, her eyes glinting. 'Believe me, I'm not bragging, but just so you know, I got straight As at Boalt Law, and I've been on the fast track with Duffy and Rogers since I graduated. I think that people's motives are critical to their performance, so you guys should understand mine.

'I've always had to prove something to myself; that smart and that super good aren't good enough.

I have to be the best. And as for Lindsay, your old friend and my new one, I know with all my heart that she's innocent.

'I'm going to prove that, too.'

Chapter Eighty-Two

Despite everything Yuki had told me about the media frenzy, I was stunned to see the square block of mosh pit at the Civic Center Plaza the next morning. TV satellite vans lined Polk on both sides of McAllister and a somewhat malevolent, shifting mob fanned out in all directions, blocking traffic to City Hall and the Civic Center Courthouse.

I parked in the garage on Van Ness, only a three-block walk to the courthouse, and tried to blend into the crowd on foot. But I didn't get away with it. Once I was spotted, reporters stampeded, shoved microphones and cameras into my face and screamed questions that I couldn't understand, let alone answer.

The 'police brutality' accusations, the baiting, the almost painful noise of the crowd made me dizzy with a kind of grief. *I was a good cop, damn it. How had it happened that the people I'd sworn to serve had turned against me like this?*

Carlos Vega from KRON-TV was on the 'Dirty

Harriet Trial' big time. He was a tiny man with a rabid style, known for interviewing people so courteously they hardly felt the evisceration. But I knew Carlos – he'd interviewed me before – and when he asked, 'Do you blame the Cabots for taking this action against you?' I almost snapped.

I was about to give Carlos an ill-advised sound bite for the six o'clock news when someone plucked me out of the mob by my elbow. I jerked away, until I saw that my rescuer was a friend in uniform.

'Conklin,' I said. 'Thank God.'

'Stick with me, Lou,' he said, steering me through the crowd to a barricaded police line that offered a narrow path to the courthouse. My heart swelled as my fellow officers, grasping hands to give me safe passage, nodded or spoke to me as I passed.

'Go get 'em, Lieutenant.'

'Hang tough, L.T.'

I picked Yuki out of the crowd on the courthouse steps and made straight for her. She took over from Officer Conklin and together we put all our weight into opening the heavy steel-and-glass doors of the Civic Center Courthouse. We climbed a flight of marble stairs and moments later stepped inside the impressive, cherry-paneled courtroom on the first floor.

Heads turned toward us as we entered. I straightened my freshly pressed collar, ran a hand over my hair, and walked with Yuki across the carpeted floor of the courtroom to the attorneys' tables at the front.

I had gained a measure of outward composure in the last few minutes, but I was absolutely seething inside.

How could this be happening to me?

Chapter Eighty-Three

Yuki stood aside as I edged behind the table and took my seat next to silver-haired-and-tongued Mickey Sherman. He half rose and shook my hand.

'How ya' doin,' Lindsay? You look terrific. You okay?'

'Never better,' I cracked.

But we both knew that no sane person would be feeling 'okay' in my shoes. My whole career was at stake and if the jury went against me, my life would go up in flames. Dr and Mrs Andrew Cabot were asking $50 million in damages, and although they'd have to get $49.99 million from the city of San Francisco, I would be financially devastated anyway and possibly known as Dirty Harriet for the rest of my life.

As Yuki sat down beside me, Chief Tracchio reached across the railing to squeeze my shoulder in support. I hadn't expected that, and I was touched. Then voices rolled across the room as the plaintiffs' 'dream team' filed in and took their seats across from us.

A moment later, Dr and Mrs Cabot came into the courtroom and sat behind their attorneys. The reed-like Dr Cabot and his blonde and visibly grieving wife immediately fixed their eyes on me.

Andrew Cabot was a trembling rock of contained rage and anguish. And Eva Cabot's face was a picture of desolation that would never end. She was a mother who'd inexplicably lost her daughter because of me, and I'd crippled her son as well. When she turned her red-rimmed gray eyes on me, all I could see was her bottomless fury.

Eva Cabot hated me.

She wished me dead.

Yuki's cool hand on my wrist broke my eye-contact with Mrs Cabot – but not before the image of our locked stare was captured on tape.

'All rise,' boomed the bailiff.

There was a deafening rustle as everyone in the courtroom stood and the small, bespectacled form of Judge Achacoso ascended to the bench. I sat down in a daze.

This was it.

My trial was about to begin.

Chapter Eighty-Four

Jury selection took almost three days. After day one, because I couldn't take the ringing phone and the media swarm outside my wee little house any longer, Martha and I packed up and moved into Yuki's two-bedroom apartment in the Crest Royal, a mini-highrise with great security.

The media swarm got bigger and more vociferous daily. The press fed the public's frenzy by detailing the ethnic and socio-economic makeup of every person picked for the jury – charging us with racial profiling, of course. In fact, it made me queasy to watch both sides choose or dismiss potential jurors based on discernible or imagined prejudice against me. When we excused four black and Latino men and women in a row, I put it to Yuki during our next break.

'Weren't you just telling me the other day about how it felt to be discriminated against because of your race?'

'This isn't about race, Lindsay. The people we excused all had negative feelings about the police.

Sometimes people aren't aware of their own bias until we ask them. Sometimes, in a hugely public case like this, people lie so that they can have their fifteen minutes of fame.

'We're working the *voir dire* process as it's our right to do. Please trust us. If we don't play hardball, we're done before we start.'

Later that same day the opposition used three peremptory challenges to excuse two middle-aged white civil servants – women who might have viewed me kindly, as if I were a daughter – as well as a fireman named McGoey who presumably wouldn't have held even a *gallon* of margaritas against me.

In the end, neither side was happy but both sides accepted the twelve men and women and three alternates. At two in the afternoon of the third day, Mason Broyles got up to make his opening statement.

In my worst dreams, I couldn't have imagined how that poor excuse for a human being would present the Cabots' case against me.

Chapter Eighty-Five

Mason Broyles looked like he'd slept his full eight hours the night before. His skin was dewy, his suit was classic, navy-blue Armani. His pale blue shirt was crisp and matched his eyes. He stood and without using notes, addressed the court and the jury.

'Your Honor. Ladies and gentlemen of the jury. In order to understand what happened on the night of May tenth, you have to go inside the minds of two kids who had a notion. Their parents weren't home. They found the keys to their father's new Mercedes and they decided to take a joy ride.

'It wasn't right, but they were kids. Sara was fifteen. Sam Cabot, an eighth grader, is only thirteen.'

Broyles turned away from the jury and faced his clients, as if to say, *Look at these people. Look at the faces of bereavement caused by police brutality.*

Broyles turned back to the jury and continued his opening statement.

'Sara Cabot was at the wheel that night. The

Cabot kids were driving around in a bad neighborhood, the high-crime area we know as the Tenderloin District, and they were driving an expensive car. Out of nowhere, another car started to chase them.

'You will hear Sam Cabot tell you that he and his sister were terrified by the police car that was in pursuit. The sirens were very loud. The grill lights and headlights were flashing, lighting up the street like a disco from hell.

'If Sara Cabot were here, she would testify that she was so afraid of the car that was chasing them that she tried to get away – and then she lost control of the Mercedes she was driving and crashed it. She would say that she was scared out of her mind because she'd run, because she'd wrecked her father's car, because she was driving without a license. And because her little brother had been hurt in the accident.

'*And she was afraid because the police had guns.*

'But Sara Cabot, who was two full grades ahead of other children her age, a girl with an IQ of 160 and almost endless promise, can't tell us anything – because she's dead. She died because the defendant, Lieutenant Lindsay Boxer, made an egregious error of judgment and shot Sarah twice through the heart.

'Lieutenant Boxer also shot Sam Cabot, barely a teenager, a bright, popular young boy who was captain of his soccer team, a champion swimmer, an athlete extraordinaire.

'Sam Cabot will never play soccer or swim again.

Nor will he stand or walk or dress himself or bathe himself. *Sam will never even hold a fork or a book in his hands.'*

Muffled gasps volleyed around the courtroom as the tragic picture Broyles had painted took hold in people's minds. Broyles stood for a long moment in the circle he'd created around himself and his bereaved clients, a kind of suspension of time, reality and truth he'd perfected during his decades as a star litigator.

He put his hands in his pockets, exposing navy-blue suspenders, and he cast his eyes down toward his shiny black wing-tips as if he, too, were absorbing the horrific tragedy he'd just described.

He almost looked as though he was praying, which I was sure he never did.

All I could do was sit there, silent, my eyes fixed on the judge's immobile face, until Broyles released us by looking toward the jury box.

Having wound up for his pitch, he delivered it, hard and fast.

'Ladies and gentlemen, you will hear testimony that Lieutenant Boxer was off duty the night of this incident and that she had been drinking. Still, she made a decision to get into a police car and to fire a gun.

'You will also hear that Sara and Sam Cabot had guns. The fact is that Lieutenant Boxer had sufficient experience to disarm two frightened children but she broke all the rules that night. Every single one.

'That's why Lieutenant Boxer is responsible for

the death of Sara Cabot, a young woman whose remarkable promise was cancelled in one shattering moment. And Lieutenant Boxer is also responsible for crippling Sam Cabot for the remainder of his life.

'We are asking that after you hear the evidence you will find Lieutenant Lindsay Boxer guilty of excessive use of force and of police misconduct resulting in the wrongful death of Sara Cabot and the crippling of Sam Cabot.

'Because of this irreparable loss, we're asking that you give the plaintiffs fifty million dollars for Sam Cabot's lifetime medical bills, for his pain and suffering and for the misery of his family. We're asking another one hundred million in punitive damages to send a message to this police community and every police community around our country that this is not acceptable behavior.

'That you don't police our streets when you're drunk.'

Chapter Eighty-Six

When I heard Sam Cabot, that cold-blooded little psycho, described as the next great sports hero, it almost made me sick to my stomach. I thought, *Champion swimmer? Soccer team captain? What the hell did that have to do with the murders he'd committed, or with the bullets he'd put into Warren Jacobi?*

I struggled to keep my expression neutral as Yuki stood and took the floor.

'The night of May tenth was a Friday night and the end of a rough week for Lieutenant Boxer,' Yuki said, her sweet, melodic voice chiming out across the courtroom. 'Two young men had been murdered in the Tenderloin, and Lieutenant Boxer was very troubled by the brutality and the lack of viable forensic evidence.'

Yuki walked over to the jury box and let her hand skim the rail as she made eye-contact with each of the jury members. They followed the thin young woman with the heart-shaped face and the luminous brown eyes, leaning forward into every word.

'As the Commanding Officer of the Homicide Detail, Lieutenant Boxer is responsible for investigating every homicide in the city. But she was especially disturbed because the victims of these murders were still in their teens.

'On the night in question,' Yuki continued, 'Lindsay Boxer was off duty, having a drink before dinner with some of her friends, when she got a call from Inspector Warren Jacobi. Inspector Jacobi was formerly Lieutenant Boxer's partner and because this was a special case, they were working it together.

'Inspector Jacobi will testify that he phoned Lieutenant Boxer to tell her that their one lead – a Mercedes Benz that had been previously seen in the vicinity of *both* homicides – had been spotted again south of Market Street.

'A lot of people in Lieutenant Boxer's situation would have said, "Forget it. I'm off duty. I don't want to sit all night in a police car." But this was Lieutenant Boxer's case and she wanted to stop whoever killed those two boys before they killed again.

'When Lieutenant Boxer got into the police car with Inspector Jacobi she told him that she had been drinking, but that her faculties were *not* impaired.

'Ladies and gentlemen, the plaintiffs will make much use of the word "drunk". But they are twisting reality.'

'Objection, Your Honor. Argumentative.'

'Overruled. Please sit down, Mr Broyles.'

'In fact,' Yuki said, standing directly in front of

the jury box, 'the Lieutenant had had a couple of drinks with her dinner. She was not inebriated, staggering around, slurring her speech, illogical or out of it.

'And Lieutenant Boxer did not drive. The drinks that she had, had absolutely nothing whatsoever to do with the events that transpired that night.

'This police officer is charged with brutally shooting down a young girl with her gun. But you will learn that Lieutenant Boxer wasn't the only person on the scene with a gun in her hand. The "victims"' – Yuki made the universal hand sign for quotemarks around the word – 'not only brought guns to the scene, but they fired *first* and with *intent to kill*.'

Chapter Eighty-Seven

Mason Broyles jumped furiously to his feet. 'Objection, Your Honor. Defense counsel is mocking the victims and she is way out of line. Sam and Sara Cabot are not on trial here. Lieutenant Boxer *is*.'

'Well, she shouldn't be,' said Yuki, pressing on. 'My client did nothing wrong. Nothing. She's here because the plaintiffs are suffering and they want someone to pay for their loss, right or wrong.'

'Objection! Your Honor! Argumentative.'

'Sustained. Ms Castellano, please hold your argument for summation.'

'Yes, Your Honor. I'm sorry.' Yuki walked over to the table and looked at her notes, then swung back around, as if she'd never been interrupted.

'On the night in question, the *exemplary* Cabot kids evaded the police by driving at over seventy-five miles per hour on crowded streets in wanton disregard for public safety; that's a felony. They were armed – another felony – and after Sara Cabot totaled her father's car, she and her brother were helped out of the wreck by two concerned police officers whose weapons were holstered, who were doing their duty to serve and protect, and above all, to render aid.

'You will hear testimony from a police ballistics expert who will tell you that the bullets that were surgically removed from Lieutenant Boxer and Inspector Jacobi were fired from Sara Cabot's and Sam Cabot's guns, respectively. And you will also hear that Sara and Sam Cabot fired upon these officers without provocation.

'On the night in question, as Lieutenant Boxer lay on the ground, losing nearly a third of her blood and close to death, she ordered the plaintiffs to drop their weapons, which they did not do. Instead, Sara Cabot fired three more shots, which mercifully missed my client.

'Only then did Lieutenant Lindsay Boxer return fire.

'If *anyone* else – a banker, a baker, even a *bookmaker* – had shot someone in *self-defense*, we wouldn't be having a trial. But if a police officer defends herself, everyone wants a piece of her—'

'Objection!!!'

But it was too late for objections. Dr Andrew Cabot's stony expression had shattered into shards of wrath. He leaped to his feet and moved toward Yuki as if he were going to throttle her. Mason Broyles restrained his client, but the courtroom boiled over even as Judge Achacoso banged her gavel again and again.

'I'm done, Your Honor,' said Yuki.

'Oh no, you're not. I will not have this trial become a free-for-all. Bailiff, clear the courtroom. I'll see both counsels in chambers,' said the judge.

Chapter Eighty-Eight

When court resumed, Yuki's eyes were sparkling. It looked to me as if she felt the butt-kicking she'd taken from the judge had been worth the points she'd scored in her opening.

Broyles put on his first witness, Betty D'Angelo, the ER nurse who'd ministered to me the night I was shot. D'Angelo reluctantly repeated what she had said during the prelim – that my blood-alcohol level had been .067. There was no way she could say if I was intoxicated, but that .067 was considered 'under the influence'.

Next up, Broyles called my friend Dr Claire Washburn. He elicited her credentials as the city's Chief Medical Examiner, and the fact that she'd performed Sara Cabot's autopsy.

'Dr Washburn, were you able to ascertain the cause of Sara Cabot's death?'

Using a line drawing of a human form, Claire pointed out where my bullets had entered Sara Cabot's body.

'Yes. I found two gunshot wounds to the chest.

Gunshot A entered on the left upper-outer chest, right here. That bullet penetrated Sara Cabot's chest cavity between left rib numbers three and four, perforated the upper lobe of the left lung, went into the pericardial sac, tore through the left ventricle and stopped in her thoracic column on the left-hand side.

'The second gunshot wound,' Claire said, tapping the chart with a pointer, 'was through the sternum, five inches below the left shoulder. It went right on through the heart, terminating in thoracic vertebra number four.'

The members of the jury were rapt as they heard about what my shots had done to Sara Cabot's heart, but when Broyles had finished examining her, Yuki was ready for Claire on cross-examination.

'Can you tell us the angles of penetration, Dr Washburn?' Yuki asked.

'The shots were fired upwards, from a few inches above the ground.'

'Doctor, was Sara Cabot killed instantly?'

'Yes.'

'So, you could say Sara was too dead to shoot anyone after she'd been shot?'

'Too dead, Ms Castellano? As far as I know, there's only dead.'

Yuki blushed. 'Let me rephrase that. Given that Lieutenant Boxer was shot twice by Sara Cabot's gun, it stands to reason that Sara Cabot fired first – because she died instantly after Lieutenant Boxer shot her.'

'Yes. Miss Cabot died instantly when she was shot.'

'One more question,' Yuki said, sounding as if it were an afterthought. 'Did you do a tox screen on Miss Cabot's blood?'

'Yes. A few days after the autopsy.'

'And what were your findings?'

'Sara Cabot had methamphetamine in her system.'

'She was high?'

'We don't use "high" as a medical term, but yes, she had .23 milligrams of methamphetamine per liter in her blood. And in that sense, it's high.'

'And what are the effects of methamphetamine?' Yuki asked Claire.

'Methamphetamine is a powerful central nervous system stimulant that produces a wide range of effects. The upside is a pleasurable rush, but longterm users suffer many of the downside effects, including paranoia and suicidal and homicidal thoughts.'

'How about homicidal *actions*?'

'Absolutely.'

'Thank you, Dr Washburn. I'm finished with this witness, Your Honor.'

Chapter Eighty-Nine

I was elated when Claire stepped down, but not for long.

I heard Mason Broyles call Dr Robert Goldman, and when the brown-haired, mustachioed man in a light blue suit had been sworn in, he began to testify about the terrible injuries Sam had received at the ugly end of my gun.

Using a chart similar to the one Claire had used, Dr Goldman pointed out that my first bullet had gone through Sam's abdominal cavity, lodging in his thoracic vertebra number eight where it still remained.

'That bullet paralyzed Sam from the waist down,' said the doctor, patting his mustache. 'The second bullet entered at the base of his neck, passing through cervical vertebra number three, paralyzing everything below his neck.'

'Doctor,' Broyles asked, 'will Sam Cabot ever walk again?'

'No.'

'Will he ever be able to have sex?'

'No.'

'Will he ever be able to breathe on his own or have the full enjoyment of his life?'

'No.'

'He's in a wheelchair for the rest of his life, correct?'

'That is correct.'

'Your witness,' Broyles said to Yuki as he returned to his chair.

'No questions of this witness,' said Yuki.

'Plaintiff calls Sam Cabot,' said Broyles.

I sent an anxious look to Yuki before we both turned to face the rear of the courtroom. Doors swung open and a young female attendant entered pushing a wheelchair, a shiny chrome Jenkinson Supreme, the Cadillac of its class.

Sam Cabot looked frail and shrunken in his little boy's sports coat and tie, nothing like the vicious freak who'd murdered a couple of people for kicks before gunning Jacobi down. Except for the venomous look in his eyes, I wouldn't have recognized him.

Sam turned those brown eyes on me now, and my heart raced as I felt horror, guilt, and even pity.

I dropped my gaze to the humming respiratory ventilator just below the seat of Sam's chair. It was a heavy metal box with dials and gauges and a thin plastic air hose snaking up from the machine to where it was clipped right beside Sam's left cheek.

A small electronically-assisted voice box was positioned in front of his lips.

Sam locked his lips around his air tube. A ghastly

sucking sound came from his ventilator as compressed air was pumped into his lungs. It was a sound that was repeated every three or four seconds, every time Sam Cabot needed to draw breath.

I watched as the attendant wheeled Sam up to the witness-stand.

'Your Honor,' Mason Broyles said, 'since we don't know how long Sam will be asked to testify, we'd like to plug his ventilator into an electric socket to preserve the battery.'

'Of course,' said the judge.

The technician snaked a long orange cord into a wall socket, and then sat down behind Andrew and Eva Cabot.

There was no place for me to look, but at Sam.

His neck was stiff and his head was braced to the back of his chair with a halo traction device strapped across his forehead. It looked like some kind of medieval torture and I'm sure it felt that way to Sam.

The bailiff, a tall young man in a green uniform, approached Sam.

'Please raise your right hand.'

Sam Cabot cast his eyes wildly from side to side. He sucked in some air and spoke into the small green voice box. The voice that came out was an eerie and unnerving mechanical sound.

'I *can't*,' Sam said.

Chapter Ninety

Sam's voice no longer sounded completely human. But his young face and his small, frail body made him seem more fragile and vulnerable than any other person in the room. The people in the gallery murmured in sympathy as the bailiff turned to Judge Achacoso.

'Judge?'

'Administer the oath, bailiff.'

'Do you swear to tell the truth, so help you God?'

'I do,' said Sam Cabot.

Broyles smiled at Sam, giving the jury enough time to really hear, see and absorb the pitiful state of Sam Cabot's body and imagine what a hell his life had become.

'Don't be nervous,' Broyles said to Sam. 'Just tell the truth. Tell us what happened that night, Sam.'

Broyles took Sam through a set of warm-up questions, waiting as the boy closed his mouth around the air tube. His answers came in broken sentences, the length of each phrase determined by the amount of air he could hold in his lungs before drawing on the mouthpiece again.

Broyles asked Sam how old he was, where he lived, what school he went to, before he got to the meat of his interrogation.

'Sam, do you remember what happened on the night of May tenth?'

'I'll never forget it . . . as long as I live,' Sam said, sucking air from the tube, expelling his words in bursts through the voice box. 'It's all I think of . . . and no matter how hard I try . . . I can't get it out of my mind . . . That's the night *she* killed my sister . . . and ruined my life too.'

'Objection, Your Honor,' Yuki rose and said.

'Young man,' said the Judge, 'I know this is difficult, but please try to confine your answers to the questions.'

'Sam, let's back up,' said Mason Broyles kindly. 'Can you tell us the events of that night and please take it step-by-step.'

'A lot of stuff happened,' Sam said. He sucked at the tube and continued. 'But I don't remember . . . all of it. I know we took Dad's car . . . and we got scared . . . We heard the sirens coming . . . Sara didn't have her license. Then the air bag burst . . . all I remember . . . is seeing that woman . . . shoot Sara . . . I don't know why she did it.'

'That's okay, Sam. That's fine.'

'I saw a flash,' the boy continued, his eyes fastened on me. 'And then my sister . . . she was dead.'

'Yes. We all know. Now, Sam. Do you remember when Lieutenant Boxer shot *you*?'

Within the small arc permitted by his restraints, Sam rolled his head from side to side. And then he started to cry. His heart-wrenching sobs were interrupted by the sucking of air and enhanced by the mechanical translation of his wails through the voice box.

It was an unearthly sound, unlike anything I'd ever heard before in my life. Chills shot up my spine and, I was quite certain, everyone else's.

Mason Broyles quickly advanced across the floor to his client, whipped a hanky out of his breast pocket, and dabbed at Sam's eyes and nose.

'Do you need a break, Sam?'

'No . . . sir . . . I'm okay,' he brayed.

'Your witness, Counsel,' said Mason Broyles, shooting us a look that was as good as a dare.

Chapter Ninety-One

Yuki approached the thirteen-year-old killer who looked even younger and more pitiable now that his face was red from weeping.

'Are you feeling a little better, Sam?' Yuki asked, putting her hands on her knees and stooping a little so that her eyes met his.

'Okay, I guess ... considering,' said Sam.

'Glad to hear it,' said Yuki, standing, taking a few steps back. 'I'll try to keep my questions brief. Why were you in the Tenderloin District on May tenth?'

'I don't know ... ma'am ... Sara was driving.'

'Your car was parked outside the Balboa Hotel. Why was that?'

'We were buying a newspaper ... I think ... We were going to go to the movies.'

'You think there's a newsstand inside the Balboa?'

'I guess so.'

'Sam, you understand the difference between a lie and the truth?'

'Of course.'

'And you know that you promised to tell the truth?'

'Sure.'

'Okay. So, can you tell all of us why you and Sara were carrying guns that night?'

'They were ... Dad's guns,' the boy said. He paused for breath and maybe for thought as well. 'I took a gun out of the glove compartment ... because I thought those people ... were going to kill us.'

'You didn't know that the police were trying to pull you over?'

'I was scared ... I wasn't driving and ... everything happened fast.'

'Sam, were you on crank that night?'

'Ma'am?'

'Methamphetamine. You know – ice, get-go, beanies.'

'I wasn't on drugs.'

'I see. Do you remember the car accident?'

'Not really.'

'Do you remember seeing Lieutenant Boxer and Inspector Jacobi help you out of the car after it crashed?'

'No, because I had blood in my eyes ... My nose broke ... All of a sudden ... I see guns and the next thing I know ... *they shot us.*'

'Do you remember shooting Inspector Jacobi?'

The kid's eyes widened. Was he surprised by the question? Or was he simply remembering the moment?

'I thought he was going to *hurt* me,' Sam croaked out at last.

'So you *do* remember shooting him?'

'Wasn't he going to arrest me?'

Yuki stood her ground as she waited for Sam's lungs to fill. 'Sam. Why did you shoot Inspector Jacobi?'

'No. I don't remember . . . doing that.'

'Tell me. Are you under a psychiatrist's care?'

'Yeah, I am . . . Because I'm having a hard time. Because I'm paralyzed . . . and because that woman murdered my sister.'

'Okay, let me ask you about that. You say that Lieutenant Boxer murdered your sister. Didn't you see your sister fire at Lieutenant Boxer first? Didn't you see the Lieutenant lying on the street?'

'That's not how I remember it.'

'Sam, you remember that you're under oath?'

'I'm telling the truth,' he said and sobbed again.

'Okay. Have you ever been inside the Lorenzo Hotel?'

'Objection, Your Honor. Where is this going?'

'Ms Castellano?'

'It'll become apparent in a second, Your Honor. I just have one more question.'

'Go ahead, then.'

'Sam, isn't it true that right now you're the prime suspect in the investigation of multiple homicides?'

Sam turned his head a few degrees away from Yuki and bellowed in his soul-searing, mechanically-aided voice, *'Mr Broyles.'*

Sam's voice tailed away as the air went out of him.

'Objection! No foundation, Your Honor,' Broyles shouted above the murmurs washing over the room and the slams of Judge Achacoso's gavel.

'I want that question struck from the record,' Broyles shouted, 'and I ask Your Honor to instruct the jury to disregard—'

Before the judge could rule, Sam's eyes wheeled frantically.

'I take the amendment,' the kid said, getting a fresh infusion of air, before speaking once more. 'I take the Fifth Amendment on the grounds—'

And with that, a horrific shrieking alarm came from beneath the wheelchair. There were screams from the gallery and from the jury as the readouts on the ventilator dropped to zero.

Andrew Cabot leaped from his chair, shoving the attendant forward.

'Do something! Do something!'

There was a collective intake of breath as the tech knelt, fiddled with knobs and reset the ventilator. At last, the alarm went silent.

A loud whoosh was heard as Sam sucked in his life-saving air.

Then the roar of the crowd's relief filled the room.

'I'm done with this witness,' Yuki said, shouting over the rumble that flowed from front to back of the courtroom.

'Court is adjourned,' said Judge Achacoso, slamming her gavel down. 'We'll resume tomorrow at nine.'

Chapter Ninety-Two

As the courtroom emptied, Yuki directed her full five-foot-two presence toward the judge.

'Your Honor! Move for a mistrial,' she said.

The judge waved her to the bench and she and Mickey as well as Broyles and his second chair clumped up to the front.

I heard Yuki say, 'The jury had to have been prejudiced by that freaking alarm.'

'You're not accusing the plaintiff of deliberately setting off that "freaking" alarm, are you?' asked the judge.

'No, of course not, Your Honor.'

'Mr Broyles?'

'Pardon my language, Judge, but shit happens and what the jury saw is an ongoing feature of Sam Cabot's life. Sometimes the ventilator malfunctions and the kid could die. The jury saw that. I don't think it made our case any stronger than the fact that Sam's in that chair and his sister is dead.'

'I agree. Motion denied, Ms Castellano. We're going forward tomorrow morning, as planned.'

Chapter Ninety-Three

I don't know who was more shell-shocked, me or Yuki. We found our way to the fire exit stairwell, clattered down the concrete stairs and opened the side door onto Polk, leaving Mickey to handle the press.

Yuki looked positively stunned, and mortified.

'Sam's testimony was beyond a nightmare,' she said, her voice cracking. 'When that alarm went off, my whole cross-examination was obliterated. It was like everyone was thinking, *What in God's name did she do to that child?*'

We took the most circuitous and least scenic route to the garage. I had to put my arm across Yuki's waist to stop her from crossing the wind tunnel of Van Ness against the light.

'My God,' Yuki said again and again, each time throwing her hands out, palms facing the sky. 'My God, my God. What a joke. What a complete travesty!'

'But Yuki,' I said, 'you got your point across. You said it all. The kids were parked in the Tenderloin.

They had no business there. They had guns. You said that Sam was the target of a homicide investigation and Sam *will* be arraigned for those murders,' I said. 'His prints were found on the lip of the bathtub where that poor kid was electrocuted. He and Sara murdered those kids, Yuki. Sam Cabot is a terror. The jury has to know that.'

'I don't know that they know. I can't get away with saying he's a suspect again because he hasn't been arraigned. The jury might have even thought I was baiting the kid, trying to get his pathetic little goat. Which, apparently, I did.'

We crossed Opera Plaza, a mixed-use development with restaurants, a bookstore and movie theaters on the ground floor. Avoiding the stares of the crowd, we took the elevator down to the garage, and after going back and forth several times between the rows of parked cars, we found Yuki's Acura, at last.

We strapped in and when Yuki turned the key, the engine jumped to life. I was already thinking ahead to tomorrow.

'You're sure it's a good idea for me to testify?' I asked my attorney.

'Absolutely. Mickey and I totally agree on this. We've got to get the jury's sympathy going toward you. And to do that, those people are going to have to see and hear what you're made of.

'And that's why you've got to testify.'

Chapter Ninety-Four

The next morning, the view from Yuki's kitchenette was gray as rain gathered for a fall from the huge thunderheads over the city. Strangely, this was the San Francisco that I loved, stormy and tempestuous.

I drank my coffee and fed Martha. Then we went for a quick walk on Jones Street.

'Gotta hurry, Boo,' I said, already feeling the mist in the air. 'Big doings today. Mama's going to be lynched.'

Twenty minutes later, Mickey picked us up in his car. We got to the courthouse at quarter to eight, cleverly missing most of the mob scene.

Inside Courtroom B, Mickey and Yuki sat next to each other and argued in whispers, Yuki's hands fluttering like frantic little birds. As for me, I stared out the courthouse window at the sheets of falling rain as tense minutes ticked off on the electric clock against the side wall.

I felt a touch on my arm.

'I'll be honest, that alarm was one of the worst

things that ever happened to me in a courtroom,'
Mickey said, leaning across Yuki to talk to me. 'I'd
hate to think that Broyles staged that event, but I
wouldn't put it past him to have rigged the electric cord.'

'You can't be serious?'

'I don't know, but we've got to do damage
control. It's our turn to put on *our* case and we have
two messages to convey. The kid's a horror even
on wheels, and you're a great cop.'

'Look, do not worry about your testimony,
Lindsay,' Yuki added. 'If you were any more
prepared, you wouldn't sound natural. When it's
time to do it, just tell the story. Take your time and
stop to think if you aren't sure of something. And
don't look guilty. Just be the great cop that you are.'

'Right,' I said. And for good measure, said it
again.

Too soon, the spectators filled the room in their
damp raincoats, some of them still shaking out
umbrellas. Then the opposition filed in and banged
their briefcases down on the table. Broyles gave us
a civil nod, barely masking his joy. The man was
in his element all right. Court TV. Network TV.
Everyone wanted to speak with Mason Broyles.

Out of the corner of my eye, I saw Broyles shake
Andrew Cabot's hand, kiss Eva Cabot on the cheek.
He even helped the medical attendant position Sam
Cabot's wheelchair just so. He orchestrated *every-
thing*, so why not that alarm yesterday?

'Sleep okay, Sam? That's great,' Broyles said to
the boy.

For me, the nightmare resumed.

The sound of Sam sucking air through his ventilator tube every few seconds was such a painful and constant reminder of what I'd done that I found it hard to breathe myself.

Suddenly, the side door to the courtroom opened and the twelve good men and women and three alternates walked to the box and took their places. The judge, carrying a cardboard cup of coffee, took hers as the court was called into session.

Chapter Ninety-Five

Yuki, looking calm, collected and sensational in a gray suit and pearls, kicked off our case by putting veteran dispatcher Carla Reyes on the stand. Yuki asked Carla some general questions about her duties and what her shift on 10 May had been like.

Then she played the tape of my radio transmissions that awful night; four and a half long minutes of my voice calling in our locations as well as radio calls from the patrol cars.

The clipped and broken transmissions surrounded by sparking static pumped adrenaline into my bloodstream and sent my mind careening around the corners of that dark night in the past, chasing the unknown suspects in a black Mercedes.

Jacobi's voice requesting paramedical help for the passengers of the wrecked car was interrupted by the hard *pops* of gunfire that cut him off midsentence.

I actually started in my seat at the sounds of the gunshots. My hands began to sweat and I felt myself tremble.

A moment later, I heard my own fading voice request ambulances, *'Two officers down. Two civilians down.'*

And the worried voice of Carla Reyes. *'Lieutenant, are you okay? Lindsay. Answer me.'*

'I really thought I'd lost her,' Carla told Yuki from the witness-stand. 'Lindsay's one of our best.'

After Mason's tepid cross, Yuki put on our next witness, Mike Hart from Ballistics, who confirmed that the slugs removed from my body were a match to Sara's gun and that the slugs taken from Jacobi had been fired by the gun found beside Sam Cabot.

Broyles had no questions for Mike, so Yuki called Jacobi to the stand.

Tears brimmed in my eyes as my old friend and partner walked to the front of the room. Jacobi's walk was heavy even though he'd lost a lot of weight. He struggled as he heaved himself up to the witness-stand.

Yuki gave him time to pour himself a full glass of water. Then she asked him some routine questions about how long he'd been with the force, how long with Homicide.

Then, 'Inspector Jacobi, how long have you known Lieutenant Boxer?'

'About seven years.'

'Have you had an occasion to work with her before the night in question?'

'Yep. We were partners for three years.'

'Have you been in other situations with her where she had to use her gun?'

'Yes. A coupla times.'

'And how would you say she reacts under pressure?'

'She's great under pressure. And you know, every time you go out on the street you're under pressure because *nothing* suddenly turns into *something* without any warning at all.'

'Inspector, when you hooked up with Lieutenant Boxer on the night of May tenth, did you smell alcohol on her breath?'

'No.'

'Did you know that she had been drinking?'

'Yes. Because she mentioned it to me.'

'Well, why did she mention it to you?'

'Because she wanted me to know, so that I could kick her out of the car if I wanted to.'

'In your opinion, having worked with her for so many years, did she have all her faculties?'

'Of course. She was sharp, just like she always is.'

'If she was in any way impaired would you have gone on this assignment with her?'

'Absolutely not.'

Yuki took Warren through the night of the tenth, from the moment he picked me up at Susie's to the last thing he remembered.

'I was glad we got those kids out of that car. I was worried that the gas tank was leaking and the whole thing could've gone *kaboom*. I was on with our dispatcher, Carla Reyes over there, telling her that Sam Cabot had a broken nose from the airbag blowing up in his face, and that those kids coulda had internal injuries. Little did I know.'

'I beg your pardon, Inspector?'

'Little did I know that while I was calling for paramedics, that little prick was going to shoot me.'

Mason Broyles blew his cork, of course, and the judge admonished Jacobi. I was ecstatic that Jacobi had had the balls to call Sam Cabot a prick. When order was restored, Yuki had a last question for my old partner.

'Inspector, are you familiar with Lieutenant Boxer's reputation in the police community and if so, what is that reputation?'

'In a word? She's a damned good cop.'

Chapter Ninety-Six

Broyles got nothing much out of Jacobi on cross. He answered 'yes' and 'no' and refused to rise to the bait when Broyles insinuated that he'd been lazy in performing his duty according to SFPD policies and procedures.

'I did the best I could do for both those kids and I'm thankful that your client wasn't a better shot,' Jacobi said. 'Otherwise I'd be dead, instead of talking to you here.'

When court adjourned for a lunch break, I found a quiet spot in a corner on the second floor between a Coke machine and a wall, and talked to Joe, our virtual hug spanning three time zones. He apologized at least a half-dozen times for being in the middle of a huge investigation involving threats to airports from Boston to Miami, which was why he couldn't be with me in San Francisco.

I had a bite of a dry ham sandwich and a sip of coffee from a machine before taking my seat beside Yuki as court was called back into session.

Then the moment I'd been dreading arrived. Yuki

called me to the witness-stand. When I was seated in the witness-box, she stood in front of me so that my view of the Cabot family was blocked, and she gave me a sunny smile.

'Lieutenant Boxer, do you believe in following police procedures?'

'I do.'

'Were you drunk on the night in question?'

'No. I was having dinner with friends. I had a couple of drinks before I got the call from Jacobi.'

'You were off duty?'

'Yes.'

'It's not against any rules to drink off duty, is it?'

'No.'

'When you got into the car with Inspector Jacobi, you officially went back on duty?'

'Yes. Still, I was sure that I had all my faculties. I stand by that now.'

'Would you say you're a "by-the-book" kind of cop?'

'Yes, but the book doesn't cover all circumstances. Sometimes you have to work with the situation at hand and use your best judgment.'

At Yuki's prompting, I told the story up to the point where Jacobi and I wrenched open the car door and freed the Cabot kids from the wreck.

'I made a mistake because those kids looked such a mess. I felt sorry for them.'

'Why did you feel sorry for them?'

'They were both crying. And Sam in particular was bleeding, throwing up and pleading with me.'

'Could you explain?'

'He said, "Please don't tell my father. He'll kill me".'

'So what did you do?'

'As Inspector Jacobi said, we had to get them out of the car. There was danger of the gas tank exploding. I put my gun away so that I could get a grip on the car door and together Inspector Jacobi and I got them out.'

'Go on, Lieutenant.'

'After they were out of the car, I should have cuffed Sara. Instead, I treated her as a victim of a bad traffic accident. When I asked to see her driver's license, she pulled a gun out of her jacket and shot me in the shoulder, then in the thigh. I went down.'

'Where was Inspector Jacobi when Sara shot you?'

'Inspector Jacobi was calling an ambulance.'

'Where was his gun?'

'It was holstered.'

'You're sure of that?'

'Yes. He was on the phone. His gun was holstered. I yelled "Gun!" just before Sara shot me. I saw Jacobi turn and see me fall. Just then Sam Cabot fired on him – hitting him twice.'

'You're sure you saw all this, Lieutenant? You didn't lose consciousness?'

'No. I was conscious throughout.'

'Did Inspector Jacobi lose consciousness?'

'Yes. I thought he was dead. I saw Sam Cabot kick him in the head and he didn't move or try to protect himself.'

'You saw Sam Cabot kick Inspector Jacobi in the head? Please continue.'

'Maybe they thought I was dead, because they seemed to have forgotten all about me.'

'Objection. The witness is speculating.'

'Sustained.'

'Just tell us what you saw and heard and did,' Yuki said. 'You're doing very well.'

I dipped my head and tried to remember.

'I heard Sara tell Sam that they should leave the scene,' I said. 'I got my gun out of my holster and demanded that Sara Cabot drop her weapon. She called me a bitch, then fired several more shots at me. Then I returned fire.'

'What happened after that?'

'Sara dropped to the ground and Sam started screaming at me that I'd shot his sister. Again, I demanded that he drop his gun which he refused to do. I shot him also.'

'Tell me, Lieutenant, did you want to hurt those children?'

'No, of course not. I wish with all my heart that none of this had ever happened.'

'In your opinion, if Sam and Sara Cabot hadn't been carrying guns, could this tragedy have happened?'

'Objection,' Broyles shouted. 'Calls for a conclusion on the part of the witness.'

The judge leaned back in her chair and stared up at the ceiling through her thick, black-rimmed glasses. Then having decided, she snapped back upright.

'Sustained.'

'Lindsay. Is it true that in your ten years in Homicide, you've been cited for excellent arrests on thirty-seven occasions and received fifteen unit citations and twenty meritorious service commendations?'

'I didn't keep count, but that sounds about right.'

'In short, Lieutenant Boxer, the San Francisco Police Department would agree with Inspector Jacobi's description of you. You're "a damned good cop".'

'Objection. Counsel is making a speech.'

'Thanks, Lindsay. I'm done, Your Honor.'

Chapter Ninety-Seven

I forgot about Yuki as soon as she turned away from me. I was falling backwards in time, feeling the pain of that horrifying night. The whooshing sound of Sam's breathing was like the sound of salt water washing over my open wounds and the courtroom was a slick sea of faces, reflecting back what must have been my own pained and stricken expression.

I picked out six members of the Cabot family by their resemblance to Sara and Sam and the fury in their eyes. And I saw cops everywhere, men and women I'd known and worked with for years. My eyes locked on Jacobi and his eyes held mine. He gave me a thumbs-up and I wanted to smile but Mason Broyles was coming toward me.

He wasted no time with amenities.

'Lieutenant Boxer, when you shot my client and his sister, did you shoot to kill?'

There was a loud ringing in my ears as I tried to understand his question. *Had I shot to kill? Yes. But how could I say that I had meant to kill those kids?*

'I'm sorry, Mr Broyles. Could you repeat the question?'

'Let me ask it another way. If this incident happened as you say, that Sara and Sam Cabot refused to put down their guns, why didn't you simply disable them? Shoot them in the arms or legs, for instance.'

I hesitated, trying to imagine it. Sara standing squarely facing me on the pavement. Those shots pounding into my body. Falling to the street. The shock. The pain. The shame.

'Lieutenant?'

'Mr Broyles, I fired in self-defense.'

'Amazing that your aim was so good. Drunk as you were.'

'Objection. He's badgering Lieutenant Boxer.'

'Sustained. Watch yourself, Mr Broyles.'

'Yes, Judge. Lieutenant, I don't understand. You shot two bullets into Sara's heart – a pretty small target, wouldn't you say? Why couldn't you have shot her so that she'd survive? Why didn't you shoot Sam Cabot's gun out of his hand?'

'Your Honor! Asked and answered.'

'I withdraw the question. We understand what you did, Lieutenant,' Broyles sneered. 'We understand *exactly* what happened.'

Chapter Ninety-Eight

I heard Yuki say, 'Redirect, Your Honor.' Then she approached me, moving quickly out of her seat. She waited until I was looking into her eyes.

'Lindsay, when you fired on Sam and Sara Cabot, was your life in danger?'

'Yes.'

'What's proper police procedure for that situation? What's "by-the-book"?'

'You shoot to center mass to alleviate the threat and once the threat is alleviated, you cease firing. Often those center-mass shots are fatal. You can't take any chances by shooting at extremities. You could miss. The individual might still be able to shoot and you've got to make sure the shooter can't hurt you or other people.'

'Did you have any other choice but to shoot the way you did?'

'No. None at all once the Cabots introduced lethal force.'

'Thank you, Lieutenant. *Now* we understand exactly what happened.'

I was weak with relief when I stepped down from the stand. As soon as I took my seat, I heard the judge dismiss the court.

'See you all tomorrow at nine,' she said.

Yuki and Mickey and several attorneys from his office formed a buffer zone around me as we left the courthouse by the back door and entered the black Lincoln town car that was waiting for us on Polk.

Through the car's smoked windows, I saw the angry, chanting crowd holding posters with my picture and the slogans *Loose Cannon* and *Dirty Harriet*.

'You did great, Lindsay,' Mickey said, reaching over from the front seat and patting my arm. But his brown eyes didn't smile and the lower half of his face looked frozen.

'I shouldn't have hesitated. I – just didn't know what to say.'

'No harm done. We're going to dinner now. Yuki and I have to spend some time going over her closing. You're welcome to come with us.'

'If you don't need me, why don't you drop me off at Yuki's place. Let you guys work in peace.'

I clutched Yuki's keys in my hand and watched the city I knew so well fly by the darkened car windows. I knew that I'd blown it. A few seconds of hesitation and everyone in the room had read my mind.

The impression that jury walked away with today was that I'd shot those kids to kill.

And, of course, they were right.

Chapter Ninety-Nine

A shrill alarm shattered whatever nightmare had gripped me in its vise lock. I lay stiff and immobile, trying to get my bearings when the alarm went off again, less strident now, less jarring.

I grabbed my cell phone from the night table and flipped it open – but the caller had disconnected.

Awake and grouchy at 6:00 a.m., I moved piles of Yuki's stuff in the small second bedroom until I found my tracksuit and running shoes. I dressed quietly, collared and leashed Martha, and together we slipped out of the Crest Royal into dawn's early light.

I ran through the route in my mind, pretty sure that I could do two miles on gentle hills and flatlands. Then Martha and I headed north for the straight-away of Jones Street at a slow jog, the twinge in my joints reminding me how much I really hated to run.

Slipping the lead from Martha's collar so that she wouldn't wrap her leash around my legs and herd me into a pratfall, I forced myself into a faster pace on the downhill side of Jones, until the still irksome pain from my shoulder and leg dissolved into an overall ache of my rusty muscles.

As much as I hated it, running was my only hope of escaping my obsession with the trial because it was the best way to shift from a mental state to a more manageable physical one. And even though my tendons screamed, it was good to feel my sneakers pounding the sidewalk, my sweat drying in the cool air as the dawn faded into morning.

I kept running north on Jones across Vallejo Street until I reached the summit of Russian Hill. Straight ahead was Alcatraz Island with its flashing lighthouse and the glorious view of Angel Island.

It was there that my mind floated free and my heart hammered from exertion rather than from stress and fear.

I blew through the wall as I crossed onto Hyde and the wonderful endorphins warmed me. To my right was the crooked block of Lombard, an endlessly charming street that runs down the hill to Leavenworth. I pumped my arms and jogged in place waiting for a red light to change, delighted that I was still ahead of the commuter crowd that a half-hour from now would totally clog the streets and sidewalks.

The light changed and I pushed off. The path I'd chosen took me through some of the city's prettiest blocks of gorgeous old homes and postcard views, even with the fog still drifting around the Bay. Martha and I had reached the edge of Chinatown when I heard the *shushing* of car wheels following close on my heels.

Someone called out, 'Miss, you have to put your dog on a leash.'

I was ticked-off at the interruption of my new blissful mood and swung around to see a black-and-white unit dogging me. I stopped running and called Martha to my side.

'Oh, my gosh, Lieutenant. It's you.'

'Good morning, Nicolo,' I panted to the young officer riding shotgun. 'Hello, Friedman,' I said to the driver.

'We're all behind you, Lou,' Friedman said. 'I don't mean like literally this moment,' he sputtered. 'I mean we really miss you, man – uh, Lieutenant.'

'Thanks.' I smiled. 'That means a lot. Especially today.'

'Never mind about the dog, okay?'

'Hey, you were right the first time, Nicolo. She stays on the leash.'

'Following procedures?'

'Yup, that's me.'

'Good luck, okay, Lieutenant?'

'Thanks, guys.'

Friedman flashed the car's headlights as they pulled past me. Holding Martha's lead with both hands so that it crossed tightly against my body, I turned up Clay Street and headed back up the hill toward Jones.

By the time I stumbled into the lobby of Yuki's building, all of the knots and snarls had melted out of my system. Minutes later I soaked under the hot shower I'd earned and it was a stupendous reward.

I toweled myself off with one of Yuki's giant terrycloth bath jobbies and then I wiped the condensation off the mirror.

I gave myself a good hard look.

My skin was pink. My eyes were clear. I'd run my miles in decent time, including the dog-leash stop. I was okay. Win or lose, I was still the same person I'd always been.

Even Mason Broyles couldn't take *that* away from me.

Chapter One Hundred

Apart from the sound of Sam Cabot's laborious breathing, the courtroom was quiet as Broyles stood at his table, eyes on the screen of his laptop, waiting for the last excruciating moment to begin his closing statement.

Finally, he stepped over to the jury box and after greeting the jury members in his usual greasily gracious manner, he launched into his summation.

'I'm sure we all appreciate that the police have a difficult job. To tell you the truth, it's not a job I'd like to do. The police deal with rough people and ugly situations routinely, and they have to make tough, split-second decisions every day.

'These are all conditions of the job Lieutenant Lindsay Boxer took on when she put on her badge. She swore an oath to uphold the law and to protect our citizens.

'And it's indisputable that you can't do those things properly when you're drunk.'

Someone in the back of the room stepped on his rhetoric with a coughing fit. Broyles stood patiently, hands in his pockets, and waited for the hacking to cease.

When the room was quiet once more, he picked right up where he'd left off.

'We all heard Lieutenant Boxer's testimony yesterday and I find it interesting that she denies what she can't admit – and admits what she can't deny.

'Lieutenant Boxer *denies* that she should never have gotten in that car; that she should never have assumed the position of a police officer when she'd had too much to drink. But she *must admit* that she didn't follow procedures. And she *must admit* that she killed Sara Cabot and destroyed Sam Cabot's life.

'Ladies and gentlemen, we have police procedures in place to prevent deadly shoot-outs like the one that happened on the night of May tenth.

'Those procedures weren't made up after this tragic incident occurred. They're time tested and have been in effect for decades for a reason. Every cop alive knows that you approach a suspect vehicle with your gun drawn so as to show the person you're approaching that you mean business.

'And you disarm suspects so that no one gets hurt.'

Broyles walked over to his table and drank from a tall glass of water. I wanted to jump up and call him out on his perversion of the truth, but instead I watched in silence as he turned toward the cameras before walking back to the jury, all of whom seemed transfixed by what he was saying.

'Sam and Sara Cabot were young, cocky kids, and they took liberties with the law. They borrowed their dad's car without permission, and they fled from a police pursuit. They lacked maturity and they lacked good judgment. What that means to me is that despite their intelligence, they needed more protection than adults would have needed in a similar situation.

'And Lieutenant Boxer failed to provide that protection because she didn't follow the most basic police procedures. She decided to "serve and protect" when she was intoxicated.

'As a result of that decision, an exceptional young woman is dead, and a young man who could have been anything he wanted to be is going to sit in a wheelchair for the rest of his life.'

Mason Broyles pressed his hands together, adopting a prayer-like pose, and, damn it, it was moving. He took a deep breath and released it, nearly sighing his sorrowful conclusion to the jury.

'We can't bring Sara Cabot back,' he said. 'And you've seen what's left of Sam's life. Our legal system can't reverse the damage done to these children, but you *are* empowered to compensate Sam Cabot and his parents for their loss and suffering.

'Ladies and gentlemen of the jury, I ask you please to do the right thing and find for my client in the amount of one hundred and fifty million dollars.

'Don't just do it for the Cabot family.

'Do it for your family and mine, for every family and every person in this city of ours.

'Finding the defendant guilty is the only way we can make sure a tragedy like this one *never* happens again.'

Chapter One Hundred and One

Yuki closed her notebook and stepped out onto the courtroom floor. She turned her lovely face to the jury and greeted them. I clasped my hands tightly together and tried to think past Mason Broyles's powerful closing speech.

'This is a very emotional case,' Yuki said. 'On the one hand we have a tragedy that will remain with the Cabot family forever.

'On the other hand, a damned good cop has been unfairly accused of causing this incident.

'Because this case is so emotional, because the Cabot kids are and were so young, I want to state the facts again, because your job is to decide this case based on facts, not emotion.

'It's a fact that if a cop wants to have a couple of margaritas on a Friday night when she's off duty, there is absolutely nothing wrong with that. Cops are people too. And while police officers are there for the public twenty-four hours a day, it would have been perfectly okay for Lieutenant Boxer to have told Inspector Jacobi that she was busy.

'But this officer cared intensely about her work and went beyond the call of duty and in so doing she put herself in harm's way.

'You've heard the plaintiffs say over and over again that Lieutenant Boxer was drunk. In fact, she was not intoxicated. And while her alcohol consumption may have been a *condition* of this incident, it was not the *cause*.

'Please don't lose sight of this distinction.

'Lieutenant Boxer did not make any errors of judgment on the night of May tenth because her reactions were slow or her thinking was faulty. If Lieutenant Lindsay Boxer did anything wrong that night, it was because she showed *too much* compassion for the plaintiffs.

'The two people who were the cause of the death and injuries to Sara and Sam Cabot were the Cabot children themselves. The fact is that two young, spoiled rich kids had nothing better to do on the night in question, but go out and cause injury and misery to other people, and eventually to themselves.

'Ladies and gentlemen, Sam and Sara Cabot caused the events of May tenth with their reckless behavior and with their use of deadly force. *They* introduced deadly force into this affair, not Lieutenant Boxer. And that is the crucial fact.'

Yuki paused, and for a terrible second, I thought she might have forgotten where her closing statement was headed. She lifted her pearls from the front of her silk blouse and ran her fingers over them, then she turned back to the jury and I realized she was simply gathering her thoughts.

'Usually when a cop goes on trial it's a Rodney King or Abner Louima type affair. A cop pulled the trigger too quickly or beat the hell out of someone or abused his or her authority.

'Lindsay Boxer is being accused of doing just the opposite. She holstered her gun because the Cabot children seemed helpless and in fact they were in danger. And the prosecution wants to turn her humanity toward these children into a "failure to follow police procedures".

'Forgive me, but this is bull.

'Lieutenant Boxer followed procedures when she approached the car in question with her gun drawn. Then, based on the visible injuries to Sam Cabot, she rendered aid to the victims of a car accident.

'That was the right thing to do.

'Inspector Jacobi, another damned good cop with over twenty-five years on the SFPD, did the same thing. You heard him. He holstered his gun. After he and Lieutenant Boxer freed the Cabot kids from their vehicle, he tried to get them medical assistance.

'Isn't this the kind of behavior we all want from our police force? If you were in an accident? If these had been your kids?

'But instead of thanking these officers, the Cabot children fired guns at them, with intent to kill. Sam kicked Inspector Jacobi in the head after he'd been shot. Was their vicious and potentially lethal aggression caused by the use of drugs? Or were they just bent on murder?

'We don't know.

'But we do know that Lieutenant Boxer was shot first and that she returned fire in self-defense. That's a fact. And defending herself, ladies and gentlemen, is "proper police procedure".

'Lieutenant Boxer told you she'd give anything in the world to have Sara Cabot alive today and for this young man to have the full use of his body.

'But the fact is, the events of May tenth did not happen because of a fire that Lindsay Boxer set. She tried to put that fire out.'

I felt a rush of gratitude that almost spilled from my eyes. My God, to be defended with such heart and eloquence. I bit my lower lip and watched Yuki as she finished her summation.

'Ladies and gentlemen of the jury, you've been very patient this week through a lot of testimony and harassment at home and on the streets from the media. I know you are looking forward to your deliberation.

'We ask that you find Lieutenant Lindsay Boxer guilty of being the kind of cop we should all be proud of – a compassionate, dedicated, selfless officer of the law.

'And we ask that you find her innocent of the outrageous charges that have been brought against her.'

Chapter One Hundred
and Two

'What do you say we go out the front door today?' Mickey said, taking my arm. 'It's Friday. The case will be on hold throughout the weekend and that makes me think this is a good time to "meet the press".'

I walked between my attorneys into the hallway and from there down the marble stairs and out onto McAllister. The corner of the Civic Center Courthouse is cut on an angle so that the building faces both the wide intersection and the manicured park across from Civic Center Plaza.

By contrast to the dark of the courthouse, the sunshine was blinding. And, as it had been since the beginning of my trial, McAllister was so jammed, I couldn't see over the press and the satellite vans that were lining the curb.

It was like the scene outside the O.J. Simpson courtroom. The same kind of adrenaline-fueled madness that masked the truth, whatever that might be. This trial wasn't worthy of the world stage. The media exposure was all about viewership, ratings, advertising dollars. Be that as it may, today I was 'it'.

Like hounds on a rabbit, the press saw me coming down the steps and closed in for the kill. Mickey was ready with his statement, but he never got to deliver it.

'How long do you think the jury will be out, Mr Sherman?'

'I don't know, but I'm sure, however long it takes, the jury will find Lieutenant Boxer innocent of all charges.'

'Lieutenant Boxer, if the jury finds against you—'

'That's unlikely to happen,' Yuki answered for me.

'Ms Castellano, this is your first high-profile case. How do you think you did?'

Fifteen feet away, a crowd was also forming around Mason Broyles, his clients and his deputies. Film rolled as the medical attendant pushed Sam Cabot down a wooden ramp and loaded him into a van. Reporters followed, firing questions at Sam as his father did his best to shield the boy.

I picked Cindy out of the crowd. She was shouldering through the sardine-can-packed bodies, trying to get closer to me. And that's why I wasn't paying much attention to Mickey when he answered his cell phone.

Then his hand was on my shoulder. His face was totally gray.

'I just got a heads-up from the Clerk's Office,' he shouted into my ear. 'The jury has a couple of questions.'

We pressed through the crowd, making our way to the street and Mickey's waiting car. Yuki and I got into the back seat and Mickey got in front beside his driver.

'What do they want to know?' Yuki asked as soon as the doors closed. The car moved slowly through the crowd, heading toward Redwood.

'They want to see the evidence of Lindsay's alcohol intake,' Mickey said, turning to face us.

'Christ,' Yuki said. 'How could they still be stuck on that?'

'What else?' I asked urgently. 'You said there were two things.'

I saw Mickey hesitate. He didn't want to tell me, but he had to do it.

'They wanted to know if there was a limit on how much money they could award the plaintiffs,' he said.

Chapter One Hundred and Three

It was a gut shot and the shock resonated from my solar plexus throughout my body. I felt my stomach drop and bile rise into my throat. I had envisioned losing this case in terms of a fanciful, theoretical aftermath; working at street fairs, reading books on the deck of some beach house, la-de-da. But I hadn't taken into account the full emotional impact of the reality of losing.

Beside me, Yuki squealed, 'Oh my God, it's all my fault. I shouldn't have said "find her guilty of being a good cop blah-blah". It was a flourish! I thought it was good, but I was wrong.'

'You did a great job,' I said, my voice as heavy as stone. 'This has nothing to do with what you said.'

I wrapped my arms around myself and lowered my head. Mickey and Yuki were talking together. I heard Mickey assure her that the fat lady hadn't yet sung, but the voice in my mind was a needle stuck in an old-fashioned record groove.

One question kept repeating.
How could this be?
How could this be?

Chapter One Hundred
and Four

When I tuned back into the conversation in the car, Mickey was explaining something to Yuki.

'The judge gave them the paperwork from the hospital and the transcript from the nurse. And she told them not to worry about limiting the award. That's her job and need not concern them.'

Mickey ran his hand over his face in what I took to be exasperation. 'Yuki, you did a fantastic job – I mean it. I can't believe that the jury bought Mason Broyles's act,' he said. 'I just *don't* believe it. I don't know how we could have done better.'

And that's when Yuki's cell phone rang.

'The jury is back,' she said. She folded her phone, clutching it until her knuckles whitened. 'They have a verdict.'

My mind spaced. I saw the word 'verdict' in front of my eyes and tried to parse it, looking between the letters and syllables for something to hope for.

I knew from past days in court that the Latin roots of the word 'verdict' mean to speak the truth.

Would this verdict be the truth?

In the minds of the people of San Francisco, it would be.

Mickey directed his driver to turn around, which he did, and a few minutes later I was saying 'No comment, no comment, please,' and following Yuki and Mickey through the mob, up the steep stairs and into the courthouse once again.

We took our places in Courtroom B and the opposition took theirs.

I heard my name pierce the moment as if it had come from another time and place. I turned to look behind me.

'Joe!'

'I just got in, Lindsay. I came straight from the airport.'

We reached out and for a brief moment entwined our fingers across the shoulders of the people sitting behind me. Then I had to let go and turn away.

Along the sides of the room, cameramen focused their lenses – then, only an hour since we'd left this room, the judge entered from her chambers and the jury filed back in.

The bailiff called the court back into session.

Chapter One Hundred and Five

It took the members of the jury long moments to fix their skirts, put down their bags and get comfortable in their seats. Finally, they were at attention. I noticed that only two of them had looked at me.

I listened numbly as the judge asked the jury if they'd arrived at a verdict. Then the foreman, a fifty-something African-American man named Arnold Benoit, straightened the lines of his sports jacket and spoke.

'We have, Your Honor.'

'Please pass your verdict to the bailiff.'

Across the aisle, Sam Cabot's breathing quickened, as did mine, keeping double time along with my pounding heart as the judge opened the single sheet of paper.

She scanned it, and without expression passed it back to the bailiff, who returned it to the jury foreman.

'I caution all present not to react to whatever the foreman says,' said the judge. 'All right, Mr Foreman. Please pronounce the verdict.'

The foreman took his glasses out of his jacket pocket, flipped them open and set them on his nose. Finally, he began to read.

'"We, the jury in the above entitled action find the accused, Lieutenant Lindsay Boxer . . . *not guilty* of the charges against her".'

'So say you all?'

'We do.'

I was so numb, I wasn't sure I'd heard correctly. And when I played the statement back in my mind, I half-expected the judge to overrule what the foreman had just said.

Yuki grasped my wrist tightly and only when I saw the smile lighting her face did I fully realize that I wasn't imagining anything. The jury had found in my favor.

A voice shouted; *'No! No! You can't do this!'*

It was Andrew Cabot, on his feet, holding onto the chair-back in front of him where Mason Broyles sat, white-faced and grim, and beaten.

Broyles's request that the jury be polled was a demand, and the judge complied.

'As you hear your seat number called, please tell the court how you voted,' said Judge Achacoso.

One at a time the jurors spoke.

'Not guilty.'

'Not guilty.'

'Not guilty . . .'

I had heard the expression, but I'm not sure I

understood it until that moment. With both my attorneys' arms around me, I floated in a feeling of relief so complete that it was in a dimension of its own. Perhaps this feeling was reserved only for moments of redemption, moments like this.

I was free, *and my heart took flight.*

PART FIVE

The Cat's Meow

Chapter One Hundred and Six

There was a moody gray sky overhead when Martha and I left my apartment and headed out of San Francisco. I turned on the car radio and caught the weather report, listening with half an ear as I negotiated the stop-and-go snarl of the usual commuter traffic.

As I bumped along Potrero Street, I was thinking about Chief Tracchio. Yesterday, when we'd met at the Hall of Justice, he'd asked me to come back to work and I'd gotten as flustered as if he'd asked me for a date.

All I'd had to do was shake his hand on it.

If I'd done that, I would have been driving to the Hall this morning, making a speech to the troops about going forward, diving into the mountain of paperwork on my desk, unsolved cases. I would've taken back my command.

But although the Chief had laid it on really thick, I'd turned him down.

'I still have some vacation time, Chief. I need to take it.'

He said he understood, but how could he? I still didn't know what I wanted to do with my life, and I had a sense that I wouldn't know until I'd gotten to the bottom of the killings in Half Moon Bay.

Those unsolved murders were a part of me now, too.

My gut told me that if I did what I was good at, if I persevered, I would find the s.o.b. who had killed my John Doe and all those others.

Right now, that was all I really cared about.

I took 280 southbound and, once clear of the city, I rolled down the windows and changed the channel.

By 10:00 a.m., my hair was whipping across my face and Sue Hall was spinning my favorite oldies on 99.7 FM.

'It's not raining this morning,' she purred. 'It's the first of July, a beautiful, gray, San Francisco day – just floating in pearly fog. And isn't the fog something that we love about San Francisco?'

Then the perfect song poured through the speakers: 'Fly Like an Eagle'.

I sang along in full voice, the tune pumping oxygen into my blood, sending my mood right through the ozone layer.

I was free.

The horrific trial was in my rear-view mirror and suddenly my future was as open as the highway ahead.

Eighteen miles out of the city, Martha needed a

rest stop so I pulled over into the parking lot of a Taco Bell in Pacifica. It was a wooden shack built in the 1960s before the zoning commission knew what was happening. And now there stood one of the tackiest buildings in the world on one of the most beautiful spots on the coastline.

Unlike most of the highway, which streamed high above the ocean, the fast-food restaurant parking lot was at sea level. A row of rocks separated the asphalt from the beach and beyond it, the deep blue Pacific flowed over the rim of the horizon.

I bought an irresistible cinnamon-sugared churro and a container of black coffee and took a seat on the boulders. I watched tattooed, hard-bodied surfers riding the waves as Martha ran over the luminous gray sand until the sun had nearly burned off the fog.

When this great moment was sealed in my memory, I called Martha back to the car. Twenty minutes later, we entered the outskirts of Half Moon Bay.

Chapter One Hundred and Seven

I drove across the air-bell on the apron of the *Man in the Moon Garage* and honked a little 'shave and a haircut' until Keith came out of his office. He lifted off his baseball cap, shook out his golden hair, stuck the cap back on, smiled my way and sauntered on over.

'Well, well. Lookit who's here. The Woman of the Year,' Keith said, putting his hand on Martha's head.

'Oh, that's me, all right,' I said, laughing. 'I'm just glad it's over.'

'Yeah, I totally get it. I saw that Sam Cabot on the news. He was so pitiful. I was really scared for you, Lindsay, but it's water over the hill now. Congratulations are in order.'

I murmured my thanks for his interest and asked Keith to fill up the tank. Meanwhile, I took the squeegee from a bucket and cleaned the windshield.

'So, what're you up to, Lindsay? Don't you have to go back to work in the big city?'

'Not right away. You know, I'm just not ready yet . . .'

As the words left my mouth, a red blur breezed across the intersection. The driver slowed and looked right at me before gunning the engine and tearing down Main.

I'd been in town for less than five minutes and Dennis Agnew was back in my face.

'I left the Bonneville at my sister's house,' I said as I observed the Porsche's contrail. 'And I have a little unfinished business here in town.'

Keith turned and saw that I was watching Agnew's Porsche disappear down the street.

'I've never understood it,' he said, jacking the gas gun into my tank, shaking his head. A bell rang as the gas meter racked up the gallons. 'He's a really bad dude. I just don't understand why women are so attracted to trouble.'

'You're kidding me,' I said. 'You think I'm interested in that guy?'

'Aren't you?'

'Very. But not in the way you mean. My interest in Dennis Agnew is purely professional.'

Chapter One Hundred and Eight

As we headed to Cat's house, Martha jumped around from back seat to front, barking like a fool. And when I parked in the driveway, she leaped through the car's open window and ran up to the front door, where she stood wagging her tail and singing in a high key.

'Be cool, Boo,' I said. 'Show a little restraint.'

I jiggled the key in the lock, opened the front door and Martha trotted inside.

I called Joe and left him a message: 'Hey, Molinari, I'm at Cat's house. Call when you can.' Then I left a message for Carolee, telling her that she and Allison could stand down from pig-sitting detail.

I spent the day thinking about the Half Moon Bay murders while I cleaned up around the house. I cooked up some spaghetti and canned baby peas for dinner, making a mental note to do some grocery shopping in the morning.

Then I took my laptop into my nieces' room and set it up on their shelf of a desk. I noticed that the sweet potato vines had sent another couple of inches across the windowsill, but the notes Joe and I had tacked up on the girls' cork board were unchanged.

Our little scribblings detailing the circumstances and the savagery done to the Whittakers, Daltrys, Sarduccis and O'Malleys still led nowhere. And of course my lone John Doe remained pinned to the wall.

I booted up my laptop and went into the FBI's VICAP database. The Violent Criminal Apprehension Program was a national website with one purpose: to help law-enforcement agents link up scattered bits of intel related to serial homicides. The site has a kick-ass search engine and new information was always being plugged in by cops around the country.

Now I typed in key words that might make the tumblers spin, some answers fall into place.

I tried them all: whippings administered cummortem, couples killed in bed, and of course slashed throats, which sent up a storm of information. Too much.

Hours passed and my vision started to blur, so I put the computer on 'hibernate' and dropped down onto one of my nieces' small beds to rest for a few minutes.

When I woke up, it was pitch black outside. It felt as though something had awoken me. A slight noise that didn't belong. According to the time flashing on the kids' VCR, it was 2:17 a.m. and I had a prickly sense that I couldn't nail down, as if I were being watched.

I blinked in the blackness and saw a red blur shoot across my vision. It was the afterimage of that red Porsche and it called up snatches of the disturbing scenes I'd had with Agnew. The set-to at The Cormorant and the one at Keith's garage. The near-collision on the road.

I was still thinking about Agnew. It was the only thing that explained the sensation of being watched.

I was about to get up and go to my room for what remained of the night, when the sound of splintering glass, followed by a series of hard pops shattered the still night air.

Shards of the window fell all around me.

Gun! Gun! Where the hell was my gun?

Chapter One Hundred and Nine

M artha's reflexes were quicker than mine. She dove off the bed and crawled under it. I was right behind her, rolling onto the floor while riffling through my shocked mind, trying to remember where I'd put my weapon.

Then I knew.

It was in my handbag in the living room and the closest phone was there, too. How could I be so vulnerable? Was I going to die trapped in this room? My heart pounded so hard it hurt.

I lifted my head just inches off the floor and by the faint green light of the VCR clock, I took inventory.

I focused on every surface and object in the room, looking for something – anything I could use to protect myself.

The place was littered with big stuffed animals and a dozen dolls, but there wasn't a single baseball bat or hockey stick, nothing I could use in a fight. I couldn't even throw the TV because it was bolted to the wall.

I pulled myself across the hardwood floor on my forearms, reached up and locked the bedroom door.

Just then, another fusillade of shots rang out – automatic gunfire raking the front of the house, again striking the living room and the spare room at the end of the hall. Then the true intent of the assault finally sunk in.

I could have been – should have been – sleeping in that bedroom.

Inching forward on my stomach, I clasped the leg of a wooden chair, pushed at it, angled the chair onto its rear legs and wedged its back under the door knob. Then I picked up its twin and swung it against the dresser.

With a length of chair leg in my hand, I crouched with my back to the wall.

It was just pathetic. Forget the dog under the bed, my only line of defense was a chair leg.

If anyone came through the door aiming to kill me, I was dead.

Chapter One Hundred
and Ten

As I listened for the sound of feet on the floor-
boards outside the bedroom, I imagined the
door being kicked open and me swinging at the
intruder with my stick, hoping to God that I could
somehow knock his brains out.

But as the VCR clock blinked away the minutes
and the silence grew longer, my adrenaline ebbed.

And I started to get mad.

I stood, listened at the door and when I heard
nothing, I opened it and worked my way down the
long hallway, using doorways and walls as barri-
cades.

When I got to the living room, I grabbed my bag
from where it leaned against the sofa.

I reached in and closed my hand around my gun.
Thank You, God.

As I called 911, I peeked through slits in the
window blinds. The street looked empty but I

thought I saw something glinting on the front lawn. What was it?

I told the dispatcher my name, rank and shield number and that shots had been fired at 265 Sea View.

'Anyone hurt?'

'No, I'm fine, but call Chief Stark on this.'

'It's already been called in, Lieutenant. The cavalry is on the way.'

Chapter One Hundred and Eleven

I heard sirens and saw flashing lights approaching Sea View. As the first cruiser arrived, I opened the front door and Martha bolted past me. She ran straight over to a snake-like object that was lying in the moonlight.

She gave it a sniff.

'Martha, what have you found? What is it, girl?'

I was hunkered down beside Martha when Chief Peter Stark got out of his squad car. He walked over with his flashlight and knelt down next to me.

'You okay?'

'Yep. I'm good.'

'Is that what I think it is?' he asked.

Together, we looked at a man's belt. It was about 36 inches long and a half-inch wide, narrow brown leather with a squared, dull silver buckle. It was such an ordinary belt; probably half the people in the state had one like it in their closet somewhere.

But this particular belt seemed to have some brownish-red stains on the metalwork.

'Wouldn't it be grand,' I said, refusing to dwell on the terror of the last few minutes – how those shots had surely been meant for me. 'Wouldn't it be something,' I said to Chief Stark, 'if this belt was evidence?'

Chapter One Hundred
and Twelve

Three squad cars had pulled up to the curb. Radios sputtered and crackled and all along Sea View lights went on in houses and people came out onto their doorsteps wearing PJs and robes, T-shirts and shorts, hair standing up, fear overriding the lines in their sleep-creased faces.

Cat's front yard was lit by headlights and as the cops exited their cars, they conferred with the Chief and spread out. A couple of uniforms started collecting shell casings and a pair of detectives began to canvass the neighbors.

I took Stark into the house, and together we examined the shattered windows, the splintered furniture and the bullet-pocked headboard in 'my' bedroom.

'Any thoughts on who did this?' Stark asked me.

'None,' I said. 'My car's in the driveway where anyone can see it, but I didn't let anyone know I'd be in town.'

'And why *are* you here, Lieutenant?'

I was considering the best way to answer that when I heard Allison and Carolee calling out my name. A young cop with ruddy, protruding ears came to the threshold and told Stark that I had visitors.

'They can't come in here,' Stark said. 'Jesus Christ, is someone roping off the street?'

The uniformed cop's face colored completely as he shook his head, no.

'Why the hell not? Number one. *Stabilize the scene.* Get on it.'

I followed the patrolman as far as the front doorstep, where Carolee and Allison grabbed me in a much-needed two-tier hug.

'One of my kids monitors the police band,' Carolee said. 'I got over here as soon as I heard. Oh my God, Lindsay. *Your arms.*'

I glanced down. Broken glass had made a few cuts in my forearms and blood had streaked down and stained my T-shirt.

It looked a lot worse than it was.

'I'm fine,' I told Carolee. 'Just a few scratches, I'm sure.'

'You don't plan to stay here, do you, Lindsay? Because that's crazy,' Carolee said, her face showing how mad she was and how scared. 'I've got plenty of room for you at the house.'

'Good idea,' Stark said, coming up behind me. 'Go with your nice friend. I've got calls in to the CSU techs and they're going to be prying slugs out of your walls and combing the place for the rest of the night.'

'That's fine. I'll be okay here,' I told him. 'This is my sister's house. I'm not going to leave.'

'All right. But don't forget that this is our case, Lieutenant. You're still out of your jurisdiction. Don't go all cowgirl on us, okay?'

'Go all *cowgirl*? Who do you think you're talking to?'

'*Look*. I'm sorry, but someone just tried to kill you.'

'Thanks. I got that.'

The Chief patted down his hair out of habit. 'I'll keep a patrol car posted in the driveway tonight. Maybe longer.'

As I said good-night to Carolee and Allison, the Chief went to his car and returned with a paper bag. He was using a ball-point pen to lift the belt into the bag as I wrapped my dignity tightly around myself and closed the front door.

I went to bed, but of course I couldn't sleep. Cops were coming and going through the house, slamming doors and laughing, and besides, my mind was spinning.

I stroked Martha's head absently as she shivered beside me. Someone had shot up this house and left a calling card.

Was it a warning to stay away from Half Moon Bay?

Or had the shooter really tried to kill me?

What would happen when I turned up alive?

Chapter One Hundred and Thirteen

A sunbeam slipped through the window at an unaccustomed angle and pried my eyes open. I saw blue wallpaper, a picture of my mother over the dresser – and it all came together.

I was in Cat's bed – because at 2:00 a.m. bullets had thudded through the house, plugging the headboard in the spare room inches above where my head would have been.

Martha pushed her wet nose at my hand until I swung my feet out of bed. I pulled on some of Cat's clothes – a faded pair of jeans and a coral-colored blouse with a deep, ruffled neckline. Not my color and definitely not my style.

I ran a comb through my hair, brushed my teeth and stepped out into the living room.

The CSU techs were still digging bullets out of the walls, so I made coffee and toast for everyone and asked pointed questions that yielded the basic facts.

Twelve 9mm shots had been fired, evenly distributed through the living room and spare bedroom, one through the kids' room's small, high window. The bullets and spent cases had been bagged and tagged, the rest no doubt were inside the back seat of the shooter's car.

The bullet holes in the walls and furniture had been photographed and as soon as those slugs were extracted, the forensic team would be wrapping up. In an hour, the whole kit and caboodle would be sent to the lab.

'You doing okay, Lieutenant?' asked one of the techs, a tall, thirty-ish guy with big hazel eyes and a toothy smile.

I looked around at the destruction; the glass and plaster dust over everything.

'No. I'm not. This makes me sick,' I said. 'I've got to sweep up, get the windows fixed, do something about this mess.'

'I'm Artie, by the way,' the tech said, stretching out his hand.

'Nice to meet you,' I said, shaking it.

'My uncle Chris has a Disaster Master franchise. You want me to call him? He can get this place cleaned up, like pronto. I mean, you'll go to the head of the line, Lieutenant. You're one of us.'

I thanked Artie and took him up on his offer. Then I grabbed my handbag and took Martha out the back way. I fed Miss Piggy, then circled around to the patrol car in the driveway and ducked my head to window level.

'Noonan, right?'

'Yes, ma'am.'

'Still on duty?'

'Yes, ma'am. We'll be here for a while. The whole squad is watching out for you, Lieutenant. The Chief and all of us. This really stinks.'

'I appreciate the concern.'

And I did. Harsh daylight only made the shooting more real. Someone had driven down this sweet suburban street raking Cat's house with automatic gunfire.

I was unnerved and until I got my composure back, I had to get away from here. I jingled my car keys so that Martha flattened her ears and nearly wagged her tail off.

'We need groceries,' I said to her. 'What do you say we take the Bonneville on a shake-down cruise?'

Chapter One Hundred and Fourteen

M artha jumped onto the bench-style front seat of the 'big gold boat'. I strapped in and turned the key. The engine caught on the second try and I pointed the Bonneville's aristocratic nose toward town.

I was going to the gourmet grocer on Main Street, but as I made my way along the crosshatched streets of Cat's neighborhood, I gradually became aware of a blue Taurus sedan in my rear-view mirror. It seemed to be deliberately lagging behind me, but keeping up all the same.

That creepy feeling of being watched tickled my spine again.

Was I being tailed?

Or was I in such a state I just kept seeing myself as a pop-up figure in a shooting gallery?

I took Magnolia across the highway and onto Main where I whizzed past all the little shops: the Music Hut, the Moon News, the Feed and Fuel store. I wanted to convince myself that I was just being skittish, but damn, if I lost that Taurus for a block or two, it was behind me at the next turn.

'Hang on tight. We're going for a ride,' I said to Martha, who was smiling broadly into the wind.

Toward the end of Main, I hooked a right onto Route 92, Half Moon Bay's umbilical cord to the rest of California.

Traffic was going fast on this winding two-laner and I merged into a bumper-to-bumper chain of cars going 50 in a 25 mph zone. The double yellow line went the distance – a full five miles of no passing lane.

I drove on, dimly aware of the hillside of scrubby trees and chaparral on my left and the twenty-foot drop a few feet from the right side of my car. Three cars behind, the blue sedan kept me in sight.

I wasn't crazy. I had a tail.

Was it a scare tactic?

Or was the shooter inside that car, waiting for an opportunity for a clear hit?

The end of 92 intersected with Skyline – and at the near right-hand corner was a rest stop with five picnic tables and a gravel parking lot.

I didn't signal for a turn, just hauled right on my steering-wheel. I wanted to get off the road, let that Taurus pass me so that I could see his face, get his plate-number. Get out of his sights.

But instead of gripping the road as my Explorer would have done, the Bonneville fishtailed across the gravel, sending me back out onto 92, across the double yellow line and into the stream of oncoming traffic.

The Taurus must have passed me, but I never saw it.

I was hanging onto the wheel of my spinning car when the lights on the dashboard freaked out.

My power steering and brakes were gone, the alternator was dead, the engine was heating up, and I was skidding around in the middle of the roadway.

I pumped the brakes and a black pick-up truck swerved to avoid creaming me broadside. The driver leaned on his horn and yelled obscenities out his window – but I was so glad he'd missed me, I wanted to kiss him.

By the time I skidded to a stop on the roadside, a cloud of dust billowed around me and I couldn't see beyond the windshield.

I got out of the Bonneville and leaned against it. My legs were rubbery and my hands shaking.

For now, the chase was over.

But I knew it wasn't really over.

Someone had me in his crosshairs and I had no idea who it was, or why.

Chapter One Hundred and Fifteen

I phoned the *Man in the Moon Garage* on my cell phone and got Keith's answering machine.

'Keith, I'm in a little jam. It's Lindsay. Please pick up.'

When Keith answered, I gave him my coordinates. Twenty minutes felt like an hour before he pulled up in his jouncing tow truck. He hooked up the Bonneville for her ignominious return home, and I climbed up into the passenger side of the cab.

'It's a *luxury* car, Lindsay,' Keith chastised me. 'You're not supposed to do loop-de-loops with this thing. It's more than twenty years old, for God's sake.'

'I know, I know.'

Long silence.

'Nice blouse.'

'Thank you.'

'No, really,' he said, making me laugh. 'You should wear more stuff like that.'

Back at the garage, Keith flipped open the Bonneville's hood.

'Ha. Your fan belt snapped,' he said.

'Ha. I know that.'

'Did you know that in a pinch you could fix this with a length of pantyhose?'

'Yes, I did. But, strange as it may seem, I didn't have any tights in my roadside emergency kit.'

'I have an idea. Why don't I buy this car back from you? Give you a hundred bucks more than you paid me.'

'I'll think about it. No.'

Keith laughed and said he'd drive me home and I had to accept his offer. Since he was going to find out anyway, I told Keith what I hadn't told my girl-friends, hadn't even told Joe yet.

I told him about the gunfire the night before.

'And now you think someone's following you? Why don't you go home, Lindsay? Seriously.'

'Because I can't turn this murder case loose. Not now. Especially since someone threw a dozen rounds at my sister's house.'

Keith gave me a sorry look, tugged on the bill of his Giants cap, handily negotiated the turns in the road.

'Anyone ever call you "stubborn"?'

'Sure. It's considered a good trait in a cop.'

I understood what he was getting at. I no longer knew whether I was being intrepid or stupid.

But I wasn't yet ready to make the call.

Chapter One Hundred and Sixteen

When Keith and I pulled up in front of Cat's house, the driveway was full; the Explorer, a patrol car, a glazier's truck bearing the legend *We Do Windows* and a big metallic-blue van with *Disaster Master* decals on the doors.

I thanked Keith for the lift and, with Martha trotting behind me, I went inside the house, where I found a big man with a little mustache and a horseshoe of dark hair around his head, vacuuming the sofa. He turned off his power vac and 'Uncle Chris' and I exchanged introductions.

'Buncha snoopy reporters showed up,' he said. 'I told them you moved out until the house was put back together. Okay?'

'Perfect. Brilliant.'

'And Chief Stark was here a few minutes ago. Said to call him when you could.'

I ignored the 47 messages blinking on the

answering machine and called the station from the kitchen phone. I got the Duty Officer.

'The Chief's in an interview,' she said. 'Can he call you back?'

'I really wish he would.'

'I'll see to it, Lieutenant.'

I hung up and walked down the hall to my nieces' room.

The blankets were still on the floor. A window was shattered and one of those sweet potato vines was drying up on the floor. I'd dented the dresser really good when I bashed the chair against it and the whole room full of stuffed animals seemed to rebuke me.

What if the kids had been here?

What then, Lindsay?

I dragged the unbroken chair over to the corkboard, sat down and stared at my notations on the murders. My eyes went right to the thing that disturbed me most.

Sometimes the most telling facts hide in plain sight until you're ready to see them.

I had tunnel vision now – *on the peepholes in the O'Malleys' closet.*

I changed my clothes and put Martha outside with Penelope. 'You two play nice.' Then I carefully angled the Explorer around the glazier's truck and out to the street.

I drove back into town.

Chapter One Hundred
and Seventeen

The Watcher took the blue Taurus north on 280, sticking to the freeway through Hillsborough. His thoughts were varied, but most of them centered on Lindsay Boxer.

Thinking about Lindsay gave the Watcher a complex set of feelings. He was kind of weirdly proud of her, the way she kept surviving, kept snapping back. The way she refused to back off, stand down, go back to where she came from. But it was bad news that she insisted on being their problem. Bad news for her.

When it came right down to it, they didn't want to kill her. Killing a cop, especially this particular cop, would mean an all-out manhunt. The whole SFPD would spill out of the city and work her murder. Maybe the FBI, too.

The Watcher slowed at the exit sign for Trousdale Drive, then his sturdy little car glided down the off ramp. A mile and a half later, he turned right at the huge Peninsula Hospital, and right again onto the Camino Real, heading south.

He found an Exxon station two blocks down the road and went inside the attached mini-mart. He wandered around for a couple of minutes, picking up a few small things – a bottle of spring water, a candy bar, a newspaper.

He paid the busty teenaged girl at the cash register $4.20 for his purchases and another $20 for gas. As he left the store, he unfolded the morning paper and saw the story on page one: GUNSHOTS RIP THROUGH DETECTIVE'S HOUSE.

There was a picture of Lindsay in uniform over the story and in the right-hand column was a follow-up about the Cabot case. Sam Cabot had been charged with a double homicide, *Continued on page 2*.

The Watcher put the paper neatly down on the passenger seat and filled up his tank. Then he started the car and headed toward home. He would talk to the Truth later. Maybe they wouldn't kill Lindsay the way they had the others. Maybe they would just make her disappear.

Chapter One Hundred
and Eighteen

The late Dr O'Malley's office was inside a two-story brick house on Kelly Street, his name etched on a brass plaque to the right of the doorway.

I felt a little rush as I rang the bell. I knew the Chief would kick my butt for going around him, but I had to do *something*. Better to beg forgiveness later than to ask permission and be refused.

The buzzer sounded and I pushed open the door. I found the waiting room to my left: small and square with gray upholstered furniture and yards of condolence cards strung up around the walls.

Behind the reception desk was a middle-aged woman with graying hair in a 1960s flip-up style.

'I'm Lieutenant Boxer, SFPD,' I said, showing my badge. I told her that I was working on a cold homicide case that had some similarities to Dr O'Malley's unfortunate death.

'We've already spoken to the police,' she said,

scrutinizing my badge and the winning smile I'd put on just for her. 'Hours and hours of questions.'

'I'll only need a couple of minutes.'

She slid her frosted-glass window closed and a moment later, appeared in the doorway to the inner office.

'I'm Rebecca Falcone,' she said. 'Come in.'

Two other middle-aged women were in the office behind the connecting door.

'That's Mindy Heller, RN,' she said, indicating a streaked blonde wearing nurse's whites and gobs of eye makeup, dumping platters of film-wrapped cookies into the trash can. 'And this is Harriet Schwartz, our office manager,' Rebecca said of a wide woman in red sweats sitting behind an old computer. 'We've all been with Dr Ben since before the Flood.'

I shook hands and repeated my name and why I was there. 'I'm sorry for your loss,' I said. Then I told the women that I needed their help. 'Anything you can do to shed some light.'

'You want the truth?' said Harriet Schwartz. She turned away from the computer, leaned back in her chair and warmed to her memories. 'He was like a Picasso drawing. A bunch of lines and from looking at those, you deduce a person. In between the lines, blank space—'

Mindy Heller jumped in. 'He was a decent doctor, but he was chintzy, withholding, a know-it-all. And he could be nasty to his galley slaves.' She shot a meaningful look at her co-workers. 'But I don't believe he was killed because he was a dickhead, and that's the worst he was.'

'Uh-huh. So you think the O'Malleys were just victims of opportunity.'

'Exactly. Picked at random. I've been saying that all along.'

I asked if any of the other murder victims had been patients of Dr O'Malley and I was shut right down.

'You know we have to protect patient confidentiality,' said Ms Heller, 'but I'm sure Chief Stark can tell you what you want to know.'

Okay, then.

I jotted down my cell-phone number and left it on Harriet Schwartz's desk. I thanked everyone for their time, but I felt deflated. Dr O'Malley may have been all his staff said he was, but in fact, I'd hit another dead end.

I'd just opened the door to the street, when someone gripped my arm. It was Rebecca Falcone, a look of urgency drawing her features into a line down the center of her face.

'I have to speak to you,' she said, 'in private.'

'Can you meet me somewhere?' I asked.

'The Half Moon Bay Coffee Company. Do you know the place?'

'In that little strip mall at the top of Main?'

She nodded once. 'I get off at twelve-thirty.'

'I'll be there.'

Chapter One Hundred
and Nineteen

Our knees almost touched under the small table at the back of the coffee-shop near the rest rooms. We had salads and coffee in front of us, but Rebecca wasn't eating. And she wasn't yet ready to talk.

She pulled on the little gold cross hanging from a chain around her neck, sliding it back and forth.

I thought I understood her conflict. She wanted to be the one to tell the real information, but at the same time, she didn't want to blow the whistle where her friends could hear it.

'I don't *know* anything, understand?' Rebecca said at last. 'And I certainly don't know anything about the murders. But Ben was under some kind of shadow lately.'

'Can you elaborate, Rebecca?'

'Well, he was unusually moody. Snapped at a couple of his patients which, let me tell you, was rare. When I asked him what was going on, he denied that he was having problems.'

'You knew Lorelei?'

'Sure. They met at church, and frankly I was surprised Ben married her. I think he was lonely and she looked up to him.' Rebecca sighed. 'Lorelei was pretty simple. She was a childlike woman, who liked to shop. No one hated her.'

'Interesting observation,' I said. And that was all the encouragement Rebecca needed to say what she'd wanted to say all along.

She looked as though she was standing on the edge of a diving board and the pool was far, far below.

She took a breath and dove.

'Did you know about the first Mrs O'Malley?' she asked me. 'Did you know that Sandra O'Malley killed herself? Hanged herself in her own garage?'

Chapter One Hundred and Twenty

I felt that peculiar crawly feeling at my hairline that often presaged a breakthrough.

'Yes,' I said. 'I read that Sandra O'Malley committed suicide. What do you know about it?'

'It was so unexpected,' Rebecca said. 'No one knew . . . I didn't know she was so depressed.'

'So why do you think she took her own life?'

Rebecca forked her Caesar salad around on her plate, finally putting the utensil down without eating a bite.

'I never found out,' she said. 'Ben wasn't talking, but if I had to guess, I'd say that he was abusing her.'

'Abusing her how?'

'Humiliating her. Treating her like she was nothing. When I heard him talk to her, I'd cringe.' She made the gesture now, pulling her shoulders up, lowering her chin.

'Did she complain about it?'

'No. Sandra wouldn't have done that. She was so compliant, so *nice*. She didn't even squawk when he started having an affair.'

The wheels inside my head were sure turning, but they weren't getting traction yet. Rebecca pursed her lips with distaste.

'He'd been seeing this same woman for years, was still seeing her after he married Lorelei, I'm sure of it. She was calling the office up to the day he died.'

'Rebecca,' I said patiently, although I couldn't stand the suspense for another second. 'Rebecca. What was the other woman's name?'

Rebecca leaned back in her chair as a couple of men scraped past us on the way to the bathroom. When the bathroom door closed, she leaned forward again and whispered, 'Emily Harris.'

I knew that name. I pictured her bright lipsticky mouth. Her pink patterned dress.

'Is she with Pacific Homes Real Estate?'

'That's the one.'

Chapter One Hundred and Twenty-One

Emily Harris was seated at her desk when I entered the long narrow office with a row of desks along one wall. Her pretty mouth stretched into an automatic smile, which broadened when she recognized me.

'Oh, hello,' she said. 'Didn't I meet you and your husband a couple of weeks ago at the Ocean Colony Road house? You have a beautiful dog.'

'That's right,' I told her. 'I'm Lieutenant Boxer. I'm with the SFPD.' And then I showed her my badge.

The woman's face stiffened instantly. 'I've already talked to the police.'

'That's great. So I'm sure you won't mind doing it again.'

I pulled out the chair beside her desk and sat right down.

'I understand that you and Dr O'Malley were close friends,' I said to her.

'I'm not ashamed of what you're insinuating. The man was miserable at home, but I wasn't a threat to his marriage and I damned well had nothing to do with his murder.'

As I watched, Ms Harris squared all the pads, pens and papers on her desk. Tidying up. Getting everything straight and true. What was running through this neatnik's mind right now? What did she know about the O'Malleys?

'And you're the listing broker for his house?'

'That's not a reason to murder someone, for God's sake. Are you crazy? I'm one of the top brokers in this area.'

'Take it easy, Ms Harris. I wasn't implying that you murdered anyone. I'm just trying to get a handle on the victims because I'm working another unsolved homicide.'

'Okay. I'm still a little raw, you know.'

'Sure. I understand. Have you actually sold the house?'

'Not yet, but I have an offer pending.'

'Good. How about showing the house to me, Ms Harris? I have a couple of questions that I hope you can answer. Maybe you can help solve Ben O'Malley's murder.'

Chapter One Hundred and Twenty-Two

Pacific Homes flyers were fanned out on a table in the foyer, and the flowers had been changed since Joe and I had taken our self-guided tour of this pretty house on Ocean Colony Road.

'Mind coming upstairs with me?' I asked the realtor.

Ms Harris shrugged, tossed the keys down next to the lilies and started up the stairs ahead of me.

When we got to the entrance to the master bedroom, she hung back.

'I don't like to go into this room,' she said, casting her gaze around the pale green bedroom with its brand new green carpet.

I could imagine the murder scene almost as well as she could. Only three weeks before, the body of Lorelei O'Malley had lain gutted about ten feet from where we stood.

Emily Harris swallowed hard, then joined me reluctantly in front of the walk-in closet. I showed her the faint, painted-over outline of the peephole in the door, and the still visible crescent where Joe's thumbnail had left its impression in the wood filler.

'What do you make of *this*?' I asked her.

Emily's voice thinned and became scratchy. 'This *kills* me, that's what I make of it,' she said. 'It's obvious, isn't it? He was video-taping sex with Lorelei. He told me he wasn't sleeping with her anymore, but I guess he lied.'

Then her face crumpled and she started to cry softly into a bouquet of pale blue tissues she pulled from her handbag.

'Oh God, oh God,' she sobbed.

After a while she blew her nose, cleared her throat and said, 'My relationship with Ben has no bearing on his murder. Can we get out of here, now?'

Not if I could stop her. Whatever I might learn from Emily Harris, there was no better time than now, no better place than right here.

'Ms Harris.'

'Jesus Christ. Call me Emily. I'm telling you all this personal stuff.'

'Emily. I really need to know your side of the story.'

'Fine. You know about Sandra?'

I nodded my assent, and as if I had pulled the plug, she spilled.

'Don't you think I worried that she killed herself because Ben was seeing me?' She dabbed at her swollen eyes and more tears came.

'Ben said Sandra was a *head case*, which is why

he didn't leave her. But after she killed herself, I stopped seeing him for a year.

'Then Lorelei came into the picture. The Princess. Ben thought the sooner he got married, the better for Caitlin, so what could I say? I was still married, Lieutenant.

'Then, we started up again. My place, mostly. Motels once in a while. Funnily enough, I don't think Lorelei gave a damn about Caitlin.

'But Ben and I made the best of the situation. Played a game with it. He called me Camilla. I called him Charles. His Royal *Highness*. It was fun. And I miss him so much. I know Ben loved me. I know he did.'

I didn't say, 'As much as a scurvy, cheating prick can love someone,' but I did open the door to the walk-in closet, and invited the real-estate broker inside.

'Please, Emily.'

I showed her the second peephole in the back wall.

'This hole goes through the wall . . . to Caitlin's room.'

Emily gasped and put both hands to her face.

'I never saw that. *I know nothing about it!* I have to go,' she said, turning and running out of the bedroom. I could hear her high heels clacking as she ran down the stairs.

I caught up to Emily as she grabbed the keys from the hall table and opened the front door. She stepped outside.

'Emily.'

'I'm done,' she said, her chest heaving, pulling the door closed and locking it behind us. 'This is too painful. Don't you understand? I loved him!'

'I can see that,' I said, walking beside her, then standing next to the driver's side door as she fired up her engine.

'Just tell me one more thing,' I persisted. 'Did Ben know a man named Dennis Agnew?'

Emily released her emergency brake and turned her tear-streaked face toward me.

'What? What are you saying? Did he sell our videos to that *slime*?'

Without waiting for an answer, she yanked on the steering-wheel and jammed down the accelerator.

'I'll take that as a "yes",' I said to the retreating Lincoln.

Chapter One Hundred and Twenty-Three

I cruised by the idling patrol car at the end of Sea View Avenue, lifting my hand in greeting as I passed. Then I hooked a right into Cat's driveway and parked the Explorer next to the Bonneville. Apparently, Keith had returned the old girl while I was away.

I let Martha into the house and gave her a biscuit. Then I turned my attention to the blinking answering machine. I pressed 'play' and started making notes on a scratch pad.

Joe, Claire and Cindy had all phoned in with worried requests for me to call back. Message number four was from Carolee Brown, inviting me to dinner at the school that night.

Then, a message from Chief Stark, his voice weary as it came through the speaker.

'Boxer, we got the labs back on that belt. Call me.'

Chief Stark and I had been playing phone tag all

day. I swore as I flipped through the scratch pad looking for his number. Then I dialed.

'Hang on, Lieutenant,' said the Duty Officer. 'I'll page him.'

I heard the sound of the police band sputtering in the background. I tapped my nails on the kitchen counter and counted to seventy-nine before the Chief got on the line.

'Boxer.'

'That was a fast return on the lab report,' I said. 'What have we got?'

'It was fast for a reason. There were no prints, not that that surprises me. But unless you count bovine DNA, there was nothing else, either. Lindsay, the bastards dripped a little beef blood on the buckle.'

'Aw, give me a break!'

'I know. Shit. Look, I gotta go. Our Mayor wants a few words with me.'

The Chief hung up and, by God, I felt sorry for him.

I walked out to the deck, took a seat in a plastic chair and hung my ankles over the railing as Claire had recently advised me to do. I stared out beyond my sandals and the neighbors' backyards to the aqua-blue line of the Bay.

I thought again about that belt lying on the lawn this morning, and the bloodstain that had turned out to be nothing.

One thing was clear.

The killers hadn't tried to kill me.

The belt was a warning meant to scare me away.

I wondered why they'd bothered.

I hadn't solved John Doe's murder and ten years later I was still sucking swampwater here.

Meanwhile, the killers were out there, and all the white hats had was a tantalizing handful of 'what ifs' and 'how comes' that went nowhere.

We didn't know *why*.

We didn't know *who*.

And we didn't know *where* they would strike again.

Other than that, everything was the cat's meow.

Chapter One Hundred and Twenty-Four

*F*amilies, the bane of modern civilization, where the scum of the past are kept alive, cultivated, and refined. At least, that was the Watcher's perspective tonight.

He opened the mudroom door and entered the pink stucco house, high up on Cliff Road. The Farleys were out for the night, so secure in their cocoon of wealth and privilege that they never even bothered to lock the door.

The mudroom led into a glassed-in kitchen that was glowing with the last rays of sunset.

This is just surveillance, the Watcher reminded himself. *Get in and out in under five. Same as always.*

He took his camera from the inside pocket of his soft leather jacket and panned the room, taking a series of digital photos of the many tall glass panes, the mullions wide enough for a person to enter.

Zzzzt, zzzzt, zzzzt.

He moved quickly through the kitchen to the

Farley family room, which cantilevered out over the mountainside. Amber light filled the woods, giving the shaggy eucalyptus bark an almost human presence, the trees like elderly men watching his movements. As though they understood and approved.

Just surveillance, he told himself again. Things were too complex, too hot right now to go forward with their plans.

He rapidly mounted the back stairs to the bedrooms, noting the steps that creaked the loudest, the solid banister. He proceeded down the hallway of the upper floor, stepping inside each of the opened doors, taking his photos, memorizing the details. Frisking the rooms as if he were a cop patting down suspects.

The Watcher checked his watch as he entered the master bedroom. *Nearly three minutes gone.* He quickly opened the closets, sniffed the scents of Vera Wang and Hermès, closed the doors.

He ran down the steps to the kitchen and was about to leave when he thought of the basement. There was enough time for a quick look.

He opened the door and skittered down.

There was an extensive wine cellar to his left and the laundry room was in front of him. But his eyes gravitated to a door on his right.

The door was in shadow, secured with a combination padlock. The Watcher was good with combination locks. He was very good with his hands. He turned the dial left until he felt the minute resistance, then right and left again. The lock sprung open and the Watcher unlatched the door.

He identified the equipment in the basement's half light: The computer, the laser printer and reams of high quality photo paper. The video and digital cameras with night vision capability.

A thick stack of photo prints were neatly piled on a counter.

He stepped quickly inside and closed the door behind him. Flipped the switch that turned on the lights.

It was just a harmless surveillance mission, that was all, one of many.

But what he saw when the lights went on, almost sent him over the edge.

Chapter One Hundred and Twenty-Five

Marinara sauce was in the air as I came up the walk to Carolee's Victorian live-in school-house. I shielded my eyes against the last rays of sun flashing off the many-paned windows and dropped the brass knocker on the big front door.

A dark-skinned boy of about twelve opened up and said, 'Greetings, police lady.'

'You're Eddie, right?'

'*Ready*-Eddie,' he said, grinning. 'How'd you know that?'

'I've got a pretty good memory,' I told him.

'That's good, since you're a cop.'

A cheer went up as I entered the 'mess hall', a large, open and airy dining room facing the highway.

Carolee gave me a hug and told me to sit at the head of the table. 'That's the "honored guest" spot,' she said. With Allison grabbing the chair to my left and Fern, a small red-haired girl, fighting for the chair to my right, I felt welcomed and at home in this huge 'family'.

Bowls of spaghetti and a tub of salad with oil and vinegar journeyed around the table and chunks of Italian bread flew across it even as the kids pelted me with questions and riddles – which I fielded and occasionally aced.

'When I grow up,' Ali whispered, 'I want to be just like you.'

'You know what I want? When you grow up, I want you to be exactly like *you*.'

Carolee clapped her hands together, laughing gaily.

'Give Lindsay a break,' she said. 'Let the poor woman eat her dinner. She's our guest, not something for you to devour along with your food.'

As she got up to bring a liter of cola from the sideboard, Carolee put her hand on my shoulder and leaned down to say, 'Do you mind? They love you.'

'I love them, too.'

When the dishes were cleared and the children had gone upstairs for their study hour, Carolee and I took our coffee mugs out to the screened-in porch facing the playground. We sat in matching rockers and listened to the crickets singing in the darkening night. It was good to have a friend in town, and I felt especially close to Carolee that night.

'Any news on whoever shot up Cat's house?' Carolee asked, concern edging into her voice.

'Nope. But you remember that guy we had a run-in with at The Cormorant?'

'Dennis Agnew?'

'Yeah. He's been harassing me, Carolee. And the Chief isn't making a secret of the fact that he likes Agnew for the murders.'

Carolee looked surprised, even shocked. 'Really? I'm having a hard time imagining *that*. I mean, he's a creep, all right,' she said, pausing. 'But I don't see him as a murderer.'

'Just what they said about Jeffrey Dahmer,' I laughed.

Then I drummed my fingers on the arm of the chair; Carolee crossed her arms over her chest and I imagine we'd both gone inside our heads to think about killers in the wind.

'It's pretty quiet here, huh?' said Carolee at last.

'Remarkably. I love it.'

'Hurry up and catch that maniac, okay?'

'Listen, if you ever get nervous about *anything*, Carolee, even if you think it's just your imagination, call 911. Then call me.'

'Sure, thanks. I will.' After a moment of silence, Carolee said, 'They always get caught eventually, don't they, Lindsay?'

'Almost always,' I answered, though that wasn't exactly the truth. The really smart ones not only didn't get caught, they weren't even noticed.

Chapter One Hundred and Twenty-Six

I had a rough night's sleep, riding my nightmares on a steeplechase of drive-by shootings and whipped corpses and faceless killers with no names. I awoke to a dismal, gray morning, the kind that makes you want to stay in bed.

But Martha and I needed exercise. So, I dressed in my blue track-suit, tucked my gun into its shoulder holster and my cell phone into the pocket of my denim jacket.

Then, Sweet Martha and I took off to the beach.

Thunderheads were moving in from the west, bringing the sky so low to the Bay that sea birds coasting through the clouds looked like airships in newsreels about the Second World War.

I noticed a few hardy souls jogging or meandering far ahead and behind us, so I let Martha off her lead. She trotted after a little flock of plovers, making them scatter, and I headed south at a moderate clip.

I'd only gone about a quarter of a mile when the rain started to fall. Soon, the intermittent drops thickened, pock-marking the sand and firming my running surface.

I turned to check on Martha, running backwards long enough to see that she was right behind a man in a hooded yellow slicker, maybe 100 yards back.

I put my face into the slanting rain and was hitting my stride when Martha's yipping bark grabbed my attention. She was nipping at the heels of the guy behind me. She was herding him!

'Martha!' I shouted. *'That'll do!'*

That was the command to return to my side, but Martha totally ignored me. Instead, she drove the guy at a right angle away from me, uphill toward the grassy tops of the dunes.

That's when I realized that Martha wasn't fooling around with him. She was protecting me.

Son of a bitch.

I'd been followed again!

Chapter One Hundred and Twenty-Seven

I yelled out, '*Hey!* Stop running and she'll back off,' but neither dog nor man paid any attention. Finally, I charged after them, but climbing the crumbling twenty-foot-high incline was a little like running underwater.

I bent low, clutched at the sand, and at last pulled myself up to the grassy plateau of the Francis Beach campground. But the driving rain plastered my hair to my face, and for a moment, I was completely blind.

In the time it took to drag the hair away from my eyes, I felt the situation slip out of control. I looked wildly around, but I couldn't even see the guy who'd been tailing me. Damn it! He'd gotten away, again.

'*Mar-thaaaa.*'

Just then, a smear of yellow shot out from behind the rest rooms, across my field of vision – with Martha still close on his heels. The guy kicked out at her, but failed to shake her off as they cut across the picnic grounds.

I pulled out my nine, and yelled: *'Freeze! Police!'* but the man in the slicker veered around the picnic tables and sprinted toward a multi-hued pick-up truck in the parking lot.

Martha stayed on him, growling, grabbing onto his leg, keeping him from getting into his vehicle. I screamed 'Police!' again, and ran with my loaded gun in front of me.

'On your knees,' I ordered when I got within range. 'Keep your hands where I can see them. Get down on your belly, Mister. Do it now!'

The guy in the slicker did what I told him and I approached quickly as the soaking rain pelted down on us. I pulled down his hood, keeping my gun muzzle pointed at his back.

I recognized the yellow hair instantly but I tried to deny what I saw. He lifted his face toward me, his eyes seeming to throw off sparks of fury.

'Keith! What are you doing? What's going on?'

'Nothing, nothing, nothing. All I was doing was trying to warn you.'

'Is that so? Why didn't you call me on the phone?' I panted.

My heart was pounding; *ba-boom, ba-boom.*

My God. I had a loaded gun in my hand – again.

I kicked Keith's legs apart and patted him down, finding a nine-inch-long Buckmaster hunting knife in a leather sheath at his hip. I removed the fearsome knife and tossed it aside. This was getting worse by the second.

'Did you say "nothing"?'

'Lindsay, let me *talk*.'

'Me first,' I said. 'You're under arrest.'

'What for?'

'For carrying a concealed weapon.'

I stood where Keith could clearly see both my gun and the look on my face that showed I would use it.

'You have the right to remain silent,' I said. 'Anything you say can and will be used against you in a court of law. If you don't have an attorney, one will be appointed for you. Do you understand your rights?'

'You've got me all wrong!'

'Do you understand your rights?'

'Yeah. I get it.'

As I fished inside my pocket for my cell phone, Keith twisted, as if he were about to make a break for it. Martha bared her teeth.

'Stay right where you are, Keith. I don't want to have to shoot you.'

Chapter One Hundred
and Twenty-Eight

The three of us were in 'the box', the small, gray-tiled interrogation room inside the police station. The Chief had already told me that he had his doubts.

He'd known Keith Howard for a dozen years as the Man-in-the-Moon automechanic with nothing more on his mind than a steady dollar and a well-tuned car.

But the Chief was going along with my instincts, thank God, because I'd seen a look in Keith's eyes that frankly scared the hell out of me. It was the same soulless look I'd seen on the faces of sociopaths before.

I sat opposite Keith at the scarred metal table, both of us dripping rainwater, while Chief Stark leaned against the wall in a corner of the room. Behind the glass, other cops watched, hoping that I was right, that soon they'd have more to go on than a knife and a hunch.

Since his arrest, Keith had regressed, seeming much younger than his twenty-seven years.

'I don't need a lawyer,' he said, directing his pitch to me. 'I was just *following* you. Girls always know when a guy likes them. You know that, so just tell them, okay?'

'You mean you were *stalking* me,' I said. 'That's your explanation?'

'No, I was following you. Big difference, Lindsay.'

'What can I say? I don't get it. Why were you following me?'

'You know why! Someone was trying to hurt you.'

'Is that why you shot at my sister's house?'

'*Me?* I didn't do that.' Keith's voice cracked and he put a steeple of fingers across the bridge of his nose. 'I *like* you, always have. And now you're going to hold that against me.'

'You're pissing me off, you little ass-wipe,' the Chief finally muttered. He stepped forward and slapped Keith across the back of his head. 'Be a man. What have you done?'

Keith seemed to fold into himself then. He dropped his head to the table, rolled it from side to side and moaned, a hollow cry that seemed to come from some bottomless place of misery and fear.

But all the moans in the world wouldn't help him. I'd been suckered by crocodile tears recently, and it was a terrible mistake I wouldn't make again.

'Keith, you're scaring me, buddy,' I said evenly.

'You're in a real jam right now, so don't be stupid. Tell us what you've done so we can help you spin the story to the DA. I'll help you, Keith. I mean it. So tell me. Are we going to find bloodstains on your knife?'

'Noooo,' he howled. 'I haven't done anything wrong.'

I relaxed the muscles in my face. Then I smiled. I covered Keith's hand with my own.

'Would you feel more comfortable if we took off those cuffs?'

I looked up at the Chief who nodded. He took keys from his shirt pocket and undid the lock. Keith regained his composure. He shook his hands, unzipped his slicker and flung it over the back of the chair. Then he peeled off the sweater he wore underneath.

If I had been standing up, my knees would have buckled and I would have dropped to the floor.

Keith was wearing an orange T-shirt emblazoned with the logo from The Distillery, the tourist restaurant on Highway 1 between Moss Beach and Half Moon Bay.

It was a carbon copy of the shirt John Doe #24 had been wearing when he was whipped and killed ten years before.

Chapter One Hundred and Twenty-Nine

Keith saw me staring at his shirt.

'You like?' he asked breezily, his smile returning as if we were back at his garage. 'This one's practically a classic,' he said. 'The Distillery doesn't even sell T-shirts anymore.'

Maybe not, but its bloody twin was locked in the evidence room at the Hall of Justice.

'Where were you the night before last, Keith?' I pressed.

'Do you own a gun?

'What did you want to warn me about?

'Tell me something I can believe.'

He was defiant at first, then giddy, then tearful, and sometimes he just went mute. As the hours crawled by, Stark took over to ask Keith if he knew the victims of the recent homicides.

Keith admitted that he knew them all.

He also knew nearly every person who lived in Half Moon Bay or had passed through his little gas station at the crossroads, he told us.

'We have a witness,' said the Chief, putting both of his hands on the table, giving Keith a stare that could have bored through steel. 'You were seen, my friend, leaving the Sarducci house on the night of their murder.'

'Come on, Pete. Don't make me laugh. That's so lame.'

We were getting nowhere, and at any minute Keith could say, 'Charge me for the knife and let me out of here,' and he'd be within his rights to post bond and walk away.

I stood up from the table and talked to the Chief over Keith's head, my voice colored with compassion.

'You know what? He didn't do it, Chief. You were right. He doesn't have it in him. Look. He's not too bright, and he's not exactly mentally stable. I mean, I'm sorry, Keith, you're a pretty good grease monkey, but it's crazy to think you have the chops to do those murders. And without leaving a clue? I don't think so.'

'Yeah, we're wasting our time,' the Chief said, following my lead. 'This little punk couldn't get away with stealing dimes out of parking meters.'

Keith swung his head to the Chief, to me, to the Chief again. 'I get what you're doing,' he said.

I ignored him, continuing to direct my remarks at the Chief.

'And I think you were right about Agnew,' I continued. 'Now, there's a guy with balls enough to knock off people at close range. Watch them squirm. Watch them die. And he has the brains to get away with it.'

'Right. Him being connected and all,' said the Chief, patting down the back of his hair. 'It only makes sense.'

'You shouldn't be talking this way,' Keith muttered.

I turned back to him with a questioning look.

'Keith, you know Agnew,' I said. 'What do you think? *Is he our guy?*'

It was as if a timer had tripped and a bomb had detonated far underground. First there was a tremor, then a rumble, then everything broke loose.

'Dennis Agnew?' Keith spat. 'That dick-for-brains freaking porno has-been. He's lucky I didn't kill *him*. And believe me, I've *thought* about it.'

Keith clasped his hands together and brought them down hard on the tabletop, making the pens, the notepad, the soda cans jump.

'Look. I'm a brighter bulb than you think, Lindsay. Killing those people was the easiest thing I ever did.'

Chapter One Hundred and Thirty

Keith wore the same coldly furious expression he'd shown me when I'd put my gun to his neck. I didn't know *this* Keith.

But I needed to.

'You're totally wrong about me, both of you,' he said. 'And even if you're playing me, that's fine. I'm sick of the whole deal. Nobody cares.'

When Keith said, 'Nobody cares,' I sat back hard in my chair. The Cabot kids had spray-painted the same words on the wall where they'd killed their victims. And so had the killer of John Doe #24, ten years ago.

'What do you mean, "nobody cares"?'

Keith fixed me with his hard blue eyes. 'You're the smart one, right? You figure it out.'

'Don't mess with me, Keith. I do care. And I'm really listening.'

As the video camera recorded his confession, it was a cop's dream come true. Keith gave it all up:

the names, the dates, the minutiae only the killer could possibly know.

He talked about using different knives, different belts, described every murder, including how he'd tricked Ben O'Malley.

'Yeah, I clubbed him with a rock before cutting his throat. I threw the knife and the rock over the side of the road.'

Keith laid out the details in an orderly fashion, like so many cards in a game of Solitaire, and they were convincing enough to convict him many times over. But it was still hard for me to believe that he'd done these bloody crimes alone.

'You killed Joe *and* Annemarie Sarducci by your-self? Without a fight? What are you – Spiderman?'

'You're *starting* to catch on, Lindsay.' He lurched forward in his seat, scraping the chair against the floor, sticking his face too close to mine.

'I *charmed* them into submission,' he said. 'And you better believe it. I worked alone. Spin *that* for the DA. Yeah, I'm Spiderman.'

'But why? What did these people ever do to you?'

Keith shook his head as if he pitied me. 'You couldn't understand, Lindsay.'

'Try me.'

'No,' he said. 'I'm through talking.'

And that was it. He ran his hands through his blond hair, guzzled down the last of his Classic Coke and smiled pleasantly, as if he were taking a curtain call.

I wanted to punch his face until he didn't look

so smug anymore. All those people slaughtered, and it made no sense at all.

Why wouldn't he say *why* he'd done it?

Still, it was a great day for the good guys. Keith Howard was booked, printed, photographed, slapped back into cuffs and taken to a holding cell pending his transport and arraignment the next day in San Francisco.

I stopped by Chief Stark's office on my way out.

'What's wrong, Boxer? Where's your party hat?'

'It's bothering me, Chief. He's protecting other people, I'm sure of it.'

'That's your *theory*. Guess what? I believe the guy. He's said he's smarter than we think and I'm gonna give him credit for being the big, bright bulb he claims to be.'

I gave the Chief a tired smile.

'Shit, Boxer. He confessed. Be happy. This goose is cooked. Let me be the first to congratulate you, Lieutenant. Great catch. Great interview. It's over now. Thank God, it's finally over.'

Chapter One Hundred
and Thirty-One

The phone rang, yanking me out of a sleep so deep, I thought I was in Kansas. I fumbled around in the dark for the receiver.

'Who is this?' I croaked.

'It's me, Lindsay. Sorry to call so early.'

'Joe.' I pulled the clock toward me; it read 5:15 a.m. in bright red numbers. I felt a jolt of alarm. 'Are you *okay*? What's wrong?'

'Everything's fine with me,' he said, his voice calm, warming, sexy. 'There's a crowd outside *your* house, though.'

'You're picking that up by GPS?'

'No, I just turned on the TV.'

'Hold on,' I said. I stepped across the room and pulled up a corner of the window shade. A couple of reporters had set up on the lawn and camera crews were stringing cables out to satellite vans that curved around the road like Conestoga wagons.

'I see them now,' I said, getting back under the covers. 'They've got me surrounded. Shit.'

I snuggled back down into the bedding and with the phone tucked between my face and my pillow, Joe felt so close, he could have been in the same time zone.

We talked for a good twenty minutes, made plans to get together when I got back to the city and winged some kisses across the phone line. Then I got out of bed, threw on some clothes and a little makeup, and stepped outside Cat's front door.

Reporters converged and pushed a posy of mikes up to my chin. I blinked in the morning light, saying only, 'Sorry to disappoint you guys, but I can't comment, you know. This is Chief Stark's case and you'll have to talk to him. *Th-th-that's all, folks!*'

I stepped back inside the house, smiled to myself, and closed the door on the fusillade of questions and the echoing sound of my name. I threw the bolt and turned off the phone's ringer. I was taking down our crime notes from the girls' corkboard, when Cindy and Claire rang in with a conference call to my cell phone.

'It's over,' I told them, repeating what the Chief had said. 'At least, that's what I've been told.'

'What's *really* going on, Lindsay?' my intuitive, highly skeptical friend Cindy asked.

'Boy, you're smart.'

'Uh-huh. So what's the deal?'

'Off the record. The kid's really proud of himself for getting into the psycho-killer hall of fame. And I'm not sure he's totally earned it.'

'Did he confess to the John Doe killing?' Claire asked.

'There you go, Butterfly,' I said. 'Another smarty.'

'Well?'

'No, he did not.'

'So where do you come out?'

'I don't know what to believe, Claire. I really thought whoever killed these people also killed John Doe. *Maybe I was wrong.*'

Chapter One Hundred
and Thirty-Two

I t was a rare place for me to be: I was sitting in the back seat of a patrol car with Martha. I rolled down the window, undid the buttons on my blazer, and took in the excitement that was building on Main Street.

A marching band tuned up on a side street where Boy Scouts and firefighters were dressing flatbed trucks as floats. Men on ladders hung banners across the roadway and flags flew from light posts. I could almost smell the hotdogs grilling. It was the Fourth of July.

My new buddy Officer Noonan let us out in front of the police station where Chief Stark was standing before a crowd of bystanders and reporters six-deep.

As I made my way through the crowd, Mayor Tom Hefferon came out of the station house wearing khaki shorts, a polo shirt, and a fishing hat covering his bald spot. He shook my hand and said,

JAMES PATTERSON & MAXINE PAETRO

'I hope you'll spend all of your vacations in Half Moon Bay, Lieutenant.'

Then he tapped on a microphone and the crowd quieted down.

'Everyone. Thanks for coming. This is truly Independence Day,' he said, a tremor cracking his voice. 'We're free – free to resume our lives.'

He put up his hand to quell the applause. 'I give you our Chief of Police, Peter Stark.'

The Chief was in full uniform complete with brass buttons, shiny badge and gun. As he shook hands with the Mayor, the corners of his mouth turned up and, yes, he smiled. Then he cleared his throat and bent over the mike.

'We have a suspect in custody and he has confessed to the murders that have terrorized the residents of Half Moon Bay.' A cheer went up into the morning mist and some people broke down and wept with relief. A little boy brought a lit sparkler up to the platform and handed it to the Chief.

'Thank you, Ryan. This is my boy,' he said to the crowd, his voice choking up. 'You hang on to that, okay?' The Chief pulled the child next to him, kept his hand on his son's shoulder as he went on with his speech.

He said that the police had done their job, that the rest was up to the DA and the justice system. Then he thanked me 'for being an invaluable resource to this Police Department' and, to more and wilder cheers, he handed a brass medal on a ribbon to his son. A patrolman held the boy's sparkler while Ryan hung the medal around Martha's neck. Her first commendation.

'Good dog,' said the Chief.

Stark then credited every officer in his command and the state police for all they had done to 'stop this one-man crime wave that took the lives of innocent citizens'.

As for me, by bringing in the killer, I'd gotten back into my own good graces.

I was still 'a damned good cop'.

But even as I basked in the moment, I had to fight down a disturbing thought. It was like the little boy who was waving his sparkler and pulling on his father's sleeve and demanding attention.

It was a thought like that.

What if the 'one-man crime wave' didn't stop?

Chapter One Hundred and Thirty-Three

That night, fireworks exploded with incessant booms and rapid-fire cracks over Pillar Point and bloomed in the sky. I put a pillow over my head, but it didn't block the noise worth a damn.

My hero dog was squashed way under the bed, her back against the wall.

'It's nothing, Boo. It'll be over soon. Chin up.'

I fell asleep only to be jolted out of it by the metallic rattle of a key in the lock.

Martha heard it, too, and streaked out of the bedroom toward the front door, barking sharply.

Someone was coming through the door.

It all happened so fast.

I wrapped my hand around my gun, lowered myself from the bed to the rag carpet, and, with my pulse hammering, I crept toward the front room.

I was touching the walls, counting the doorways between my room and the living room, my heart in my throat, when I saw the shadowy figure coming into the house.

I went into a crouch, clasped my piece with both hands in front of me and yelled out, *'Put your fucking hands where I can see them. Do it, now.'*

There was a shrill scream!

Moonlight pouring in from the open doorway lit my sister's terrified face. The small child she was carrying in her arms screamed along with her.

I almost screamed myself.

I stood up, rendering the weapon safe by removing my finger from the trigger, and let my gun hand fall to my side.

'Cat, it's me. I'm so sorry. That'll do, Martha! That'll do.'

'Lindsay?' Cat came toward me, adjusting Meredith in her arms. 'Is that gun loaded?'

Brigid, only six, trailed behind my sister. She pressed a floppy stuffed animal over her face and broke into a piercing wail.

My hands were shaking and the blood was pounding in my ears.

Oh-my-God! I could have shot my sister.

Chapter One Hundred and Thirty-Four

I put the gun down on a table and grabbed Cat and Meredith into one fierce hug.

'I'm sorry,' I said. 'I'm so sorry.'

'I called and called,' Cat said, into the crook of my shoulder. Then she pulled away from me.

'Don't *arrest* me, okay?'

I picked Brigid up and wrapped her in a hug, kissed her damp cheek, held her dear head with my hand. 'Martha and I didn't mean to scare you, honey.'

'Are you staying with us, Aunt Lindsay?'

'Just for the night, sweetie.'

Cat turned on a light and looked around at the spackled bullet holes in the wall.

'You didn't pick up,' she said. 'And the answering machine said it was full.'

'It was full of reporters,' I told her, my heart still galloping. 'Please forgive me for scaring the crap out of you.'

Cat reached out with her free arm. Hooked my head toward her face and kissed my cheek.

'You're a damned scary cop, you know?'

I walked with Cat and the girls to their room, where we calmed ourselves as well as the sniffling children. We got them into their pajamas and tucked into their beds.

'I've been listening to the news,' Cat said, as she closed the door to the girls' room behind us. 'Is it true? You caught the guy and it turns out to be Keith? I *know* Keith. I *liked* him.'

'Yeah. I liked him, too.'

'And what's that car in the driveway? It looks like Uncle Dougie's car.'

'I know. It's a present for you.'

'Come on. Really?'

'A house gift, Cat. I want you to have it.'

I hugged my sister again, really hard. I wanted to say, 'Everything's fine now. We got the bastard.' But instead I said, 'We'll go for a test drive tomorrow.'

I said good-night, took Martha down the hall and opened my bedroom door. I switched on the light and froze in the doorway.

Actually, I almost screamed again.

Chapter One Hundred and Thirty-Five

C arolee's little girl, Allison, was sitting on my bed. That was alarming enough – but how she looked alarmed me more. Ali was barefoot, wearing a thin eyelet nightgown, and she was crying her heart out.

I put down my gun and went to her, dropped to my knees and grabbed her little shoulders.

'Ali? Ali, what's wrong? What's *wrong*?'

The eight year old threw her body against me and wound her arms tightly around my neck. She was shaking, her body heaving with sobs. I hugged her and peppered her with questions, not even giving her time to answer.

'Are you hurt? How did you get here, Ali? What on earth is wrong?'

Allison said, 'The door was open so I came in.'

At that, new tears sprang from some mysterious wound that I couldn't fathom.

'Talk to me, Ali,' I said, setting her away from

me, checking her out, looking for injuries. Her feet were cut and filthy. Cat's house was a mile from the school and across the highway. Allison had walked here.

I tried again to get answers, but by now, Ali was incoherent. She clung to me, gulping air and choking out tears, making absolutely no sense.

I pulled on a pair of jeans over my blue silk pajamas and stepped into my running shoes. I slipped my Glock into my shoulder holster, and covered up with a denim jacket.

I wrapped Ali in my long hooded sweatshirt and lifted her into my arms. Leaving Martha behind in the bedroom, I went with Ali to the front door.

'Honey,' I said to the hysterical child. 'I'm taking you home.'

Chapter One Hundred and Thirty-Six

Cat's Forester was right behind the Explorer, blocking it in. The keys to the Bonneville were in the ignition and the big gold 'boat' was facing the road.

So, I buckled Ali into the back seat, got behind the wheel and turned the key. The engine *vrooom*ed smoothly to life. At Highway 1, I signaled to go north under a crackling, rocket-streaked sky, toward the schoolhouse. Shockingly, Allison shouted, *'NO!'*

I looked into the rear-view mirror and saw her pale face, utterly wide-eyed. She pointed with her finger south.

'You want me to go that way?'

'Lindsay, pleeease. Hurry.'

Ali's fear and urgency were electrifying. All I could do was trust the little girl, so I took the car south until Ali whispered from the back seat, 'Turn here' at a lonely intersection.

The rat-a-tat bangs of the Fourth of July pyrotechnics overhead pumped adrenaline into my already overloaded system. There had been too much shooting recently and I was experiencing each bang as an exploded round.

I accelerated the Bonneville up the winding dirt track that was Cliff Road, skidding around the corners like a big rig on grass. I heard Keith's chiding voice in my mind: *'You can't do this, Lindsay. This is a luxury car.'*

I drove through a starless tunnel of eucalyptus trees that finally opened into a wide mountain view. In front of and to the left of us was a round stucco house clinging to the side of the hill.

I looked again into the rear-view mirror. 'What now, Ali? How much further?'

Allison pointed to the round tower of a house. Then she clapped her hands over her eyes. Her voice was barely audible.

'We're here.'

Chapter One Hundred and Thirty-Seven

I pulled the car just off the road and looked up at the house – a two-story column of glass panes and stucco. Two thin bands of light moved sporadically on the lower floor.

Flashlight beams.

Otherwise, the house was dark.

Clearly, people were inside who didn't belong there. I slapped at the pockets of my denim jacket and got a sick feeling even before I knew that I was right; I'd left my cell phone on the table beside my bed. I could see it lying against the clock.

This was very bad news.

I had no car radio, no back-up and I wasn't wearing a vest. If a crime was in progress, going into that house alone wasn't a real good idea.

'Ali,' I said. 'I have to go for help.'

'You can't, Lindsay,' she said, her voice coming out as a whisper. *'Everyone will die.'*

I reached around and touched her face with my

hand. Ali's mouth was turned down, the trust in her eyes was heartbreaking.

'Lie down on the back seat,' I said to the little girl. 'Wait for me and don't move until I come back.'

Ali got down with her face against the seat. I put my hand on her back, patting her gently. Then I got out of the car and shut the door behind me.

Chapter One Hundred and Thirty-Eight

Bright moonlight flooded the hilly terrain, casting long shadows that fooled the eye into believing chasms were opening up underfoot. I stuck to the brush at the side of the road, rounding the clearing until I arrived at the blind side of the house on higher ground.

An upscale SUV was parked next to the house, beside a plain wooden doorway. The doorknob turned easily in my hand and the door swung open into a mudroom.

I groped my way in the dark, advanced into a spacious kitchen. From there, I entered a high-ceilinged great room, luminous with moonglow.

Keeping to the walls, I skirted the long leather sofas and large pots of palms and pampas grass. I looked up in time to see a flashlight beam disappear at the top of a staircase.

I drew my gun and loped up the carpeted staircase, taking two steps at a time, crouching at the top landing. Over the sound of my own breathing I could hear soft murmurs coming from the room at the end of the hall.

Then a high-pitched scream shattered the air. I ran to a doorway, turned the knob, kicked open the door.

I strafed the scene with my eyes. In the dimly-lit space I could see a king-sized bed, a woman sitting with her back against the headboard. A figure dressed in black was holding a knife to the woman's throat.

'Hands in the air!' I yelled. 'Drop the knife now!'

'It's too late,' the black-clad figure said. 'Just turn around and get the hell out of here.'

I reached for the wall switch and flicked on the light.

What I saw was shocking, horrifying, unbelievable.

The black-clad figure with the knife was Carolee Brown.

Chapter One Hundred and Thirty-Nine

Carolee was about to commit *murder*. My brain stalled as I tried to assimilate the unimaginable. When it kicked back into gear, I acted, barking out a command at the top of my voice.

'Back away from her, Carolee. Keep your hands where I can see them.'

'Lindsay,' she said in a maddeningly reasonable tone, 'I'm asking you to please go. She's a dead woman, no matter what. You can't stop me.'

'Last chance,' I shouted. 'Put that knife down, or I'm going to kill you.'

The woman in the bed whimpered as Carolee measured the distance between us with her eyes and calculated how long it would take to slash the woman's throat before I put a bullet through her brain.

'You're making a huge mistake,' she said with regret. 'I'm the good guy, Lindsay. This thing you see here, this Melissa Farley, is complete trash.'

'Toss the knife over here, very carefully,' I said, grasping my Glock so hard that my knuckles were white. Could I shoot Carolee if I had to? I really didn't know.

'You *aren't* going to shoot me,' she said then.

'I think you've forgotten who I am.'

Carolee started to speak again but the resolve gripping my face stopped her. I *would* shoot her and she was smart enough to get it. She smiled wanly. Then she tossed the knife underhand onto the carpet at our feet.

I kicked the knife under a bureau, then I ordered Carolee to the floor.

'On your knees!' I shouted. 'Hands in front of you!'

I took her down to the ground, told her to interlace her hands behind her neck and cross her ankles, frisked her, found nothing but a thin leather belt around her waist.

Then I darted my eyes to the woman on the bed.

'Melissa? Are you okay? Call 911. Tell them that a violent crime is in progress and a cop needs assistance.'

The woman reached for the bedside phone even as she kept her eyes on me.

'He's got my husband,' she choked. '*A man is in the bathroom with Ed.*'

Chapter One Hundred
and Forty

I followed Melissa Farley's gaze across the shadows to the door to the left of the bed.

The door opened slowly and a male walked stiffly into the bedroom, his eyes wild behind blood-speckled glasses.

I noticed everything as the man came toward me: black T-shirt soaked with blood; belt, stripped from his pants, dangling by its silver buckle from his left hand; ugly hunting knife clutched in his right.

My mind raced ahead, thinking not where the knife was *now*, but *where it would be next*.

'Drop your weapon!' I screamed at him. *'Do it now or I'll shoot.'*

The man's mouth formed a grim smile, the chilling look of someone who is ready to die. He continued coming toward me, pointing the bloody knife.

My vision narrowed so that I could concentrate on what seemed necessary to my survival. There was too much to focus on, too much to control. Carolee was behind me, unsecured.

The man with the knife knew it, too. His lip curled back.

He said, 'G-g-g-et up! We can take her.'

I calculated what would happen if I shot him. He was less than ten feet away.

Even if I got him square in the chest, even if I stopped his heart, the closing range was short.

He was still coming.

I leveled my gun, fingered the trigger, and then Melissa Farley scrambled across the bed, launching herself toward the bathroom.

'*No!*' I yelled out. 'Stay where you are.'

'I have to go to my *husband*!'

I never heard the door open *behind* me.

I never heard someone else enter the room.

But suddenly, she was there.

'*Bobby, don't!*' Allison screamed.

And for one long second, everything stood still.

Chapter One Hundred and Forty-One

The man Allison called 'Bobby' froze. He steadied himself and I watched his face seize with confusion.

'Allison,' he said, 'you're supposed to be home.'

Bobby! The stutter hadn't cued me, but now I recognized his face. It was Bob Hinton, the lawyer from town who'd run into me with his bike. I didn't have time to figure out exactly how he fit into this picture.

Allison drifted from behind me as if she were in a dream. She walked over to Bob Hinton and put her arms around his waist. I wanted to stop her, but before I could, Hinton reached his arms around her and held Allison tightly.

'Little sister,' he whispered, 'you shouldn't be here. You shouldn't see this.'

My blood pressure dropped and the sweat on my hands made the gun's trigger slippery. I continued to gauge my shot at Hinton.

I jockeyed for a better angle and Hinton turned the dazed little girl toward me. I could see that he was dazed himself.

'Bob,' I said, putting my heart into it. I wanted him to believe me. 'It's your choice. But I'll blow your head off if you don't drop that knife and get right down on your knees.'

Bob stooped, dipping his face behind Allison's head, turning her into a shield. I knew he would put his blade across her throat next, and tell me to throw down my gun. *I'd have to do it.*

I didn't expect the look of terrible sadness that came over his face as he pressed his cheek to Allison's. 'Oh Ali, Ali, you aren't old enough to understand.'

Ali shook her head.

'I know everything, Bobby. You have to give up. I have to tell Lindsay all of it.'

A flash of red tore my attention from the haunting tableau in front of me. Melissa Farley half-fell through the bathroom doorway. The front of her nightgown was dark with blood.

'Ambulance,' she panted. 'Get an ambulance. Please! Ed is still alive.'

Chapter One Hundred and Forty-Two

About ten minutes later, sirens wailed and the flashing lights of patrol cars raced up the winding road below. Medevac chopper blades roared overhead.

Melissa Farley was back in the bathroom with her husband. 'Allison,' I said. 'Please go downstairs and open the door for the police.'

Bob still held Allison tightly in his arms. She turned her round-eyed stare on me. Her lips were quivering as she held back sobs.

'Go ahead, darling,' Carolee said from where she lay on the floor. 'It's all right.'

Ten steps away from me, Bob's face sagged; his expression was that of a beaten man. He squeezed Ali's shoulders and I gasped, involuntarily. Then he released the child.

As soon as Ali was safely out of the room, my anger exploded.

'*Who are you two*? What made you think you could get away with this?'

I stepped over to Bob Hinton, ripped away the knife, and ordered him to put his hands against the wall. I Mirandized him as I frisked him.

'Do you understand your rights?'

His laughter was shrill but sardonic. 'Better than most,' he said.

I found glass-cutting tools and a camera on Hinton, which I removed. Then I forced him to the ground and sat on the edge of the king-sized bed, holding my gun on him and Carolee.

I didn't even blink until I heard heavy footsteps rumbling up the stairs.

Chapter One Hundred and Forty-Three

It was after three in the morning and I was back at the police station. Chief Stark was with Bob Hinton in the interrogation room, where Bob was describing in detail the many homicides that he, Carolee and Keith had committed in Half Moon Bay.

I sat with Carolee in the Chief's office, an old Sony tape recorder between us on Peter Stark's messy desk. A detective brought cups of coffee into the room in a cardboard box, then he took a position inside the doorway as I interviewed Carolee.

'I think I'd like to talk to my lawyer,' Carolee said flatly.

'You mean Bob? Can you wait a few minutes?' I snapped. 'He's giving you up right now and we'd like to get it all down.'

Carolee gave me a bemused smile. She flicked a strand of hair from the front of her black silk turtleneck, then folded her manicured hands in her lap. I couldn't help but stare.

Carolee had been a friend. We'd traded confidences. I'd told her to call me if she ever needed me. I idolized her daughter.

Even now, she was dignified, articulate, *seemingly* sane.

'Maybe you'd like a different lawyer,' I said.

'Never mind,' she said. 'It's not going to matter.'

'Okay, then. Why don't you talk to me?'

I switched on the tape recorder, spoke my name, the time and date, my badge number and the subject's name. Then I rewound the tape and played it back, to make sure the machine was working. Satisfied, I leaned back in the Chief's swivel chair.

'Okay, Carolee. Let's hear it,' I said.

The lovely-looking woman in her Donna Karan perfection took a moment to organize her thoughts before she spoke for the record.

'Lindsay,' she said thoughtfully, 'you need to understand that they brought it upon *themselves*. The Whittakers were making child pornography. The Daltrys were actually starving their twins. They were part of some freaking religious cult that told them their children shouldn't eat solid food.'

'And you didn't think to get Children's Services involved?'

'I reported it again and again. Jake and Alice were clever, though. They stocked their shelves with food, but they never fed the children!'

'And Doc O'Malley? What about him and his wife?'

'Doc was selling his own child on the Internet. There was a camera in her room. That stupid Lorelei knew. *Caitlin* knew. I only hope that her grandparents get her the help she needs. I wish I could do it myself.'

The more she talked, the more I understood the depths of her narcissism. Carolee and her cohorts had taken on the mission of cleaning up child abuse in Half Moon Bay – acting as the whole judicial package – judge, jury and executioners. And the way she described it, it almost made sense. If you didn't know what she'd done.

'Carolee. *You killed eight people.*'

We were interrupted by a knock on the door. The detective cracked it open a few inches and I saw the Chief outside. His face was gray with fatigue. I stepped out into the hallway.

'Coastside Hospital called,' he told me. 'Hinton administered the *coup de grace* after all.'

I stepped back into the Chief's office. Sat down in the swivel chair.

'Make that nine, Carolee. Ed Farley just died.'

'And thank God for that,' Carolee said. 'When you people open the barn at the back of the Farleys' yard you're going to have to pin a medal on me. The Farleys have been trafficking in little Mexican girls. Selling them for sex all across the country. Call the FBI, Lindsay. This is a big one.'

Carolee's posture relaxed even as I grappled with this new bombshell. She leaned forward, confidingly. The earnestness in her face was absolutely stunning.

'I've been wanting to tell you something since I met you,' she said. 'And it doesn't matter to anyone but you. Your John Doe? That terrible shit had a name. Brian Miller. And I'm the one who killed him.'

Chapter One Hundred and Forty-Four

I could hardly absorb what Carolee had just told me. *She'd killed my John Doe.*

That boy's death had been on my mind for ten full years. Carolee was my sister's friend. Now I tried to grasp that John Doe's killer and I had been traveling on adjacent paths, paths that had finally converged in this room.

'It's traditional for the condemned to have a cigarette, isn't it, Lindsay?'

'Hell, yes,' I said. 'As many as you want.'

I reached on top of a filing cabinet for a carton of Marlboros. I broke open the box and placed a pack of cigarettes and a book of matches beside Carolee's elbow with a casualness I had to fake.

I was desperate to hear about the boy whose lost life I'd been carrying with me in spirit for so many years.

'Thank you,' said Carolee, the schoolteacher, the mom, the savior of abused children.

She peeled cellophane and foil from the mouth of the packet, tapped out a cigarette. A match sparked and the smell of sulfur rose into the air.

'Keith was only twelve when he came to my school. Same age as my son Bob,' she said. 'Lovely boys, both of them. Tons of promise.'

I listened intently as Carolee described the appearance of Brian Miller, an older boy, a runaway who gained her confidence and eventually became a counselor at the school.

'Brian raped them repeatedly, both Bob and Keith, and he raped their minds, too. He had a Special Forces knife. Said he'd turn them into girls if they ever told anyone what he'd done.'

Tears slipped from Carolee's eyes. She waved at the smoke as if that was what had made her tear up. Her hand shook as she sipped at her container of coffee.

The only sound in the room was the soft sibilance of the magnetic tape spooling between the reels of the Sony.

When Carolee began speaking again, her voice was softer. I leaned toward her so that I wouldn't miss a word.

'When Brian was finished using the boys, he disappeared, taking their innocence, their dignity, their self-worth.'

'Why didn't you call the police?'

'Look, I reported it, but by the time Bobby told me what had happened, time had passed. And the police weren't so interested in my school for runaways. It took years to get Keith to smile again,'

Carolee went on. 'Bob was even more fragile. When he slashed his wrists, I had to do something.'

Carolee fooled around with her watchband – a dainty, feminine gesture, but fury contorted her features, an anger that seemed as fresh now as it had been a decade ago.

'Go on,' I said. 'I'm listening to you, Carolee.'

'I found Brian living in a transient hotel in the Tenderloin,' she told me. 'He was selling his body. I took him out for a good meal with lots of wine. I let myself remember how much I'd once really liked Brian, and he bought it. He believed that I was still his friend.

'I asked him nicely for an explanation. The way he told it, what he had with the boys was "romantic love". Can you believe it?'

Carolee laughed and tapped ashes into an aluminum foil tray.

'I went back to his place with him,' she continued. 'I'd brought his things with me; a T-shirt, a book, some other stuff. When he turned his back, I grabbed him. I slashed his throat with his own knife. He couldn't believe what I'd done. He tried to scream, but I'd cut through his vocal cords, you see. Then I whipped him with my belt as he lay dying. It was good, Lindsay. The last face Brian saw was *mine*. The last voice he heard was *mine*.'

An image of John Doe #24 came to me, animated now into a living person by Carolee's story. Even if he was everything she said he was he'd still been a victim; condemned and executed without a trial.

The final coincidence, and it was a killer, was

that Carolee had scrawled *nobody cares* on the hotel wall. It was in all the newspaper stories. Ten years later, the clippings were found in Sara Cabot's bizarre collection of true-crime stories. She and her brother had ripped off the catch-phrase.

I flipped a notepad across to Carolee's side of the desk and handed her a pen. Her hand was shaking as she started to write. She cocked her pretty head. 'I'm going to put down that I did it for the children. That I did it all for *them*.'

'Okay, Carolee. That's fine. It's your story.'

'But do you understand, Lindsay? Someone had to save them. *I'm the one. I'm a good mother.*'

Smoke curled around us as she held my gaze.

'I can understand hating people who have done terrible things to innocent children,' I said. 'But murder, no. I'll never understand that. And I'll never understand how you could have done this to Allison.'

Chapter One Hundred and Forty-Five

I walked along the dreary alley called Gold Street until I reached the neon sign *Bix* in huge blue letters. I entered through the brick-lined doorway and the blue-note chords of a baby grand thrilled me.

The high ceilings, the cigarette smoke hanging above the long sweep of mahogany bar and the Art Deco fixtures and trappings reminded me of a Hollywood version of a 1920s speakeasy.

I stepped up to the maître d', who told me that I was the first to arrive.

I followed him up the stairs to the first floor and took a seat in one of the richly upholstered horse-shoe-shaped booths overlooking the jumping bar scene below.

I ordered a Dark & Stormy – Gosling's Black Seal rum and ginger beer – and was sipping it when my best bud in the world came toward me.

'I know *you*,' Claire said, sliding into the booth

and wrapping me in a huge hug. 'You're the gal who went and solved a whole buncha murders without any help from her home girls.'

'And lived to tell the tale,' I said.

'Just barely, the way I heard it.'

'Wait,' said Cindy, scooting into the booth on my other side. 'I want to hear. For the record, if you don't mind, Lindsay. I think a little profile of our homicide ace is in order.'

I bussed her on the cheek. 'You'll have to clear it with PR,' I told her.

'You're such a pain,' she said, kissing me, too.

Claire and Cindy each ordered one of the exotic drinks the bar was famous for as Yuki arrived, straight from the office. She was still in her prim lawyer's suit, but she had a new sassy red streak in her glossy black hair.

The oysters and firecracker shrimp came and the hand-cut steak tartare was dressed by a waiter at table-side. As the food and libations were served, I told the girls about the takedown at the stucco house on the hill.

'It was so freaking weird that I thought of her as a buddy,' I said of Carolee, 'and I didn't know her at all.'

'Makes you doubt your intuition,' said Cindy.

'Really. And she fooled my sister, too.'

'You think she was just keeping tabs on you because you investigated this Brian Miller's murder?' said Claire.

'Yeah. Keeping her "friend" close and her enemy closer.'

'To John Doe Number 24. His case is closed,' said Yuki, lifting her glass.

'Case closed,' we repeated, clinking our glasses to hers.

We ordered our main courses of monkfish, skate with asparagus, Maine lobster, spaghetti and New York Black Angus steak, and somehow, between chowing down on the sensational food, and all of us trying to speak at once, everyone got her story in.

Cindy was writing a story about a bank robber who'd gotten caught because he wrote his *Stick 'em up* note on the back of his own deposit slip.

'He left the deposit slip and took off with the dough,' Cindy chuckled. 'Cops were waiting for him when he got home. This one goes to the head of my *Dumb Crooks* column,' she said.

'I've got one for you!' Yuki jumped in. 'My client – to remain nameless – is a stepson of one of the partners and I *had* to defend him.' She twirled the magenta-red streak in her hair. 'A coupla cops bang on his door looking for a robbery suspect and my guy says, "Come on in", because he doesn't know anything about a robbery. Then he says, "Look anywhere you like – except the attic".'

'Go on, go on,' we urged her. Yuki sipped her Germain-Robin Sidecar and looked around the table.

'Judge grants a search warrant and the cops find my client's set-up in the attic. Hydroponic marijuana under grow lights. Sentencing is next week,' she said over our laughter.

As the conversation swirled around the table, I felt lucky to be with this gang again. We all felt so comfortable together and had shared so much – even with our newest friend, Yuki, who'd been unanimously admitted to the group for saving my butt and my life as I knew it.

We were about to order dessert when I saw a familiar white-haired man with a slight limp coming toward us.

'Boxer,' Jacobi said, without even acknowledging the others, 'I need you now. The car's running outside.'

I put my hand over my now-empty glass reflexively. My heart-rate shot into high gear and a mental slide show of a car-chase and a shoot-up flashed before my eyes.

'What's going on?' I asked him.

He bent his head toward mine, but instead of whispering, he kissed me on the cheek.

'There's nothing going on,' he said. 'I was going to pop out of a cake, but your girls here dissuaded me.'

'Thanks, Jacobi,' I said, cracking up. I put my hand on his arm. 'Come and join us for dessert.'

'Don't mind if I do.'

Jacobi slid into the booth and we all shoved over one seat to make room for him. The waiter brought chilled Dom Perignon – thanks, Jacobi – and when our flutes were full, my friends new and old toasted my return.

'To Lindsay. Welcome home!'

EPILOGUE

Chapter One Hundred and Forty-Six

The first week back on the job blew around me like a force five hurricane.

The phone rang non-stop and cops were at my door every few minutes bringing me up to speed on several dozen active cases. Everything was a red alert.

But the overarching problem was clearer to me than ever before. The Department's average of solved cases hovered around fifty percent, which put us very close to the bottom of large city Homicide Squads.

It wasn't that we weren't good, we were simply undermanned and overwhelmed, and the Squad was burning out. In fact, people had been calling in sick all week.

When Jacobi knocked on the glass door that Friday morning, I told him to come in.

'Lieutenant, shots were fired in Ocean Beach, two men down. One car is on the scene, one on the way and the officers are still requesting back-up. The witnesses are panicky and starting to scatter.'

'Where's your partner?'

'Taking lost time.'

I could see everyone in the Squad through the glass walls of my office. The only cop without a stack of active cases on his desk was me. I grabbed my jacket from the back of my chair.

'I guess we're catching,' I said to my former partner. 'Tell me what you know.'

'Two gangs from Daly City and Oakland had it out in the parking lot near the beach,' Jacobi told me.

We hustled down the stairs, and once we were outside on McAllister, Jacobi unlocked the car and took the wheel.

'It started with knives, then a gun came out. Two vics dead at the scene, one wounded. Two perps are in custody. One of the perps waded out into the surf and buried the gun in the sand.'

I was already imagining the scene of the crime, looking ahead to putting the puzzle pieces together. 'We'll need divers,' I said, gripping the dash as we took the corner at Polk.

Jacobi gave me a rare grin.

'What's that for, Jacobi?'

'Pardon me, Lieutenant,' he said over the sound of the siren. 'I was thinking.'

'Yes?'

'I still like working with you, Boxer. It's good to have you back in the saddle again.'

Turn the page for a preview of the next compelling thriller in the Women's Murder Club series.

THE 5TH HORSEMAN

JAMES PATTERSON

AND MAXINE PAETRO

PROLOGUE

The Midnight Hour

Chapter One

Rain was drumming hard against the windows when the midnight-to-8:00 a.m. rounds began at San Francisco Municipal Hospital. Inside the ICU, thirty-year-old Jessie Falk was asleep in her hospital bed, floating on a Percocet lake of cool light.

Jessie was having the most beautiful dream she'd had in years.

She and the light of her life, three-year-old Claudia, were in Grandma's backyard swimming pool. Claudie was in her birthday suit and bright-pink water wings, slapping the water, sunlight glinting off her blond curls.

'Simon says, kiss like a butterfly, Claudie.'

'Like this, Mommy?'

Then the mother and daughter were shouting and laughing, twirling and falling down, singing out, 'Wheeeeeee,' when without warning a sharp pain pierced Jessie's chest.

She awoke with a scream – bolted upright – and clapped both of her hands to her breast.

What was happening? What was that pain?

Then Jessie realized that she was in a hospital – and that she was feeling sick again. She remembered coming here, the ambulance ride, a doctor telling her that she was going to be fine, not to worry.

Falling, nearly fainting back to the mattress, Jessie fumbled for the call button at her side. Then the device slipped from her grasp and fell. It banged against the side of the bed with a muted clang.

Oh, God, I can't breathe. What's happening? I can't get my breath. It's horrible. I'm not fine.

Tossing her head from side to side, Jessie swept the darkened hospital room with her eyes. Then she seized on a figure at the far edge of her vision.

She knew the face.

'Oh, th-thank God,' she gasped. 'Help me, please. It's my heart.'

She stretched out her hands, clutched feebly at the air, but the figure stayed in the shadows.

'Please,' Jessie pleaded.

The figure wouldn't come forward, wouldn't help. What was going on? This was a hospital. The person in the shadows worked here.

Tiny black specks gathered in front of Jessie's eyes as a crushing pain squeezed the air from her chest. Suddenly her vision tunneled to a pinprick of white light.

'Please help me. I think I'm—'

'Yes,' said the figure in the shadows, 'you are dying, Jessie. It's beautiful to watch you cross over.'

Chapter Two

Jessie's hands fluttered like a tiny bird's wings beating against the sheets. Then they were very still. Jessie was gone.

The Night Walker came forward and bent low over the hospital bed. The young woman's skin was mottled and bluish, clammy to the touch, her pupils fixed. She had no pulse. No vital signs. Where was she now? Heaven, hell, nowhere at all?

The silhouetted figure retrieved the fallen call device, then tugged the blankets into place, straightened the young woman's blond hair and the collar of her gown, and blotted the spittle from her lips with a tissue.

Nimble fingers lifted the framed photo beside the phone on the bedside table. She'd been so pretty, this young mother holding her baby. Claudia. That was the daughter's name, wasn't it?

The Night Walker put the picture down, closed the

patient's eyes, and placed what looked to be small brass coins, smaller than dimes, on each of Jessie Falk's eyelids.

The small disks were embossed with a caduceus – two serpents entwined around a winged staff, the symbol of the medical profession.

A whispered good-bye blended with the sibilance of tires speeding over the wet pavement five stories below on Pine Street.

'Good night, princess.'

PART ONE

Malice Aforethought

Chapter Three

I was at my desk sifting through a mound of case files – eighteen open homicides, to be exact – when Yuki Castellano, attorney-at-law, called on my private line.

'My mom wants to take us to lunch at the Armani Café,' said the newest member of the Women's Murder Club. 'You've gotta meet her, Lindsay. She can charm the skin off a snake, and I mean that in the nicest possible way.'

Let me see; what should I choose? Cold coffee and tuna salad in my office? Or a tasty Mediterranean luncheon, say, carpaccio over arugula with thin shavings of Parmesan and a glass of Merlot, with Yuki and her snake-charming mom?

I neatened the stack of folders, told our squad assistant, Brenda, that I'd be back in a couple of hours, and left the Hall of Justice with no need to be back until the staff meeting at 3:00.

The bright September day had broken a rainy streak in the weather and was one of the last glory days before the dank autumn chill would close in on San Francisco.

It was a joy to be outside.

I met Yuki and her mother, Keiko, in front of Saks in the upscale Union Square shopping district out by the Golden Gate Panhandle. Soon we were chattering away as the three of us headed up Maiden Lane toward Grant Avenue.

'You girls, too modern,' Keiko said. She was as cute as a bird, tiny, perfectly dressed and coiffed, shopping bags dangling from the crooks of her arms. 'No man want woman who too independent,' she told us.

'Mommm,' Yuki wailed. 'Give it a rest, willya? This is the twenty-first century. This is America.'

'Look at you, Lindsay,' Keiko said, ignoring Yuki, poking me under the arm. 'You're packing!'

Yuki and I both whooped, our shouts of laughter nearly drowning out Keiko's protestation that, 'No man want a woman with a gun.'

I wiped my eyes with the back of my hand as we stopped and waited for the light to change.

'I *do* have a boyfriend,' I said.

'Doesn't she though,' Yuki said, nearly bursting into a song about my beau. 'Joe is a very handsome Italian guy. Like Dad. And he's got a big-deal government job. Homeland Security.'

'He make you laugh?' Keiko asked, pointedly ignoring Joe's credentials.

'Uh-huh. Sometimes we laugh ourselves into fits.'

'He treat you nice?'

'He treats me sooooo nice,' I said with a grin.

Keiko nodded approvingly. 'I know that smile,' she said. 'You find a man with a slow hands.'

Again Yuki and I burst into hoots of laughter, and from the sparkle in Keiko's eyes, I could tell that she was enjoying her role as Mama Interrogator.

'When you get a ring from this Joe?'

That's when I blushed. Keiko had nailed it with a well-manicured finger. Joe lived in Washington, DC. I didn't. Couldn't. I didn't know where our relationship was going.

'We're not at the ring stage yet,' I told her.

'You love this Joe?'

'Big time,' I confessed.

'He love you?'

Yuki's mom was looking up at me with amusement, when her features froze as if she'd turned to stone. Her lively eyes glazed over, rolled back, and her knees gave way.

I reached out to grab her, but I was too late.

Keiko dropped to the pavement with a moan that made my heart buck. I couldn't believe what had happened, and I couldn't understand it. Had Keiko suffered a stroke?

Yuki screamed, then crouched beside her mother, slapping her cheeks, crying out, 'Mommy, Mommy, wake up.'

'Yuki, let me in there for a second. *Keiko.* Keiko, can you hear me?'

My heart was thudding hard as I placed my fingers to Keiko's carotid artery, tracked her pulse against the second hand of my watch.

She was breathing, but her pulse was so weak, I could barely feel it.

I grabbed at the Nextel at my waist and called Dispatch.

'Lieutenant Boxer, badge number twenty-seven twenty-one,' I barked into the phone. 'Get an EMS unit to Maiden Lane and Grant. *Make it now!*'

Chapter Four

San Francisco Municipal Hospital is huge – like a city in itself. Once a public hospital, it had been privatized a few years back, but it still took more than its share of indigents and overflow from other hospitals, treating in excess of a hundred thousand patients a year.

At that moment, Keiko Castellano was inside one of the curtained stalls that ring the perimeter of the vast, frantic emergency room.

As I sat beside Yuki in the waiting room, I could feel her terror and fear for her mother's life.

And I flashed on the last time I'd been inside an emergency room. I remembered the doctors' ghost-like hands touching my body, the loud throbbing of my heart, and wondering if I was going to get out alive.

I'd been off duty that night but went on a stakeout anyway, not thinking that one minute it would be a routine job, and the next minute I'd be down. The same was true for my friend and former partner, Inspector Warren Jacobi. We'd both taken two slugs in that desolate alley. He was unconscious and I was bleeding out on the street when somehow I found the strength to return fire.

My aim had been good, maybe even too good.

It's a sad sign of the times that public sympathy favors civilians who've been shot by police over police who've been shot by civilians. I was sued by the family of the so-called victims, and I could have lost everything.

I hardly knew Yuki then.

But Yuki Castellano was the smart, passionate, and supertalented young lawyer who came through for me when I really needed her. I would always be grateful.

I turned to Yuki now as she spoke, her voice choppy with agitation, her face corrugated with worry.

'This makes no sense, Lindsay. You saw her. She's only fifty-five, for God's sake. She's a freaking life force. What's going on? Why don't they tell me something? Or at least let me see her?'

I had no answer, but like Yuki, my patience had run out.

Where the hell was the doctor?

This was unconscionable. Not acceptable in any way.

What was taking so long?

I was gathering myself to walk into the ER and demand some answers, when a doctor finally strode into the waiting room. He looked around, then called Yuki's name.

The 6th Target

James Patterson and Maxine Paetro

A Crazed Killer

When a lone gunman goes on a shooting spree aboard a packed San Francisco ferry, Lieutenant Lindsay Boxer is called in to investigate. At the scene she finds three people dead and fellow Women's Murder Club member Claire Washburn fighting for her life. Lindsay promises to find whoever did this. But it's a promise she may not be able to keep . . .

A Missing Child

As the investigation makes its way to court, news of a child abduction comes through. Lindsay's put on the case and discovers that more children have been taken. But with no ransom demands the abductions don't seem to make sense – unless the kidnappers aren't planning on returning their hostages . . .

A Race Against Time

The clock is ticking as Lindsay tries to fit all the pieces together. She knows that if she doesn't find the children quickly it will be too late . . .

Praise for James Patterson's bestselling novels:

'Brilliantly terrifying . . . so exciting I had to stay up all night to finish it' *Daily Mail*

'Skilfully put together' *Cosmopolitan*

'James Patterson does everything but stick our finger in a light socket to give us a buzz' *New York Times*

978 0 7553 4931 9

headline

The Quickie

James Patterson and Michael Ledwidge

A WOMAN SCORNED

When Lauren Stillwell sees her husband with another woman, her perfect world is destroyed. His betrayal turns her into a woman lusting for revenge.

PAYBACK GONE BAD

It was supposed to be a way to even the score. But Lauren's one-night stand takes a shocking turn, and she witnesses an unbelievable crime. She's left torn between uncovering the truth and her fear that the truth may be unbearable. But either choice could cost her everything – even her life.

IT ONLY TAKES A MINUTE TO DIE

From the man the *Sunday Telegraph* called 'the master of the suspense genre' comes his steamiest, scariest novel since the No. 1 bestseller *Honeymoon*. *The Quickie* is a story of desires, secrets and consequences that will have your heart pounding till the final page.

Praise for James Patterson's bestselling novels:

'Pacy, sexy, high-octane stuff' *Guardian*

'A novel which makes for sleepless nights' *Daily Express*

978 0 7553 3572 5

headline

Double Cross

James Patterson

A PSYCHOTIC KILLER WHO CRAVES AN AUDIENCE

Just when Alex Cross's life is calming down, he's drawn back into the game to confront the Audience Killer – a terrifying genius who stages his killings as public spectacles in Washington DC and broadcasts them live on the net.

AND A MURDERING MASTERMIND WHO WORKS ALONE

In Colorado, another criminal mastermind is planning a triumphant return. From his maximum-security prison cell, Kyle Craig has spent years plotting his escape and revenge. Craig prefers to work alone, but if joining forces with DC's Audience Killer helps him to get the man who put him away – Alex Cross – then so be it.

BOTH ARE AFTER THE SAME DETECTIVE – ALEX CROSS

From the man the *Sunday Telegraph* called 'the master of the suspense genre', *Double Cross* has the pulse-racing momentum and electrifying thrills that have made James Patterson a No. 1 bestselling storyteller all over the world.

Praise for James Patterson's bestselling novels:

'James Patterson does everything but stick our finger in a light socket to give us a buzz' *New York Times*

'A novel which makes for sleepless nights' *Daily Express*

'Pacy, sexy, high-octane stuff' *Guardian*

978 0 7553 4941 8

headline

Judge and Jury

James Patterson and Andrew Gross

IT'S THE TRIAL OF THE DECADE

Andie DeGrasse, aspiring actress and single mother, does not want to do jury service. But despite her attempts to get dismissed, she still ends up as Juror No. 11 in a landmark trial against notorious Mafia Don Dominic Cavello.

THE JUDGE IS TERRIFIED OF THE DEFENDANT

Cavello, aka the Electrician, is linked to hundreds of unspeakable crimes and his power knows no bounds. But Senior FBI agent Nick Pellisante has been tracking him for years and conviction is a sure thing.

SO IS THE JURY

As the jury reaches its verdict, the Electrician makes a devastating move. The entire nation is reeling, and Andie's world is shattered. The hunt for Cavello just got personal, and she and Pellisante join together, determined to exact justice – at any cost.

THE VERDICT: RUN FOR YOUR LIFE

James Patterson spins a heart-pounding legal thriller that pits two people against the most vicious and powerful mobster since John Gotti.

Praise for James Patterson's bestselling novels:

'James Patterson's books might as well come with movie tickets as a bonus feature' *New York Times*

'A novel which makes for sleepless nights' *Daily Express*

978 0 7553 3049 2

headline

Now you can buy any of these other bestselling books by **James Patterson** from your bookshop or *direct from his publisher*.

FREE P&P AND UK DELIVERY
(Overseas and Ireland £3.50 per book)

Miracle on the 17th Green	
(and Peter de Jonge)	£7.99
Suzanne's Diary for Nicholas	£7.99
The Beach House *(and Peter de Jonge)*	£7.99
The Jester *(and Andrew Gross)*	£7.99
The Lake House	£7.99
Sam's Letters to Jennifer	£7.99
Honeymoon *(and Howard Roughan)*	£7.99
Lifeguard *(and Andrew Gross)*	£7.99
Beach Road *(and Peter de Jonge)*	£7.99
Judge and Jury *(and Andrew Gross)*	£7.99
Step on a Crack *(and Michael Ledwidge)*	£7.99
The Quickie *(and Michael Ledwidge)*	£7.99
You've Been Warned	
(and Howard Roughan)	£7.99

Alex Cross series

Cat and Mouse	£7.99
Pop Goes the Weasel	£7.99
Roses are Red	£7.99
Violets are Blue	£7.99
Four Blind Mice	£7.99
The Big Bad Wolf	£7.99
London Bridges	£7.99
Mary, Mary	£7.99
Cross	£7.99
Double Cross	£7.99

Women's Murder Club series

1st to Die	£7.99
2nd Chance *(and Andrew Gross)*	£7.99
3rd Degree *(and Andrew Gross)*	£7.99
4th of July *(and Maxine Paetro)*	£7.99
The 5th Horseman *(and Maxine Paetro)*	£7.99
The 6th Target *(and Maxine Paetro)*	£7.99

Maximum Ride series

Maximum Ride: The Angel Experiment	£7.99
Maximum Ride: School's Out Forever	£6.99
Maximum Ride: Saving the World and	
Other Extreme Sports	£6.99

TO ORDER SIMPLY CALL THIS NUMBER
01235 400 414
or visit our website: www.headline.co.uk

Prices and availability subject to change without notice.